Warwickshire
County Council

013471280 5

AND YOU ARE . . . ?

Simon Astaire

QUARTET

First published in 2009 by
Quartet Books Limited
A member of the Namara Group
27 Goodge Street, London W1T 2LD

This is entirely a work of fiction. The names,
characters and incidents portrayed in it are the
work of the author's imagination. Any resemblance
to actual persons, living or dead, businesses, localities
or historical events is entirely coincidental.

A catalogue record for this book
is available from the British Library

ISBN 978 0 7043 7161 3

Typeset by Antony Gray
Printed and bound in Great Britain by
T J International Ltd, Padstow, Cornwall

To

JIMMY BALFOUR

(1936–1999)

&

MICHAEL MAINWARING

(1943–2000)

with gratitude

'Hollywood for me will always evoke a contradictory mixture of certain scents. A sexual damp, I have called it, the moisture in the clean creases of a woman's flesh, combined with a challenging sea-salt smell; ... '

Arthur Miller, *Timebends*

PART ONE

8 November 1981
'Jack Lemmon, pick up the house phone . . . Mr Clint Eastwood, telephone for you. Calling Mr Eastwood.'

As soon as the names were announced, stars glided to the curved cubicle under the pink cabana. The guests of the Beverly Hills Hotel pool pretended to look the other way, but their eyes told a different story. They were enthralled by the posturing of Hollywood's biggest stars. I was turning a golden brown under the Hockney-blue sky and sipping my drink, confused and exhausted by the last twenty-four hours. The stone beneath my feet sizzled and a lizard caught the corner of my eye as it scuttled under a low table. An orchestra of clinking ice cubes in sweet white wine created the perfect background music.

'When you receive a call for Samuel Alexander, don't announce my name. Ask for Suite 302.' I was instructing the hotel operator and she was listening.

* * *

8 November 1977
I'll always remember that morning; I'll remember it until my final breath. I was in London with old school friends David Burford (who had recently inherited the title Earl of Amersham) and Neil Nimmo Smith, the two friends with whom a few months earlier I had shared the day of expulsion from public school. The rain was torrential and the wind was gale-force. Umbrellas flew across the city streets like in that scene from *Mary Poppins*. To shelter

from the elements, we ducked into the cinema in the King's Road where *The Spy Who Loved Me* was showing. We paid over the odds to sit in the posh seats, but it was worth it as they turned out to be sofa-size.

After the lights went up, we charged across the road to the oldest cafe in Chelsea, the Picasso. The rain was relentless and we crammed into one of the booths, drenched by our short sprint. We were famished so we each ordered a full English breakfast and waited patiently for the best fry-up in town to arrive. I was holding the bottle of HP, ready to spill sauce over my plate into the fried eggs. I felt a wind blow in from the street and looked out. The rain had ceased and I noticed from the lifting of people's collars that the temperature had dropped; there was no warning, the change had been sudden. My hand became stiff and I noticed the grey arteries in my wrist pulsating. My limbs seemed leaden and the way the world was spinning round was making me dizzy. After a few moments, things righted themselves and I was my normal self again.

'Anything wrong, Sam?' asked Neil. He noticed my face had become drained of colour and that I was staring at my left hand. All vital signs had vanished from my eyes; he would comment on his observation months later.

'I'm fine now, but that was weird.'

I heard a vague sound, a distant yelp coming from outside. Without another word, I rose, lit a cigarette and made my way to the payphone that hung on the wall opposite the coffee machine. I lost my first tenpence when the pips sounded and I realised, on hearing an angry Scots voice, that I'd dialled a wrong number. That was certainly not my father, I chuckled, my spirits slowly beginning to return. I dialled again and this time the ring sounded more friendly; to my surprise, Aunt Flo picked up the phone. Why I was startled to hear her voice, I didn't know.

She was more of a fixture in the house than anyone. Aunt Florence was my mother's sister and dearest friend. It must have been her tone, frightened and remote; not in the least familiar.

'Hello, is that you, auntie?'

'Sam, thank God. We've been trying to reach you all day.'

'Is mother there?'

There was a pause and the phone was passed. I overheard whispering and then my mother's voice.

'Darling, you need to come home immediately. Don't ask me why, but it's important that you are here with us now. Do you hear me?'

It sounded as if she was in the attic, calling down. Yes, I had heard what she'd said, but only just. There was a desolation; the sense of an intolerable burden weighing her down. It was difficult to decipher but I suppose I knew, surely I knew, what had happened, but I couldn't take on board something so terrible. I returned to the table and noticed the dirty floorboards and a pound note caught between the cracks. I picked it up and swept it into my pocket. Before I sat down, I told my friends that I had to return immediately to my home in Oxfordshire.

'Are you OK, Sam? Is everything all right?' asked David.

'I'm not sure,' I mumbled, trying to deal with my appetising fry up and the confusion spinning in my head. 'My mother sounded very strange, indistinct and distracted. I think I have to go home. Here's a pound . . . ' The note I'd just found fell from my hand on to the table.

Without finishing my sentence, I stumbled out into the King's Road and hailed a passing cab; it raced me past Hyde Park and on to Paddington. The station was busy as the rush hour was approaching. My eyes scanned the overhead timetable and I saw that the Charlbury train was about to leave. No time to buy a ticket; I had not reached my seat before the train was pulling out. The sky had turned black from the east and everywhere lights were coming on. Although it was a journey of well over an hour, I asked myself few questions about the need for my immediate return home. I looked out of the window and saw my reflection stare back. It wore a different expression from the one I was familiar with. I whiled away the time making funny faces, sticking out my tongue; a humourless, tweed-suited lady who was sitting near by tutted like a metronome next to a third-rate fiddler. If only she had known what agony of mind my clowning concealed.

* * *

Harold, our butler, was waiting at the station. His kind African face was solemn and his eyes were lowered; he stood to attention underneath the overhead light. I glimpsed him from my window, and as I left the train, he turned and marched briskly to the car ahead of me, without a word. The ten-minute drive home was silent. Nothing was said, which in itself was unusual as normally we would eagerly have discussed the latest soccer results and on this occasion our team's amazing 9–0 victory against Bristol Rovers a couple of weeks earlier. Harold gazed fixedly ahead as he drove through the narrow lanes in the profound darkness. The torrents of rain had ceased and the countryside breathed again. We turned into our drive, the small stones crunching loudly underneath the tyres. Harold switched off the engine but remained in his seat, motionless, and I was overwhelmed with dread. I made my way alone to the front door, the door that I had known since I was a child. I took a deep breath and walked in. The strange thing about coming home is that it looks the same and feels the same – all that is changed is you. As I moved into the hall, my mother came towards me from the kitchen. Her slight frame had become suddenly frail and she crept into my arms and held my body close to hers, weeping with an excruciating sound; a sound I never ever want to hear again.

And then I asked; I asked the question to which I already knew the answer. She lifted her face and her blue eyes were pale as ash. 'Darling, it's your brother. Thomas died this morning.'

I rocked to the throb of somewhere in my head and for an instant I came near to collapse, wailing with anguish at a catastrophe that would alter my life and change the trajectory on which I was travelling for ever. I held my mother, her body surprisingly warm, brittle and thin, and inhaled that deep smell of lavender that always emanated from her skin. The two of us sobbed uncontrollably and fell to our knees as one in a dull white light. She was stroking my hair as if to reassure herself that I was indeed her other boy, her only living son.

Aunt Flo was in the kitchen, pottering about being supportive and trying to keep busy. She gave me a firm English hug, wiped her eyes and offered to make a cup of coffee. Harold's wife Violet, our South African cook, sat at the breakfast table, immobilised like her husband by the force of the blow. I went over and kissed her cheek and she sighed but said nothing. Her usually laughing face was drained of expression. I leaned against the sideboard and drank from a mug that my parents had bought when we visited Disney World in Florida. That had been our last family holiday and the memory was, fleetingly, blissful. How I had revelled in the rides, dazzled especially by flying over London on the Peter Pan attraction with my brother Tom, six years older than me and probably quite bored, but not letting his excited eleven-year-old brother notice. I then caught the name on the mug and it was not mine but

Tom's. I choked and started to sob again, first weeping quietly and then louder and louder until I was howling, like a hound for its dead master.

I had been home for half an hour and had still not seen my father, the man who cherished and worshipped his elder son. They had between them a connection that I recognised he and I would never share. They would go for long walks and laugh at each other's jokes, and I would see them from a distance pushing each other with tenderness and collapsing into hugs; they had been the best of friends. And yet for me, my father was a remote figure, and he rarely paid me a compliment. He was a stranger in my life; a man who exchanged few words with me, and after my expulsion from his old school, regarded me with a resigned look.

'He's in the study,' my mother told me.

* * *

My father's study was never a room to inspire joy or lightness of heart; it was the place where, sitting behind his oversized desk, he would read aloud my school reports with an air of cruel derision. I had to be invited into his sanctuary and such times were rare. The room was substantial and every wall was lined with books, which my father would retreat to after dinner. He was at his most content when stretched out on his designer leather chair close to the fireplace turning the pages of the latest novel. On one side of his desk stood a large picture of my mother in Portofino, looking radiant. A smaller picture of his two boys, taken during that Florida holiday, with Tom's arm round my neck in mock strangulation, was placed on the other side. I had a wide grin and not a care. In the centre, next to a gold carriage clock, was a photo of Tom on his last day at public school, looking handsome and confident and so full of life.

My father was sitting in a dark corner with the instinct of an animal to hide when wounded. His face had turned grey, like that of some old stone crusader lying on a cathedral tomb. He made no sound, but his head quivered slightly. His appearance had changed and he no longer resembled the man – the father – I knew.

'Father?' I whispered, but he did not respond. 'Father?' raising my voice. This time his head turned sharply, as if distracted by the tiresome ringing of a phone. He looked in my direction and for a second I thought he did not recognise me. There was a silence, a still moment of suspense.

He walked towards me before putting his arms out and saying, 'My beautiful Sam; my dear, dear son,' and we hugged.

* * *

Solitude was what I needed most. The phone rang constantly as the news filtered through our social world. I had not even called my girlfriend Lana, which on the face of it would have been the most natural thing to do. Instead, I stayed in my room, gazing in the mirror and going numb from the reflected stare of my anaesthetic eyes. My father had taken his 'longest' flight, to deal with American bureaucrats and bring back my brother's body. We had bidden him farewell at the front door, and as his chauffeured black car disappeared from sight, my mother gave way to her grief and collapsed. Aunt Flo caught her as she fell. I didn't say a word, just returned to my room to be alone with the knowledge that would haunt me for ever. For I knew from my visit to New York earlier in the year that my older brother had been a junkie.

I had discovered his drug use when I found him smelling of vomit, lying overdosed in his damp bathroom. His body was sprawled next to a discarded needle, dripping heroin.

He crawled back to the land of the living that night and in the days that followed admitted that he had lied to our father in order to raise funds to continue his habit. He told him that he needed cash to pay for an abortion for his girlfriend, he said that he been mugged and his recently drawn funds had been snatched from his bag, he even lied that the restaurant he had been employed by had gone bankrupt, having failed to pay him for three months. My father did not even get suspicious; Tom was above suspicion; by return he sent off a cheque. 'Don't ever tell dad about any of this, you promise me,' Tom had begged; I never did.

It was during those hours of closeness, after St Vincent's Hospital in Greenwich Village had saved his life, that I saw the way the terrifying habit had ravaged his body. I smelled the stench of the drug seeping from his skin. I believed him when he looked deep into my eyes and said that he would not take the drug again. I believed him and, yes, I trusted him to act on his words; surely nobody would want to repeat that hell?

And, finally, my brother and I had a shared secret. He needed my faith and understanding. Who was I to go running to the two people he would want to be the last to know? If they ever found out, it would not be from me. At last my hero brother was my equal and, although shocked by his weakness and the shattering of my illusion, I left the city with a slice of satisfaction that he was not the demigod that my father made him out to be. My brother, my dear darling brother, was like the rest of us.

* * *

Lana had called and called again. My parents did not approve of our relationship. She had been an accessory in my final rebellious act at public school. Two members of the Royal Family had been coming to open a new wing.

The day was described at the time as being one of the 'more important days' in the school's history. I had stripped myself of my school uniform and dressed as a Sioux Indian, with Lana costumed as my squaw. We rode to meet the visiting dignitaries on a chestnut mare. They thought it was charming; the headmaster and governors thought otherwise and I was expelled before night had fallen.

'I never liked her,' my father had bellowed when he found out about Lana's involvement. That was a lie, for he had been clearly smitten by her beauty and vivacity when I had first brought her to the house.

When I finally came to the phone, Lana spoke with words of solace chosen with a compassion beyond her years. She offered unwavering support, and by the time our conversation came to a close, I had agreed that I would travel from our Oxfordshire home to spend a few days with her family. My mother was all for it. 'It will do you some good,' she said. 'Give her our love.'

As the train approached Paddington, passing serried ranks of drab terraced houses, I thought about the fact that I'd be revisiting the vicinity of my old school. Lana was a local girl whom I had met in the Rose and Crown, close to the town's cricket pitch. I had fallen in love with her at first sight. I know I had, for the rush of feeling was overwhelming. The sensation was almost like a physical assault and I literally staggered in the same way as when I heard the news of my brother's death. I gasped for air and paused before the room came back to its senses.

At Paddington, I changed on to the tube, and as the Metropolitan Line train rattled into the familiar station my stomach lurched, in spite of my grief-stricken state. Then I remembered that this time I didn't have to return to school to endure the torture that had blighted my everyday existence there during those long three years.

I handed in my ticket and thought I recognised the West Indian ticket collector.

'Thank you very much, it's good to be back,' I said, reverting to my cocky schoolboy persona, but he didn't take up my remark or even show a glimmer of recognition, and before I reached the street I had settled back into the reality of the present. Lana's house was not far from the station and yet far enough from the gates of the school to make the chance of bumping into a master only a remote possibility. In the many illegal excursions that I had made from school I had never been caught, and only perhaps twice glimpsed a figure of authority who could have landed me in trouble.

As I walked by the cinema, I stopped and remembered my escapes to that place. How the films had transported me into another world, so distant from the place of grim despair a mile up the road. The hard upright red seats, the musty smell, the stamped popcorn beneath the feet. I allowed myself a chuckle, but then I noticed that they were showing *The Spy Who Loved Me*, the film I had seen only days (or was it a lifetime?) before. My chuckle subsided into sudden tears and I hastened away from the scene – straight into the path of my former geography master Gripper Yates.

'Hello, sir,' I said, instinctively reverting again to pupil mode.

'Ah, Alexander. I didn't expect to be seeing you again so soon.'

My tears gave way to embarrassment at meeting a former teacher. I avoided his gaze, feeling as if I had been caught playing truant with a cigarette in my mouth.

'I am sorry to hear of your brother's death . . . it was announced today at morning assembly, and as he was a former head boy, we observed a minute's silence.'

'Thank you, sir,' I answered, woodenly.

There followed an awkward pause. At last, he said, 'Well,

I must be going. You take care of yourself.' And he disappeared from my life into the suburban high street.

* * *

There was no sense of not feeling sorry or ignoring the pain, but Lana and her family felt that 'life must go on'.

Lana opened the door; seeing her smile made my rehearsed 'stiff upper lip' quiver, and when she gave me a hug, I felt a wave of reassurance.

'Would you like a cup of tea?' asked her mum, already pouring one into a David Cassidy mug. 'He's my favourite,' she said, and started to sing 'How Can I Be Sure'. There was no question of sparing me her tuneless rendition, no sense that she should not be behaving frivolously when I was in mourning: her attitude was a relief.

The strong PG Tips was the English remedy for all ills. I felt strength returning as the teapot was placed under the tea-cosy and Lana turned up the radio to Baccara's 'Yes, Sir, I Can Boogie'.

With the music blaring, and mother and daughter gyrating to the sound, there was a remarkable atmosphere of ordinariness. I remembered, when I visited Lana's parents for the first time the previous year, dressed in my school uniform, how different her background had seemed from my own. I lived in a house of minimal communication, where what needed to be said was never said. Here it was the opposite. There was honesty and openness, in word and in deed. Those days were intrinsically important in the jigsaw of my life. When I drifted back into my realm of avoidance, I tried to recollect the spark of that time, and that lesson in sharing stood me in good stead.

'How is your team playing? Any more 9–0s?' Lana's dad asked, taking off his tie and throwing it on to the sofa. 'I don't usually have to put on this muck, but I had a union meeting and needed to look the part.' He walked over to his daughter and gave her a teasing hug. Then he turned to me again, his large face more florid than I remembered, 'Sorry to hear about your brother . . . bloody waste.' He lit up a Player's No. 6 and started puffing away as though it were a large cigar.

'Out you go!' ordered his wife, as if commanding a dog to leave the room after it had just pissed on the carpet. There was to be no smoking inside, although inside permanently smelled of burned toast.

Outside, without warning, the heavens opened. 'Come in, you idiot,' called Lana, and her father ducked back in, drenched by the sudden downpour. 'Don't know where that came from. It was a fine evening a moment ago,' Lana laughed.

'It's God's tears,' I said without thinking, and there followed a silence. 'But I suppose anyone in mourning would say the same.'

* * *

We had dinner in front of the box; a total 'no no' in our house.

'Only yobs watch the television when eating,' my father used to retort when I asked if I could watch *Sportsnight with Coleman* with a tray on my lap.

Lana's family's favourite show *M*A*S*H* was on and they weren't going to miss that. They laughed together in unison, enjoying Alan Alda's 'Hawkeye' Pierce character as soon as he appeared on screen. The more Hawkeye baited his whining colleague Frank Burns, the louder the laughs grew. Lana held my hand in a firm grasp, and although I wanted to resist, I left it where it was. The reluctance came from my awareness of the tortured breathing of the father, who was sitting on her other side. He had been welcoming and generous since we first met, but fathers are fathers, especially when it comes to their daughters; that much I did know.

Keith, the nineteen-year-old delinquent brother, was staying out for the night, so I naturally assumed that I would be crashing in his room. As the *M*A*S*H* credits started to roll, Lana's mother said that she had put a hot-water bottle in *our* bed to warm the sheets.

'They don't need no bloody hot-water bottle.' And her dad nudged his elbow into my ribs with considerable force.

'Thank you, that's very kind of you,' and I backed out of their front room as if I were leaving the presence of Royalty.

* * *

'Well, that's a first, my parents letting my boyfriend share my bed.' Lana giggled.

We were silent for a moment, submerged by an invisible spirit, call it sentimentality. I was grateful for the ease of the evening. They were decent, good people and the lack of conversation about my grief was a godsend, obviously deliberate on their part. I felt as if I were halfway through a marathon and had just hit the wall. I was wondering how to move on another step, let alone another mile.

'Come here,' Lana whispered and pulled me towards her. We started to kiss, at first gently and then more and more passionately. Throughout our lovemaking, my mind was in turmoil, and it seemed to me I glimpsed my own death. I found myself gasping for air in the intensity of the moment. As I reached my orgasm, I collapsed on to Lana's breast, like a body being thrown into a grave. She stroked my back and as if reclaiming me said, 'I have you again, my love. I have you again, my . . . I have you again . . . I have you . . . I have . . . I . . . '

And with my mournful heart soothed, I fell into a deep sleep, away from the reality of those woeful days.

* * *

Tom was buried two weeks later at our local church in Chadlington. As father was Jewish and mother was a Protestant, there was a slight uncertainty as to where we stood spiritually. At school it was beneficial to announce that you were Jewish as that curtailed chapel attendance and there was extra time to pursue outside activities. In the end, the decision rested with us, and it seemed Thomas had once made it plain to his girlfriend Suzy that 'should he die' he wanted his body to lie in an English churchyard. There was to be no argument.

Suzy had accompanied my father back from the bureaucrats in New York City with Tom's body. She had been living with my brother in New York throughout his battle with drugs and I had witnessed the torture she endured during the process. She loved my brother with a heart full of grace and care. Yet there was nothing she could do to halt his slide to destruction.

'He'd got no better since the last time I saw him . . . had he, Suzy?' I asked.

'He tried, I promise you he tried,' she spoke quietly and sorrowfully. 'But he just couldn't pull out of it. After his second overdose, he vowed that he would never go near the drug again, but I had heard that before. This time I grew firmer, and promised that if he did, I would leave him and never come back . . . it made no difference.' She broke down, remembering her helplessness. Her stunning face seemed even more mesmerising as it reflected the trauma of those events. 'I truly believe that he didn't touch a thing until that final morning.'

'Look what you've done, Thomas,' I thought. 'Look at

the misery on all our faces. Surely you wouldn't have given way if you could have seen the devastation it would cause?'

In his final hour, he had hailed a cab outside their apartment on Hudson and Perry Street to Penn Station to meet some stranger. That stranger murdered my brother; for murder it was. Thomas scored more heroin than his body could stand. He had resisted his habit for sixty-two days until that morning; injecting his usual amount proved fatal. An attendant found him just before one o'clock in the afternoon. He was slumped on the dirty floor, his handsome face lying in a pool of vomit.

* * *

The funeral was a modest gathering on a brilliant November day under an ice-blue sky. My brother's coffin was carried along the narrow path by the pallbearers, undertaker's men walking with measured steps. Why were we not carrying him? Who were these pale strangers in dark suits? The moment was silent and still, except for the march of their polished black shoes. I followed behind with my parents, each step as painful as if splinters of glass were sticking into my feet; I felt physically tired and emotionally drained. The church was cold, in spite of the shafts of sunlight slanting through the stained-glass windows. 'I have not been in here for years,' I thought. My mind was surprisingly alert, I could even now remember where each person was sitting. I glimpsed Lana, her golden hair tied back as a mark of respect, those green eyes sparkling in the gloom, her white shirt under her blue jacket perhaps opened a button too far.

Uncle Louis, my father's brother, was wonderfully strong and a pillar throughout. A self-made man of mystery, he had, like my father, the knack of buying winning tickets in the lottery of life. His mere presence gave comfort to a family that was finding the upset of those hours achingly traumatic. Aunt Flo, wearing a black hat that looked more like a flowerpot, sat with her pompous son Rupert; she was stoical throughout and read the lesson.

William Carmichael, Tom's dearest friend, spoke of his school memories and described Tom flying down the wing for the 1st XV. He spoke of how he looked as a schoolboy: his long tangled brown hair, impish smile and wicked humour. When he imitated my brother's raucous laugh, the sobbing drowned the mimicry. We would never hear Tom laugh again . . . William had not seen Tom for the last year of his life, and, like many gathered there, he felt guilty for not being around during those final desperate days.

'I didn't visit him in New York last Christmas because I wanted to go skiing. Skiing, would you believe? I feel ashamed. I am a fool.' And he punched the side of his leg in frustration and remorse.

We all felt somehow complicit in the tragedy.

My closest school friends, the Earl of Amersham and 'Spit' Nimmo Smith, had asked whether they could come and I was glad they were there. The two sat together in their best suits with 'I'm terribly sorry' faces. When I left my place in the front pew beside my inconsolable parents and walked up to address the congregation, I glanced at them and they both gently nodded.

I had wanted to read Dylan Thomas's 'And death shall have no dominion', especially as Tom and Suzy had lived in an apartment on the same block as the White Horse Tavern, where the Welsh poet spent many a day drinking himself to an early grave, but decided against it; I chose a simple American Indian prayer instead:

'When I am dead
Cry for me a little,
Think of me sometimes
But not too much,
Think of me now and again
As I was in life.
At some moments it's pleasant to recall
But not for long.
Leave me in peace
And I shall leave you in peace,
And while you live
Let your thoughts be with the living.'

It was as if my brother's spirit had spoken the words. I saw his smile when reading and as I finished I beamed back. I crossed my father's path as he quietly went up to speak, opening with the passage from *Anna Karenina*, Tom's favourite, 'All happy families resemble one another; but each unhappy family is unhappy in its own way . . . ' He groped for my hand and clasped it briefly. The anguish etched on his face was unbearable; my mother, sitting by my side as he read, cried and cried.

* * *

The wind had picked up by the time we walked to my brother's grave. Near to the oak tree was the place where he would rest. I wanted to say, 'What a perfect spot!' but I resisted. How smart everyone looked, how the English stand tall when suffering! As the coffin was lowered, I thought that one day I would join my brother. The plain understanding that we have no choice and that we are all doomed to die was comforting as the casket was lowered.

We regrouped back at home to eat sandwiches and drink tea or, for a few, a measure of whisky. The conversation was unguarded, the consciousness of grief allowing everyone to talk openly about their lives and Tom's. Perhaps that was why Lana could tell, why it was so obvious. I was standing with Lana, when my statuesque Italian friend Chiara walked over to offer her condolences. Our encounter was defensive and constrained in contrast to the others going on in the room. She had arrived that morning from New York to support her best friend Suzy. She didn't look the least bit tired. She stroked my cheek and gave it a sympathetic kiss. 'I'm so sorry, Samuel. I understand the pain you feel. I loved your brother very much.' Our meeting was stilted, rigid in movement, slow in speech. I had had sex with her while visiting my brother in New York and I did not have the strength that day to pretend otherwise.

* * *

'I know you slept with that Italian tart,' Lana accused on the phone the following week.

'Don't be so silly, she's far too old.' I lied and badly.

'That woman is one of the most successful models in the world. She's been on the cover of countless magazines.'

'It meant nothing. I promise, I promise.'

'You just broke my heart, Samuel.'

'But I love you and want to be with you. Do you hear me?'

'You said that I was the first girl you'd had sex with. Don't you understand what your lie has done? Do you fucking well understand? You're a bastard!'

'But it meant nothing,' I kept repeating.

'You broke my bloody heart, Samuel.'

Lana didn't utter another word and slammed down the phone. I glared at the innocent receiver and bit my lip until I tasted blood. Then I bit my tongue in further self-punishment and more blood started to seep from my mouth.

I went to my bathroom and spat it out into the basin, watching it as it slowly disappeared down the plughole. I was mesmerised by the particles which visibly expanded, the deep red colour redder than I had ever noticed before. It reminded me of the red cloak a matador holds aloft at the stage of the contest when the picador places his lance at the back of the bull's neck and draws the first blood. There were no tears that day, not even a panicked return call to ask for forgiveness. My tears had run dry and my face remained frozen in the rictus of grief it had worn since the day of the funeral.

Lana wrote a letter that I received the following week:

Darling Samuel – There are so many words I wish to share with you but for now I have no desire to see your face. That may hurt too much.

Thank you for all the beautiful memories in all the beautiful places, but most of all I remember simply being with you, no matter where we were. I have loved you so much and I am grateful for everything we shared. You were my first love and that will remain within my heart for ever. But your selfish act has spoilt everything for me. I can't come to terms with your dishonesty or your feeble defence on the telephone last week. I deserve more than that, and my anger turns to pity as I realise that you don't have the honour to apologise. It is not only about you, Samuel; now you are in the outside world you have to deal with other people's emotions. You clearly can't!

Anyway, I am getting angry and that it not what this was meant to be.

I loved you, Samuel, but I do not want to see you again. As I said on the phone, you broke my heart.

I am sorry for the pain you must be suffering from the

loss of Tom, and hope in time the wound will heal. I truly believe you are a good person, Samuel, but I also know you are a foolish one.

Lana X

I folded the letter and placed it in a small drawer by my bed. Was I a fool? Selfish? Perhaps she never really loved me, if this is all it took? I knew the answers to my questions, but they were being asked at the wrong time. It was hard enough right now even to decide whether I wanted butter on my toast. I knew it would take many months, even years, to heal. A numbing chill descended upon me, a sense of detachment that would take a long time to thaw.

* * *

Lana ran to her room after hanging up and flung herself on her bed. There she sobbed uncontrollably into her banked-up pillows. She was strong in herself, but the betrayal was unbearable and for the moment she could not believe the amount of pain she was suffering. Her parents left her alone. They knew better than to knock on her door; when the strains of a soulful or heartbreaking record broke the silence, they looked at each other with a short grimace and continued their day.

Just before her mother was going to call Lana down for dinner, she appeared in the kitchen. Her naturally olive complexion was drained of colour and her eyes bespoke such devastation that her father hugged her to his barrel chest. The dinner of fish pie was her favourite though, and she surprised herself by eating it all up, with shrugged shoulders and few words. She did not want to discuss what had happened and was not looking for advice. Thank God her annoying brother Keith was out. He would have been insensitive and undoubtedly made things worse. After dinner she rose and gave each parent a kiss. 'We are down here if you need us,' her mother told her. Lana withdrew to her bedroom to listen to Rod Stewart's Atlantic Crossing *album, and when that got too painful, she changed to David Bowie, who lifted her spirits out of their melancholy state. She thought of the day when she had watched a school cricket match with Sam and of how they had walked to the Arts building afterwards and there finally made love. 'The first time' – that was a shameful lie. Lana could not understand how someone she loved could have deceived her so wickedly.*

Since the summer, she had worked in W.H.Smith's. It was meant to be for a few weeks, but weeks rolled into months, and although she did not feel stretched, it was comfortable and would have remained so if her world had not crashed. Before, boys from Montgomery were simply part of the backdrop; now they were irritants. The weeks passed quickly but the interval of time only increased the pain. She thought of calling Sam at Christmas, knowing the grief he must have been suffering. But she didn't, fearful that it would be too upsetting for everyone. Instead, she rang in early January when the trees were leafless and the streets in the town were bleak and deserted. She was thinking that it had been long enough for sorrow and it was time to move on. The streets were wet from a morning fall of snow and the air was cold and clammy. On walking to the nearby sandwich bar, she caught sight of a Montgomery boy very like Sam who was sauntering in her direction. She was surprised how high her heart leapt. She lingered as so often over the memory of Sam, remembering his laugh and his wickedness. As she passed the boy, she believed for a moment that it really was Sam, and as he turned, she caught his eye and said, 'Sam?' She blushed deeply and scurried away to the nearest pub to recover from her embarrassment. Lana ordered a drink and heard the jukebox playing Chicago's 'If You Leave Me Now'. She suddenly felt the need to break the cycle of torment and said to herself, 'I will give Sam a ring.'

Sam happened to be at home in Oxfordshire and picked up the phone, but as he was on his way out of the door to his mother's waiting car, their conversation was stilted and awkward.

* * *

It was an early evening in late September, still warm after a pleasant sunny day. Lana had arranged to meet a friend in Notting Hill before maybe going dancing in the West End. Stella had moved to central London to work for an advertising agency in Soho. She had been a friend of Lana's since childhood and although they tried hard to see more of each other, this was their first meeting in ages.

Stella was sitting outside the Champion close to Kensington Church Street. Exhaling a cloud of smoke and coughing, she stubbed out her cigarette to welcome her friend. She was sitting with a man whom at first Lana hardly noticed. He immediately stood up and offered to buy her a drink, but Lana said that she would get her own. She liked the gratifying sense of independence that she had these days.

The bar was quite full that Saturday evening and as Lana edged her way through the smoky pub she thought about the man who had been sitting with Stella. He was very attractive and something inside had come alive again. She felt rather peculiar and leaned her elbows on the bar to gain some balance.

'Can I have a gin and tonic, please?'

The barman pushed a glass up to the optic.

'Oh, could I have it in a straight glass, please?' Lana asked.

'Nothing straight here,' he replied. And he was right; she

found she was in the middle of a group of gay men in an obviously gay pub.

When she returned to the table, James Hurst made to stand up. Lana, embarrassed by his movement to rise, sat down quickly, fiddled with her hair and stared at Stella's over-painted face. He was clearly a gentleman and very handsome, with brown eyes and a flurry of brown hair. He had an open expression and a kind tone.

'James was at Montgomery,' Stella announced.

'When was that?' Lana asked, perhaps a little too quickly.

'I left seven years ago this July. I was glad to leave, to be honest. Did you know anyone there?' James asked.

'My ex-boyfriend; but he was expelled last year!'

'And what was his name?'

'Sam . . . Sam Alexander,' she replied slowly.

James, as he talked, was attracted to the freshness of her beauty. 'I knew his brother Thomas. What a tragedy! To lose your life so young and to drugs. Strange – he was the last person in the world that I would have imagined taking that road.'

Lana made no comment. 'So where are we going to eat?' she demanded, changing the subject.

James felt his heart sink and realised that this must be a sensitive topic. He would tread more carefully in future.

They remained at the pub until closing time, missing out on food except for the occasional bag of salt-and-vinegar crisps. The alcohol made the talk easy, and by the time the landlord called for everyone to drink up, Lana and James were drunkenly falling for one another. How predictable that Lana would go out with another 'posh' boy from Montgomery. The world is small and it is said that we never stray far from our first love. Very soon, they would spend more and more time together. It would be only occasionally that James would remind Lana of Sam, but that was mostly when he became defensive about his family and privileged upbringing.

Over dinner three months later, James asked Lana to move in with him in the New Year. She agreed, and decided to quit her job and find something better paid in central London. Before she took this important step in her life, however, she knew that she would have to make peace with herself and get in touch with Sam one final time.

* * *

Christmas Eve 1978

The first Christmas after Thomas's death we had been deep in mourning. My parents had fled to the Caribbean to avoid the intensity of the day and I was packed off to share the week with Aunt Flo and her son Rupert in East Sussex. It was a wearisome, forlorn time, and even though they tried to be generous and sweet, I was bereft and in pain. This year was, I very much hoped, going to be different.

'There's a call for you, Sam!' bellowed my father, as I lay watching a new, rather dubious double-act called Cannon and Ball. They were former welders from Oldham, one funny man and the other straight. They were clearly going to be a bit like Morecambe and Wise who had been in the news that year for defecting from the BBC to Thames Television. The *TV Times*, lying on the floor in front of the television, crowed at ITV's success in stealing the famous duo with the headline 'Christmas wouldn't be Christmas without Eric and Ernie'.

I chose a toffee with purple wrapping from the tin of Quality Street and picked up the phone. It was Lana's familiar voice. I had heard from Lana only twice over the past twelve months and neither of the calls had gone well. She remained angry that I had cheated and lied. 'You betrayed my trust,' she repeated reproachfully. However hard I tried, I was unable to respond to her scolding. Instead, I remained silent and didn't try to apologise. Emotionally, I had changed from being open and sensitive and now maintained an unresponsive, imperturbable facade in cold defence of my own vulnerability.

'How is your family?' Lana asked.

'It's still difficult, but we'll be fine,' my words were guarded.

'Shall we see each other next week, before the New Year?' she asked.

'Yes, let's do that. See you in Chelsea the day after Boxing Day.'

Her voice had seemed drained of affection. Surely, I could be forgiven for the one mistake, even if we were no longer together? I had responded to her questions with wooden replies, but below the surface I was consumed with delicious expectations strong enough to carry me through the next few days.

* * *

I was woken quite late on Christmas morning by my mother knocking on my door.

On the bedside table was Jack Kerouac's *On the Road*. It was as wrinkled as an old woman's face. When I had picked it up the previous night, pieces of paper had fallen out of the book. Pieces of a photograph. I had bent down, picking them up like a man who's not sure if a snake is dead or not. I pieced the photo together. It was a photo of me and Lana.

'Sam, may I come in?'

I groaned as she walked in, carrying a cup of milky tea.

'Come on, you have to get up! We're going to open our presents and afterwards you are walking with your father to the pub before our lunch guests arrive.'

The sight of my brother arm in arm with my father walking to the 'local' was one of the indelible images I had of childhood and indeed of Christmas. I remembered gazing from the tall drawing-room window, avalanches of melting snow falling from our rooftop. How I had yearned to be older so that I could be part of their intimacy. I was still grasping for that fatherly connection. Then, I was not resentful at being excluded, because I always thought it was my age that got in the way. When my mother spoke of the walk, I knew that this was likely to be a defining moment in my young life.

I rose from my rumpled bed and dressed in the clean clothes that had been left on my chair: black jeans, suede cowboy boots, white shirt and a navy-blue cashmere jumper, a birthday present I had been given the previous winter. I gazed into the mirror and saw I looked tired. Dark lines had appeared under my eyes overnight and my hair was dishevelled. I decided to give the shave a miss; I had yet to reach the point where the morning scrape was a necessity. I picked up the wooden hairbrush and attacked my hair vigorously, drifting into speculation as to how the day ahead was going to shape up. I noticed a mouthwash that was lurking in my medicine cupboard and had a swig that I regretted immediately: it was stale and I spat it out in horror – the mint had turned to sulphur. I swallowed a glass of tap water and, as my mother's voice was calling, scampered down the stairs to face the day.

My mother had bought me a Schott leather jacket which I had seen in a magazine a few weeks before and admired. Excitedly I pulled it on and when I felt the caress of the soft black leather I fell in love with a piece of clothing for the first time. She could see I was thrilled. I went over to give her a kiss. She pulled me to her and held me close and I laid my head against her heart, my mother's heart, and heard it beating fast. Violet and Harold had left the kitchen to join us for the present ceremony and my father handed them each a gift. 'We will open them later, sir, if that's all right?' Harold smiled, and the two backed away and returned to the task of preparing the lunch.

'What did you get them?' I asked.

'Photograph frames from a lovely shop in Burlington Arcade because . . . ' mother began.

Father finished the sentence, ' . . . they wanted a picture of you and Tom. So we had one copied. The one at Cousin Sophia's wedding where you and Tom are caught laughing at the dreadful best man's speech.' There was a pause, a desolate silence marking a poignant memory. It was not going to be the last of the day.

'Right, shall we go to the pub?' my father asked, ending the moment of sadness and clapping his hands in eager anticipation.

* * *

The morning was chill and the sunlight blindingly bright. Underfoot, the grass was wet and I felt my suede boots soaking up water. We left by the front door and walked quickly down the dirt track on to the main road through the village. My father was dressed in an expensive camel-hair coat and had my mother's Christmas present knotted loosely around his neck. The ends of the blue scarf were tucked in and protected him from the elements; he had a recurring cold and his cough had become nagging and persistent, so whenever he left the house my mother made sure he was dressed warmly.

We followed the same path that I imagined my father had taken with my brother over the years. He was deep in thought, perhaps the memory of previous times so strong that words were difficult. The pub was occupied by just a few drinkers as most of the village chose to remain by their own firesides on Christmas Day. A stationary shroud of cigarette smoke hung above our heads. I noticed George our postman sitting in the corner with a man looking remarkably like him. I gave him a wave and he raised his pint in acknowledgement. Father asked Ray, the amiable landlord, to send over the same again to George and his companion. 'It's his twin,' the publican told us.

My father had been George's hero ever since he arranged a demonstration to have George reinstated in his job. Driven by the injustice of his firing, he had galvanised the locals to rally against the decision. Drink was to blame, it seemed, and there were also rumours of a broken heart when a dalliance with a buxom conductress from Summertown in Oxford came to a sudden end. 'I have always received my post and with the kindest of smiles,' my father had said at the time, and that was why he intervened. There could not have been many complaints from locals; the entire village gathered to support George's reinstatement. We marched with banners from our house to the pub, chanting impassioned slogans like 'Hands off our postman!' Within the week, the local sorting-office manager had relented and given George his job back. The whole village met again in the pub to celebrate the success of the campaign, and still today I remember the pride I felt when the crowd toasted my father's efforts.

Raymond Chambers had owned the White Bear since the year I was born. He was Welsh, and although now in his seventies, he looked fitter than most who walked through his door. He was a large, kindly man, with a full head of coarse grey hair, who in his youth had been a fine rugby player, and if you gave him half a chance he told you all about it. His pub, like many around the British Isles, was the beating heart of the community.

As the taps filled our glasses with draught Guinness, he placed one hand on my father's shoulder and with the other downed a schooner of sherry in one go: 'For Thomas, God bless,' and father raised a desolate smile and thanked him for his moving gesture.

'Go sit over there by the fire, gentlemen. I will bring your drinks over and they are on the house.'

Burning logs spluttered and crackled in the grate and I stared into the flames. I was in a state of undefined expectancy. Opposite, my father wheezed and coughed. We sat and drank our beer wordlessly. I munched my salt-and-vinegar crisps rather too loudly. I picked up an old newspaper from the neighbouring table, read a headline and replaced it. Still nothing was said. I excused myself and went to the gents. On my return, the silence was finally broken.

'I have been wanting to ask you this for a long time.' My father's voice was soft. 'When you visited your brother in New York last year, did you know that he was taking drugs?'

I knew that question would one day be asked and had debated how I would answer. There was total silence for a split second; the question floated in the white dull air.

'No, father, I did not,' I lied.

And for the first time that I could remember he took my hand and squeezed it and squeezed it again.

'Sorry, I had to ask that. I am in such agony of mind that it's hard to go on. Your poor mother is having to be the strong one. I don't think I shall ever recover from the blow.' My father was so vulnerable.

It was then I spoke words that I believed many times in the past would never ever fall from my mouth, 'I love you, daddy. I love you with all my heart.' And my father wept quietly as he bent his head to his drink. I stood to buy another round. I walked to the bar and breathed in the wood smoke and felt a heavy burden lift from my shoulders; my world was changing for the better and I began to carry myself more like a man.

* * *

When we got back to the house, Uncle Louis had arrived with his latest girlfriend. 'Gorgeous, isn't she?' he said, giving me a wink. His full head of hair, recently dyed to a matt black, was combed back from his worn but handsome face. My father's older brother, with his Bentley parked outside and his property fortune, had countless skeletons in his cupboard. His date was an Australian from Sydney called Sharon. She was tanned, long-legged and, yes, gorgeous – but about forty years younger than my roguish uncle.

Aunt Flo had arrived, too, and was helping to lay the table. She had often had a rather disapproving attitude towards me in the past, but she had been far kinder since Tom died, and my love for her had deepened when I'd seen her grip my mother's hand throughout Tom's funeral. Her son, my cousin Rupert, pranced about as if he had a severe dose of piles, and prattled on about this and that in London society. 'They both slept with him . . . and, would you believe, at the same time!' I overheard him gossiping, but I was too busy mixing a Bloody Mary to pay any attention.

'Was it all right with daddy in the pub?' asked mother, as I was adding the Worcestershire sauce to my concoction.

'Yes, mother. I told father I loved him.'

My mother's lips trembled, and to hide her tears she walked away back into the kitchen.

* * *

We had a late lunch after the Queen's Speech at precisely ten past three. The speech was always watched by the family but it was not discussed and fifteen minutes later the content was forgotten.

Harold served and Violet watched from the door, making sure that everyone was enjoying her fine cooking. We used the crested knives and forks and somehow every bite coincided with a memory from previous years. Uncle Louis poured a torrent of gravy over his plate and Aunt Flo criticised his manners. His girlfriend said little but gave a sweet smile to anyone who caught her eye. The room was calm and Rupert again took centre stage with tales from the tabloids. After the main course was consumed, my father stood up, regaining some of his old strength. He raised his glass of wine: 'To Harold and to Violet! Thank you for preparing the most wonderful lunch, and thank you for being so kind to us over the years. Your support and friendship mean everything.' Harold bowed modestly and an embarrassed Violet hid her face in her apron. There was a ripple of spontaneous applause. My father then spoke to the guests: 'Thank you for being close to us and especially over the last twelve months. You have been with us in our grief. You have given us strength; without it, I'm not sure how we would have pulled through. Thank you.' We raised our glasses, and with the clinking of crystal, the sadness that had hovered over the day receded.

We gathered in the drawing room, each helping ourselves to coffee from a silver tray Harold had left on the sideboard. Rupert lit up a cigarette and offered me one, which I refused. I still felt uncomfortable smoking in front of my parents. The mantelpiece was full of Christmas cards and Rupert was looking to see if any were from people worth knowing. Without warning, my uncle's girlfriend walked over to the grand piano. It had remained almost untouched since a previous Christmas when Tom had orchestrated a singsong. She sat thoughtfully and began to play Satie's

Gymnopédie, Number 1, Variation 1. Her beauty and the grace of her musicianship, combined with the sublimely sad piece of music, transfixed us all. I silently said a prayer for forgiveness for the mistakes I had made and for the strength to be a good son. I glanced at my parents and they beckoned me over. And there by the fireplace the three of us hugged so warmly it was hard to ever let go.

* * *

The stilted phone call on Christmas Eve was a distant memory. From the moment I caught Lana by the waist and drew her towards me, all the ambivalence of those lost months miraculously vanished. She walked into the Markham Arms, her thick golden-brown hair falling over to one side, and I melted before the flash of her green eyes. The pub was spacious and warm. A large group was smoking incessantly around a table of half-emptied glasses. We chose to sit away from the party, at a place by the big bay window. The King's Road was home to the music and fashion worlds and that day there was room for all. The Christmas decorations already looked tired and ready to be taken down. On the jukebox Slade's Christmas anthem played again and again. I spoke of my long lonely months with thoughtless self-pity.

Lana's face suddenly changed expression. She looked up like a startled thrush and her sad eyes said, 'Didn't you think for one moment, Samuel, that it might have been difficult for me? It isn't always about you!'

I reached for her hand. She withdrew it and turned away.

'Don't forget you are the fool that cheated. I was ready to give you everything. I gave you my virginity!'

'I'm ashamed. I have no excuse. But believe me, I am very sorry.'

My mind drifted and I thought I heard people whisper,

'Poor boy, you are a fool.' I looked around but there was no one there. My imagination was snapping like the gentle click of train wheels.

'Where were you for Christmas?' I asked, taking her hand, successfully this time. A glimmer of hope like a fleck of light through a dull autumn sky.

'We went down to Bournemouth, of all places, to one of those seafront hotels. My dad's sister died last June and left some money. Not a lot, but enough for a good family piss up.'

Lana said she'd watched the elderly residents walking gingerly from Boscombe Pier to the Cumberland Hotel, which was 'the sort of gaff you would stay in!'

I laughed and remembered how she used to tease me about my posh voice and privileged upbringing. She pulled my fingers and started to massage my palm, each dig conveying a message. I stared at her face and regretted our lost days. She had given up on me because she couldn't trust me. Would I have cheated on her if I had known I would eventually be discovered? I had no answer; which might have been an answer in itself.

We drank some more and reminisced about my schooldays. We had some sausages for lunch from the hot plate at the end of the bar. She complimented me on my new leather jacket and I smiled with childish pride. I offered her a cigarette but she had given up when her aunt had died from lung cancer. 'Those fags are killers, you know. My aunt was only forty-six.'

I lit another and agreed.

We left the pub and turned to our right, plunging into the white noise of the street. There was no hesitancy in our step. The Chelsea Potter was full and drinkers spilled on to Radnor Walk. Many faces, so many colours of hair and complexion, so many differences of build and height. We walked by the Picasso cafe and I averted my eyes. The place was for ever going to be associated with the news of my brother's death. We walked by Flood Street and headed for Boy, the punk/rock boutique where punks went to show off their attitude and their wares. In the shop, business was brisk. I bought a T-shirt with Sham 69's 'If The Kids Are United' scrawled all over and Lana took a camera from her bag and shot a photograph outside.

Directly opposite I saw the place for us, a familiar cinema with a neon sign. We bought popcorn and a mug of coffee each to warm us up. We drank it quickly as *Superman* was about to begin and hot drinks were not allowed inside. No sooner had the opening credits rolled than I was struggling to control my excitement and not tear the small buttons off her blouse. The smell of her hair, the sound of her breath; I just sat as she turned her head and the light from the screen was reflected in her green eyes; a reflection of thick summer leaves. By some miracle, I was kissing my first love again. How I remembered her!

'Lana is back now,' I thought, 'and we are together again. How stupid to have wasted so much time.' My heart would mend quickly and I could return to the boy I was. Excitedly, I moved my hands under her skirt and felt her knickers and the soft inside of her thighs. She did not resist and I felt how wet she had become. I was so gloriously happy that the thought that the last time I had been in that cinema was before I heard that Tom had died didn't cross my mind. Yes, I was that happy.

We stumbled out into the busy King's Road and walked hand in hand towards Sloane Square under a cold and darkening sky. We passed the grand facade of the Pheasantry, which had been the place to be in the 1960s. Then, without warning, Lana pulled me into a side road, Lincoln Street, and the deeper blackness of a further turning.

'I need to tell you something, Sam;' she paused and took a deep breath before going on. 'I have a boyfriend now and we are about to move in together. He lives in town and I care for him.'

Her words were like the strokes of a whip.

'I had to see you again to tell you.'

I felt numbness somewhere above my neck, my mind pickled, throat dry as a desert.

'And in doing so, let me hold and touch you?'

'Sam, you have to understand. We hadn't seen each other for ages. What was I supposed to do?' She shook her head and started to cry – but were they real tears I wondered.

How could she have been so cruel? I lit a cigarette and welcomed the mix of tobacco with the night air. Only an hour ago I was content, consumed with desire, looking to the future with the girl I believed I loved. Fuck it. I pulled away from her restraining hand and strode back to where there were lights and people, a crowd to lose myself in. I jumped on to a number 22 bus and ran up to the top deck. I glanced out of the window and glimpsed her abandoned face, intent on a desperate search for someone she once loved. But I was the one abandoned, the one sitting on a London bus. The conductor asked where I was going. I stared at him, mutely. He asked again and impatiently I gave him a tenpence piece and jumped off at Glebe Place. It was far enough not to bump into her again. How bitter I felt, how betrayed! I retreated into the crowds. I was detached again and sat silently on a bench in Paultons Square in the false sanctuary of my isolation. I saw a scrumpled pound note lying forlornly in the middle of the pavement. I picked it up and pocketed it. I remembered the last time I had found some money, in the Picasso cafe on that saddest day. I lit another cigarette and tried to make myself believe that I would not see Lana ever again. As I sat I imagined a light but insistent knocking. It grew like a pulse on the brain.

* * *

3 October 1980

It stood out like the Hollywood sign. I had bought the first edition of the *Evening News* outside South Kensington tube station. I was sipping hot coffee in Dino's, a small Italian bar, scouring the paper in my search for a job. The advertisement jumped out at me:

ESTABLISHED THEATRICAL AGENCY
CENTRAL LONDON
TELEPHONIST NEEDED
GOOD SPEAKING-VOICE ESSENTIAL

I knew instinctively it was aimed at me. I spoke well and enjoyed talking to strangers. It would be the perfect first job; at the thought of show business, I immediately fell into a daydream of the movies, the stars and the United States of America.

Dino's was packed as usual. It always made me think of the Thin Lizzy lines in 'The Boys Are Back In Town': 'Friday night they'll be dressed to kill, Down at Dino's bar and grill'. I tried to attract the attention of the busty waitress, but she was being kept busy by the leather-clad bikers ordering their beans on toast. She did not notice my impatient hand waving in the air. Finally, with a sigh, she approached in her pink pinafore, her huge bosom way ahead of her; her slim ochre-coloured legs disappeared under a short black skirt, her hands were long and delicate and her voice cockney and impatient. My eyes stalked her like a jealous husband's.

'What are you staring at, lovely?'

'Can I have another cup of coffee, please?'

'Speak up, posh boy. Did you say "coooffee"?'

I nodded, gazing at her in a semi-trance.

'Are you all right? Looks like someone's turned your head.'

'Yes, you have, but I'm fine,' I answered, snapping out of my stupor.

'That will be fifteen pence, please.'

I pulled out my newly acquired Coutts chequebook, wrote a total of twenty-five pence and filled out the stub. I was quite proud of myself. I had been yearning to sign one ever since the book arrived in a plain brown envelope on that Monday morning.

'That's the Queen's bank, isn't it, dear? You don't look old enough to have an account.'

'I certainly am old enough. I'm hoping to go for my first-ever job interview and need a good-luck charm.' I raised my eyebrows and plucked up courage. 'Can you give me a good-luck kiss?'

The waitress was not shocked by my forward request and gave my cheek a gentle peck. How surreal and wonderful life can be!

'Can I have your number?' I asked.

'No, you can't,' she replied coquettishly, and mockingly slapped my hand.

I shrugged and sauntered out, away from the smell of sausages and fried eggs. Before reaching the street, I turned and caught sight of her fresh lipstick mouthing the words, 'Good . . . luck.'

* * *

The nearest red telephone box on the edge of Onslow Square had no door and smelled of last night's pub. The black receiver was tangled; I slowly unfurled the cord and put the phone to my ear. I stared at my paper, lit my first cigarette of the day and dialled the digits slowly, watching the dial rotate back into position each time. A bright and breezy voice answered after five rings: 'The Bernard Kurzner Agency. Good-morning.'

'I'm applying for the job advertised in today's paper.' I spoke with my best public-school accent.

'Excellent,' said the voice at the other end. 'Come in at three o'clock. Our address is 82 Berkeley Square, above a nightclub, on the top floor. Quite a climb, but you sound young and fit so there should be no problem.'

Instead of catching the tube to Green Park Station, I decided to walk through Knightsbridge, past Harrods and into the Park. Brompton Road was bustling with shoppers. The surprisingly warm October morning gave their steps a spring unusual for the time of year. How different I thought England would be if it had a Mediterranean-type climate. How optimistic as a nation we would become. I walked under Bowater House, passing the Jacob Epstein statue, *Rush of Green*. I glanced at Pan, charming the family away from the claustrophobic offices and crowded shops into the green expanses of Hyde Park, and imagined that the faun gave me a wink.

David Bowie's 'Ashes to Ashes' drifted from a radio across the grass where a pale man without a shirt was sitting on an old tartan rug reading Kingsley Amis's *Lucky Jim*. Even the turf underfoot felt different. A puff of cloud drifted low over the trees and momentarily hid the sun. I dared to hope that perhaps my 'difficult' years were firmly behind me. This was a clean slate and criticism from relations and family friends following my expulsion from school would soon be forgotten. I remained angry at the lack of understanding that still dogged my life. I stamped my foot in an outburst of frustration at the thought, and by mistake squashed a snail that had crawled into my path. Was this a sign? I stopped to see if I could save the poor creature (I had no wish to attract bad karma), but the broken shell had penetrated the grey flesh. My mood changed from being very confident into being able to see nothing ahead but failure and ruin. 'Bloody snail,' I cursed out loud.

* * *

The Dorchester Hotel was bustling; expensive cars with tinted windows were pulling up to the entrance and dropping passengers in well-tailored suits. That day was more hectic than usual. A crowd of middle-aged women had gathered round the shallow steps, each of them clutching a pen and a glossy ten-by-eight-inch photograph of their hero. Somewhere in the scrum was probably one of the world's biggest television stars, a bald ugly-attractive Greek American, Telly Savalas. In the police drama *Kojak*, he had captivated the public with a lollipop forever stuck in his mouth and his trademark catchphrase, 'Who loves ya, baby?'

'He is such a star!' purred a woman with thin lips and nose held ever so slightly in the air.

'Great man,' agreed an unkempt man, rolling his cigarette with tobacco pulled from his green Golden Virginia pouch. He hawked and spat his phlegm on to the pavement. His sour body odour forced me to edge away, and I headed towards the pack to get a better view of everyone's hero. The great man was busily signing autographs in an ill-fitting crimson tracksuit, sporting a hairy chest and oversized gold sunglasses. That was all I needed to see and I walked away, but not before I yelled out, 'Who loves ya, baby?'

Telly stopped the signing, took off his shades, grinned and shouted back, 'D'you think you're the first wise-ass prick to throw that at me?'

* * *

82 Berkeley Square looked down towards the Ritz and Piccadilly. Cars cut corners as if they were in a chase. The square typified privileged London, with its grandeur and echoes of history. The good weather had packed the garden square with people, stacked together like bicycles in a bicycle shed. So close they shared each other's stories. Half listening to something never said, half saying something never heard. I continued my gentle climb to the Guinea Grill pub on Bruton Street. The pub was packed with over-aged schoolboys laughing raucously at bad jokes; their jackets had been discarded because of the heat and cigarettes and drinks were clasped in their hands. I ordered a large cognac and stood detached from the type of people I had spent three years with at public school. It turned out to be a wise decision; before long a bar brawl developed when one fat oaf accused another of shagging his wife. To the sound of glass crashing against walls, I quietly drifted away to meet my future.

* * *

Mrs Kurzner had run the theatrical agency with her husband for half a century and experience was written in every one of the lines on her wrinkled face. In her late sixties, with thick white hair and watery blue eyes, she sat facing me with an air of curiosity that reminded me of my former headmistress, Miss Andrews. Her face was not beautiful but expressed good humour and goodwill. The cognac I had drunk only minutes before had made my mouth slightly dry and my brain as unfit for purpose as a crumpled old suit. My head and neck moved about as if they were stiff, as if they had been underwater for a long time.

Her husband Bernard, dressed in a white flannel two-piece, sat at the desk directly next to hers in a vast room that smelled like a French cafe; he paid little attention to the interview and took continuous sips of black coffee as he dictated letters into a hand-held microphone; he had a strong east-European accent. He looked tiny and frail in his huge throne of a chair and seemed but a breath away from meeting his maker.

'Your name is Samuel Alexander, aged nineteen. Where were you educated, Mr Alexander?' Mrs Kurzner asked in a long one-note accelerando, as if to make up for lost time.

'I attended Montgomery House,' I replied.

'So I see. For a relatively short time. Were you expelled?'

I had hurriedly scribbled down my CV in the empty nightclub below and clearly had not taken the time to read it through. 'Well, I was there for three years, but in the end I felt I had outgrown the establishment. I knew I would learn far more about the world by getting myself a job.'

'Were you expelled?'

'It was agreed that I would not return for the following term.'

'He was expelled!' Mr Kurzner piped up from his desk.

'Mind your own business,' I thought. He had clearly taken an instant dislike to me. But his wife was kind, ignored her husband's remark and did not hammer out further questions on the matter.

'Why do you think you will be good at this job?'

'People will like my manner. I am always friendly and like to be frank. If a young man isn't frank, what can he be? I won't let you down, Mrs Kurzner.'

She sighed, glanced at her watch and looked surprised by the time.

'All right, Samuel, we plan to give you a try. Start on Monday at ten o'clock sharp. You will be paid forty pounds a week. Don't be late, I can't bear unpunctuality.'

She stood to reveal bloated ankles and to shake my hand.

'Oh yes,' she added as I was leaving. 'In future, Samuel, don't write down "girls" under your list of interests. It won't impress.'

I acted surprise like a startled hare pricking up its ears at a hunter. As I was closing the large oak door, I heard Mr Kurzner moan, 'You gave that boy the job? He seemed like a fool to me.'

'Yes, a fool he may be,' she replied, 'but a charming one, at least.'

* * *

The square was like the Garden of Eden. People still talking with glimmers of hope in their stories like flecks of light through a dull autumn sky. 'I just got a job,' I squealed and raised my arm in triumph to a stupefied stranger who was waiting for our number 14 bus. I sat on the top deck, smoking and daydreaming about how familiar this route would soon be. The bus crawled up the Fulham Road to the stop opposite my local record store. I bought Marvin Gaye's LP *What's Going On* as a self-congratulatory present and Simon, the kind owner, slipped me a Joy Division single as a freebie. That was a good day. I felt a sense of reprieve as if the firing squad had been stood down. Maybe I wasn't so useless after all. I virtually ran all the way home, eager to call my parents.

* * *

My father answered the phone from, I presumed, his study, his voice still distant as it had been ever since Tom's death. Yet it was different now because it wasn't for lack of interest in my welfare but because over the months he had retreated deeper and deeper into a mournful void. He had lost his zest for life and was unlikely to recover it.

'Hello, father,' I said. 'I have some good news. I got myself a job this morning.'

There was a silence down the phone, no immediate response.

I filled the gap. 'It's for a theatrical agency and I will be answering the telephone.' Still no reply. 'Well it's a start, father, isn't it?'

'I am happy for you,' he replied in a cheerless monotone, 'As you say, you have to start somewhere.'

'Is mum there?'

The phone was handed over without a goodbye.

'Father sounds terrible. I thought things were getting better.'

'He's just a little tired, but we are both looking forward to getting away.'

I told mother my good news and she was delighted, 'Whatever you do, Samuel, don't just walk out. We would prefer you to be sacked rather than give up.'

I promised that I would not 'abandon ship'. 'Have a wonderful holiday, mum, I'll be thinking of you.'

They were taking a trip to Italy – to Forte dei Marmi, a 1950s seaside town on the Tuscan coast, where they had spent their honeymoon; they were in dire need of a time away from England, where they had shared their life with their lost son. Italy, they hoped, would give them renewed strength.

* * *

I had made the call from an apartment on the first floor of a tall town house on the outskirts of Chelsea. I shared with Billy Naylor, a twenty-five-year-old Old Etonian with an enormous appetite for food, life and boys. For him, every day was a feast for the senses which he approached with the kindest of hearts and most capacious of stomachs. We had been introduced by chance at a dreary country weekend near Ipswich; his good-humoured superiority, as if he was talking to a new boy at school, tickled my imagination and I immediately turned to him for friendship. When travelling down by train on the Sunday night in a dusty carriage, he asked whether, for a nominal rent, I would like to move into his home.

'It's far cleaner than this,' he said, opening his mouth into a grin – slowly as if he were opening a tin of corned beef. I didn't hesitate, made it plain I liked women, crammed my bags and said goodbye to the parents.

Billy arrived home with a slam of the door and an extra large slice of pizza. He collapsed on to the sofa, sighed and flashed me a warm smile. Exhausted by his day, he grumbled about how awful his customers were. 'They are so bloody demanding,' he sighed, demonstrating that it was possible to eat an 'American Hot' and hold up one end of a conversation at the same time. He had been selling cassettes in Chappell's of Bond Street for the last year, and although he regularly complained about it, clearly loved showing off his knowledge of music. He offered to cook dinner to celebrate my newly found employment, but I had arranged to meet a group of friends at the Phoenix in Chelsea on Smith Street.

'Why don't you come with me?' I asked.

'I would not be seen dead there. That stuck-up public-school den . . . p–lease! I am going to the Sombrero Club tonight like every night . . . *Olé!*' And he clicked his fingers in mock flamenco style.

The following morning, I clambered out of bed, yawned hugely and took a much needed pee. In my semi-conscious state I meandered to the kitchen and there found someone about my age sitting at the table. It was not the first time that Billy had brought a stranger home. I said hello but got no reply. I went to the fridge and poured an orange juice and I offered him a glass, but again he did not answer. He was the most exotic of creatures: part American Indian maybe, touch of Chinese and a glimmer of Aborigine – a ravishing international mix.

'Isn't he lovely?' Billy asked, appearing at the door dressed in a navy-blue silk dressing gown, white stomach bursting out.

'Yes, gorgeous, Billy. Where is he from?'

'I'm still not sure. I asked, but he didn't want to answer.'

'I know how to find out. Don't move.'

In the living room a huge globe had been gathering dust since I moved in. His wealthy grandfather had left it to Billy in his will. He'd owned practically a whole English county up north, although all Billy inherited was 'that fucking lousy globe'. I slipped it from its axis and rolled the planet into the kitchen.

'Where are you from?' I spoke loudly, clearly and VERY slowly to our stranger. 'Put your finger on the country or city where you come from.' I was treating him like a simpleton, but it seemed the only way. He understood and began to search the globe, turning it around. He finally rested his middle finger on a city; I went in for a closer inspection.

'Brighton!' I shrieked. 'You are from Brighton?'

'Yes. B–rr–ight–on.'

I paused and it sank in with a thud. 'Billy, you fucking idiot, this guy is as deaf as a door knob!'

'That's strange,' Billy replied. 'I had a two-hour conversation with him at the club last night and he seemed absorbed.'

* * *

'The Kurzner Agency, can I help you? Just putting you through . . . thank you.'

This mantra fell from my mouth countless times in the

first few weeks of my very first job. I sat on an upright chair facing a small switchboard. The room had a mothball impersonality. It reminded me of a dentist's waiting-room, even a morgue. It had grey steel filing cabinets pushed against each wall and a sea-green overused carpet. It was painted like a hangover.

I was on time that first day, punctuality being a positive from my public-school training. Mrs Kurzner, as generous and welcoming as in the interview, greeted me warmly. Mr Kurzner kept his distance and continued to convey an air of disapproval. He said little, except for the occasional grunt when he shuffled by my desk every hour to have a pee in the lavatory by the small kitchen down a dark red corridor. He had a shock of ivory-coloured tousled hair and a deluge of dandruff drifted across the shoulders of his ill-fitting suit. His glasses hung around his neck and the knot of his tie fell to his second button. He had a habit of muttering to himself and it took a few days to realise that he was not talking to me as he walked past.

His secretary, Jackie, was always busy and dealt with everything with composure; she was the linchpin of the office, picking up the tapes from Mr Kurzner's dictating machine and typing out the letters with a speed that was a wonder to behold. As the previous telephonist had left on the Friday, it was Jackie's duty to talk me through the switchboard drill.

'If only one line is ringing, count to five and only after that respond. Never pick up immediately as it sounds desperate.'

She had an efficiency that was very attractive. She also had a habit of flicking back her long thick auburn hair and hitching her dress slightly above the knee when in conversation, and she sometimes used a scolding tone that I found most agreeable. The sharpness in her voice was, I believed, the legacy of an unhappy love affair. It was far too early to pry into such matters, so I left that observation on hold for the moment. It was, obvious, however, that a healthy competition existed between Jackie and Mrs Kurzner's secretary.

Margaret was well spoken, in her late twenties, slim, with short jet-black hair and eyes so blue they were almost violet. She dropped names: not the theatrical kind, but those of aristocrats and the rich socialites she regularly partied with.

'You must know Viscount Missenden, darling. He said the most disgusting thing on the phone to me the other day. Really, I had only met him once,' she warbled at our first meeting.

But it was only for effect and I liked her immediately. She was so damned attractive that I could only gaze wonderingly at her; fool that I was.

'What did that naughty man say to you?' I heard myself ask.

'You are far too young to hear such things,' came her flirtatious reply.

She had worked for Mrs Kurzner for ten years and clearly enjoyed the role. 'Mrs Kurzner is brilliant. Doesn't do much agency work any more, mind you, just plays the market with astute judgement and immense style. She regularly triples the funds that Mr Kurzner makes from the business.' She lowered her voice, 'They're Jews, of course, but the more attractive type, and to be sure I have nothing against the Hebes.' I let her foolish remark go; I believed she meant nothing by it.

The hours were relaxed. Lines opened at ten o'clock (a theatrical agency starts a little later than the average business), I had an hour for lunch and we closed at six. My first week skipped by, so occupied was I with answering the moderately busy phone, and when on the Friday I asked when I would receive my very first pay-packet, I found that we were not paid until the last Friday of the month. Luckily, I had some funds still hovering above the red in my bank account, so I decided that night I would go and celebrate not only that I had completed my first week of work but that I had also enjoyed it. I left the office feeling mighty pleased with myself.

*   *   *

The Phoenix public house on Smith Street, just off the King's Road in Chelsea, had become a meeting place for ex-public-school boys and girls. Being a member of that tribe, I gravitated to this long, smoky bar, loud with haughty voices, drawn to the 'posh' girls and the pool table in the back. More of a club than a pub, the place was full of regulars drinking their shorts and laughing at chinless jokes. But I was comfortable with the familiarity of language and of background. I had been educated among these people, and although I had spent most days trying to escape them, I was drawn to their world.

A regular there called Bella had caught my eye. She had a boy's haircut but that was the only thing about her that was masculine. She possessed a body that had me stumbling over my words, and in the weeks that I had been visiting the pub she was there every evening, looking even more tempting than the night before. Even so, I had yet to introduce myself. She was an outsider and that was attractive. I was daunted by the arrogance of her manner and the nonchalant way she avoided conversation with anyone who made an approach.

That night, I walked to the bar.

'Gin and tonic?' the barman suggested.

'Ah, no,' I answered. 'Pernod on the rocks, please, and make it a double.'

He took the green bottle of colourless liquid and carefully measured the amount. I drank the French pastis slowly, savouring it, meeting it for the first time and beginning to find out what it was really like.

The bitter drink hit the spot. 'Another one, please.' Instead of joining the signalling Earl of Amersham on the far side, I lingered at the bar. This was the night I was going to meet Bella. It was not long before all the gesturing enticed her. She walked over and oddly stuck out her tongue.

I puffed on my cigarette. 'What did you do that for?' I asked.

She chose not to answer and instinct immediately told me to keep clear; I could see either madness in her eyes or a disturbing absence of sensitivity. I ignored the warnings and bought her a drink, a large vodka and orange. We talked for some time in a desultory way. She was a little sullen and unforthcoming, perhaps because I could not keep my gaze off her breasts. We walked out into the dark night, along from the pub and down a side turning, Woodfall Street. We began to kiss under the street sign and its name jumped out at me every time I came up for air. Woodfall had been a most obnoxious twit at school, with a squeaky voice and dreary jokes. I cursed his memory – it was spoiling this high-octane moment.

Bella stroked my hair and kissed my mouth gently. I lowered my head and started to kiss those breasts; how flawless. I wondered if she knew how sublime her body was. How many boys had worshipped her after touching this skin? I wanted her right there, but she pushed me away as I became more and more teenage in my excitement.

'I don't think that this is the appropriate spot, do you?' she said, suddenly becoming a schoolmistress.

'Would you like to come back to my place then?' I asked, tucking my shirt back into my trousers.

'Not before I know your name.'

'My name is Sam, or Samuel if you prefer.'

'Sam will do . . . by the way, my name is Bella.'

'Bella it is.' And we walked away from the pub with a quickened step, ready to have sex.

* * *

I went into the kitchen to fetch her a glass of wine and was glad when she made short work of it. I was in a hurry, as only young boys know how to be. We undressed quickly; in fact, Bella was swifter, as I was unable to slip my boots off easily. One of them got stuck, and in my desperation to dislodge it, I kicked far too aggressively and it flew high into the air and on its way down struck the lamp perched on the side table; it fell and splintered. I smiled, as if that was all part of my act, avoided the smashed glass and jumped into the bed to hold her close and keep her from the draught that swept under my door. I started to kiss her mouth and as the minutes went by ventured on a fantasy I had entertained countless times at school.

'Can I call you "matron"?' I asked hestitantly.

'You can call me what you like!'

I ran my fingers through her hair and she dug her long fingernails into my back like thorns. My eyes focused on her languid face. She played her role like a seasoned actress, and when we had finished, I was ready to go on the next act

'God, you are so beautiful,' I whispered.

'And you talk too much,' she said, moving away from me. Her sulky demeanour had returned and she lit a cigarette. Her dark and wounded look suggested the brooding detachment of one returning to the cellars of a traumatic childhood. A sense of self-loathing permeated the room. I moved over to offer my hand, but she drew back and said, 'Don't be silly, I am not drunk any more.'

I retreated to my side of the bed, turned my back and tried to understand her pain.

* * *

My head was beneath the sheets the next morning. I lay there half asleep, but aware that Bella had gone to the bathroom to run herself a bath. The smell of her hair was still on the sheets.

I had returned to my dreams when a terrifying scream from the bathroom shattered the peace. Bella scrambled back into the bedroom and literally dived into the bed and under the covers; her face had turned white. She was uttering indecipherable sounds.

'Calm down and tell me what's wrong.'

She pointed to the bathroom, her index finger shaking with agitation.

'A snake! A bloody *snake* was in my bath!' she screamed.

'Hey, hold on, snakes don't hang out in West London. Or perhaps you have been seeing snakes all night and it's all in your mind?'

'This is not the time to joke. Go in there and see for yourself and then get rid of it!'

She was genuinely petrified. I left the bed and decided to pull on my jeans and boots, just in case there *was* a snake . . . As I approached the bathroom, I heard running water. Bella in her panic must have forgotten to turn off the tap. I pushed open the door and hurried to the overflowing bath. I pulled the plug and the water started to drain. I checked the medicine cabinet and pulled the clothes from the laundry basket. The washbasin was empty. There was definitely no snake, just a pool of water on the floor.

'Not a snake in sight.' I wrapped my arms around her waist and hungered for more sex.

She shoved me away in distaste and returned to the

crime scene. 'Well it was there and it was long – endless – and had hideous green and blue markings. Jesus, it was horrible . . . what sort of weird apartment is this?'

She stifled a yawn, looked at her watch and saw it was eight o'clock. She had flown before ten past. 'Next time, let's go to my place.' And she slammed the door behind her, without a kiss or a thank-you.

'How ungrateful!' I thought and lit an early cigarette before making myself a black coffee. I deduced that she had made the whole thing up just to get out of the apartment . . . double quick. Was I that uncharismatic?

Later that evening, Billy had again gone to fetch some takeaway pizza from the Pizza Express on the corner of the Fulham Road. We were munching away on our American Hot, with capers, and half-watching an episode of *The Old Grey Whistle Test*. Our legs stretched out, we gossiped about our jobs and the vacillation of my friend's love life. Billy was drinking from a bottle of 7-Up and occasionally picking up *The Times* to pencil a solution into the crossword puzzle. Without warning, he said in a calm voice, 'Samuel, there is a huge snake under the television set!'

I lowered my eyes and indeed there was, and it was at least two feet long. This was no ordinary grass snake; it looked like a killer. Clearly, it was lost, angry and not keen to hang out in a Chelsea apartment, however warm and well appointed.

I threw my pizza over my shoulder and darted through the door of the living room, which I slammed behind me. I thought I had no fear of snakes, but I was wrong.

'Get rid of it,' I shouted at Billy through the door.

'Let me out, do you hear, Samuel. Let me out NOW!'

I opened the door a fraction and threw in a saucepan, which I had grabbed from the kitchen. 'Use this,' I ordered and quickly slammed the door again.

I heard cursing and the sound of furniture being moved. Then came the crash of tables being overturned, lights smashing and the tumbling of books. The clamour grew louder and louder. Then, wallop, the sound of the saucepan clearly missing its target. Billy's breathing was becoming audible – and then suddenly there was silence. I gingerly opened the door, half-expecting that it was Billy who had fallen. He was exhausted but fine, sweating profusely all over his red bloated face.

'It is done,' he puffed.

The flat snake lay motionless, inches from where we'd first seen it.

'What have you done?' I asked.

'Don't give me that. I did the dirty work, now you can get rid of the evidence.'

I went to the kitchen and found a black plastic bag. I rolled up my sleeves and with yellow washing-up gloves picked up the dead snake.

'Where shall I put it?'

'Anywhere, but not in this apartment.' Billy's voice was steady but uncompromising.

I went into the cold, darkened street and lifted up one of the gratings. I threw the snake down the deep black drain into the sewer, and before walking away, crossed myself. The splash of water confirmed that the job was done.

'Where do you think it came from?' I asked.

'Probably from the zoo.'

'Maybe we should have called the RSPCA,' I wondered, beginning to feel a little guilty.

'Well, it's too late now – and don't forget, if the RSPCA turns up, it was your idea to kill it,' replied Billy, pigging into his cold pizza.

* * *

The bus took thirty minutes to reach Green Park tube station and work. Christmas was looming and skimpy decorations hung along our route. The Fulham Road so early looked cold and deserted. Harrods in Brompton Road was dressed like an old tart trying to lure a punter through the door.

I thought of the time when my mother took my brother and me to the toy department to meet Father Christmas. I must have been six as my brother had just passed his Common Entrance to his public school, Montgomery House. That night he was going to his first black-tie ball, the Feathers at the Lyceum in the Aldwych.

'Don't be long now,' instructed my mother as my brother took hold of my hand to search for Father Christmas. We found him on the fifth floor and joined the slow-moving queue.

'What would you like for Christmas?' the jovial over-fed gentleman asked me.

'To go to the Feathers Ball tonight with my brother,' I answered.

He gave a curious twitch of a smile and spoke softly. 'One day, when you are older, I'm sure your brother will take you.'

And my brother gave me a kiss that lingered on my cheek and said, 'That won't be long, Sam. We'll go together very soon.' And the memory of the warm generosity in his voice stirred within me as the bus passed Harrods that day. I choked and wept silently, my face turned towards the window so that no one could see my tears – just like I did when I was sent away to preparatory school at the age of nine.

* * *

'Just putting you through . . . ' I was becoming good at dealing with irritating incoming calls while having a gossip with one of the girls.

'I really think, Samuel, that you should have called

animal rescue. I mean, it was as good as murder.' Margaret was upset at hearing my account of the previous evening.

'But you should have seen the size of it! Billy had to act quickly.'

'Yes, with you urging him on, that I can see.'

'You're right. Sorry. I suppose I wasn't thinking.'

'Well, you should have thought,' and she wagged her index finger close to my face. I pinched her firm bottom as she turned; I couldn't resist.

'Don't touch what you can't afford, young man.'

'I have more cash than you think.'

I gave a half-smile but Margaret ignored my overture. Her check-tweed suit fitted tightly over her curves. Her hair was brushed back and her face was open and intelligent. I sighed too loudly and felt a longing that was beginning to feel uncomfortable. She turned on her heel to continue her day. I remained grimacing at my lack of maturity. Oh, to be a man and no longer a callow boy.

* * *

As I turned into our street that evening, a chill December wind gusted into my face, and I cupped my hands and blew warm air on them. I searched for the house keys while walking. I did not want to have to stop to find them and freeze when I got to the front door of the building; it had turned that cold. I was roused from my daydreaming by the sound of someone knocking on a window. I jumped and look around in alarm. It was my neighbour on the first floor. Lady Eliston was trying to attract my attention.

Lord and Lady Eliston owned the entire house next door. When most of the buildings in the street had been converted into apartments, the Elistons had been wealthy enough to resist exorbitant offers from speculators keen to transform their town house into flats. They were wonderfully friendly, wildly eccentric and were never short of a kind word or offer of help. Both in their mid-fifties, they had two children, Sarah, a sixteen-year-old with 'trouble' stamped on her forehead, and fourteen-year-old Charlie, who attended Eton in accordance with family tradition.

'Sam, can I have a word?' Her ladyship, braving the cold, had opened the window. She was now calling down to the street. 'My poor dear Charlie is distraught.' I was beginning to feel a twisted knot of apprehension in my stomach. 'The unfortunate boy has lost his pet snake. If you see it, do please let us know; it's large, very rare and perfectly harmless.'

I was standing on top of the grating. 'Absolutely, Lady Eliston. I will keep my eyes open.'

She wished me a good evening and closed the window. In an agony of guilt, I let myself into my building.

* * *

Margaret and Jackie decorated the Christmas tree with elaborate taste. It became their passion for a full two days. The girls described it as having a country theme: silver tinsel on every branch; painted glass baubles originally manufactured in the Ore Mountains over eighty years before; popcorn scattered within the fir; and solid-silver Asprey trinkets hanging on the stouter branches. There were sweets, wax dolls, strings of almonds and raisins. The candles were to be lit only for one night when the Kurzners had their Christmas office party.

'Mrs Kurzner wants the finest decorated tree in England,' announced Margaret.

Underneath the tree, presents had already begun to accumulate. I could see most were from the Kurzners to their staff and to their wayward son Ian, whom I had yet to meet, but who, by reputation, was a creep.

'You've got one,' Margaret said, delving into the pile and finding a small box with my name on it: ' "For Sam. Thank you for all you do. Happy Christmas." ' The box could not have been more than four inches long and three inches wide. She shook it, but there was no sound. 'It's clearly very expensive. None of their presents are cheap, and yours . . . well, it's probably Cartier cuff-links or something like that. Must have a cost a fortune. You'll have to buy them something special.'

'They like a generous present,' Jackie concurred.

I lifted the box to my nose: it smelled of wealth. Mrs Kurzner must like me far more than I had imagined. I had to reciprocate in similar style. So, during my lunch break, I visited Billy at his record store seeking advice.

'Give them a Barry Manilow album! Marvellous present.'

'They have probably bought me Cartier cuff-links and you're suggesting a Barry Manilow record. Are you crazy?'

I hurried out of the store and headed to Asprey. Snow had fallen all morning and the roof-tops were covered in a thick layer. A man slowed my pace as he spread grit on the pavement. Everyone was muffled up against the cold. The store was very welcoming, with a gust of warm air greeting my entrance. The prices were way above my budget, but I didn't want to be perceived as a man lacking in taste. The pale, heart-shape-faced assistant with finely pencilled eyebrows offered discreet advice. Her high cheekbones gave her an air of infallibility and after a good fifty minutes she had sold me a stately cigarette lighter – the type that sits on your coffee table and never works: expensive and bloody useless. I returned to the office clutching the gift-wrapped box, and tucked it under the tree, poorer but confident I had done the right thing.

* * *

'Let's open the presents!' squealed an excited Margaret, when the entire staff was gathered round the tree before the office Christmas party. Mr Kurzner had offered us warm punch in plastic glasses. It was our second serving and we were already seasonably merry. The Kurzners' only son, twenty-five-year-old oddball Ian, had joined us. He ran an antiquarian bookshop in Upper Street in Islington that by all accounts sold little and was bankrolled by his parents. His grey suit gave the appearance of having been slept in for weeks and his tie had dried milk splashes all over it. The expression on his face was hard to read and his skin was as pale as the snow outside. He stood far too close to Jackie, and when he attempted conversation she retreated with distaste.

'I hardly ever leave my shop. I even sleep there,' he told me, and I knew he wasn't kidding. He was a creep and I, too, backed away from his ugly smell, hanging in the air like a fog out of season.

'Yes, open yours, Samuel . . . ' Jackie pleaded.

'No, I think it's the tradition for my parents to open their presents first,' Ian interrupted.

I looked under the tree and found the expensively wrapped violet box. I handed it to Mrs Kurzner.

'Thank you, Samuel. You really shouldn't have.'

'It's my pleasure.'

In one wrench my highly priced offering was revealed. Her eyes widened and she sighed, 'An Asprey lighter. What a thoughtful present. Far too generous and so expensive, but thank you, Samuel. I shall put it just there.' She pushed a pile of files aside and the lighter sat in the middle of her desk.

'You should open yours now, Samuel.' Mrs Kurzner, on her fifth glass of punch, found it lying to the side of the tree, sitting divinely small at the bottom of a heap. And like the way Charlie unwrapped his chocolate bar in *Charlie and the Chocolate Factory* to discover his golden ticket, I peeled the silver wrapping paper slowly and carefully at first and then, in the rush of excitement, lost control and ripped it right off – to find, yes, to find a pack of Camel cigarettes.

'I heard they were your favourite,' beamed Mrs Kurzner.

* * *

Actors drowned their sorrows in top-heavy drinks and mingled through the main room. For most, it had not been a good year, months out of work and few interviews. The Christmas party was an excuse to get drunk and complain about everything and anything, especially their hosts.

'And you are . . . ?' asked an ageing theatrical roué who looked spookily like Clark Gable. We spoke near to the Christmas tree, which now had its candles lit and was a credit to the girls' hard work.

'I joined the company in October.'

'Ah, you are that charming boy who picks up the phone. You do a marvellous job.' Without pausing, he piled into his résumé. 'I am an actor, you know? Of course, you know. I have worked with Kubrick, Lean and – the greatest of them – old Hitch.'

'Old Hitch?' I asked.

'Hitchcock, you silly boy. You know, *North by North West*, *Strangers on a Train*, *Vertigo*.'

'You have worked with Alfred Hitchcock?'

'Yes, not big parts mind you. More like walk-ons, but he was definitely fond of me. You see, I have a mysterious face.' There was a restlessness about him, as if he were in search of a more important person to talk too.

I started to scan the room for rescue. 'These candles give off a really soft light. Very flattering to your features,' I said, my mind on escape.

'Do you think so?' the actor asked, warming to the theme. 'In rep they are so lazy with the lighting. I have just completed *Henry V* at the De Montfort Theatre in Leicester and really . . . '

A hand grabbed mine and pulled me away to safety. It was Margaret, now changed into an elegant black dress and looking more alluring than ever.

'Do you think I am too young for you?' I asked.

'For what?' she replied with an evident smile.

She guided me around the room and introduced the growing number of clients looking for attention. She taught me that night that actors were fundamentally never happy, even if you found them the best job in the world. 'The next day they'll be sure they'll never work again,'

I laughed, not believing she was serious.

She was serious and said firmly, 'It's no laughing matter.'

'But how do you know? Have you ever found an actor a great job?'

'Yes! Ronnie Allen over there has been in *Crossroads* for some years now.' And she pointed to a slim, tanned, handsome forty-something holding court in the corner. I could not argue with that.

Suddenly, without warning, the temperature in the room changed. The agency's leading actor, the Star, had arrived. The whole balance of the room shifted as this famous British Film Star made his entrance. Mrs Kurzner dropped her conversation with an over-eager playwright mid-sentence and walked over to greet him. His ten per cent paid for the year's rent and part of our wages. I had been briefed in my first week that, should the Film Star call, I must drop everything else and put him through as fast as possible. I watched as he walked around the room with a manner that was both modest and dignified. He was perfectly relaxed inside his skin and I admired the aura of success surrounding him. Yes, he was a star, and I loved the way he knew it without showing a hint of arrogance (well, a bit, but it was well hidden).

I went over and asked whether he would like a drink. He replied in a voice familiar from the screen, 'Just a glass of champagne, thank you.'

I went into the kitchen to find the waiter who was pouring the Dom Perignon into fresh glasses.

'You can't have that!' the waiter snarled.

'It's not for me, you fool, it's for the Star,' I snapped, grabbed one and delivered it swiftly.

The Film Star thanked me and remarked what a smart jacket I had on. I thanked him back and said it was a gift from my father. 'Fine style,' he said. 'Fine style.' He shook my hand and moved on; it was like meeting a ruling monarch.

'He liked you, that's for sure,' Margaret whispered and ordered me to follow her. I went like a stray dog in hope of a morsel of food. We walked through the side door of the office and found the script room. Banks of scripts, in alphabetical order, were arranged on wooden shelves.

She leaned towards me and started to kiss my mouth. She was older and I felt comfortable that she was in control. Our kisses built with affection followed by enthusiasm. My heart was beating a drum roll. She groaned and then bit my neck and I drew her close. I lifted her dress and could see her black panties out of the corner of my eye. In one firm action I peeled them down and off. I felt like a magician who conjures a bird from his hand. (Yes, it was a trick that worked like magic, but it was one that I have never been able to repeat or even get near to again.) The panties ended up on the script of *Buck Rogers in the Twenty-Fifth Century*. She unbuckled my belt and pulled my trousers down to my knees. How I had dreamed of this ever since I began working in the office: the illicit sex, the rush of blood, the headiness of a furtive affair; I was with someone I had long desired and the tension and pleasure were overwhelming.

'I want to go to the ocean and feel the sand on my back and your . . . '

She stopped me talking by kissing me again. I was about to pull her body closer to mine when a stampede of feet thundered outside our hiding place. The sound of panic was unmistakable and we dressed hastily without a word. Opening the door, I bumped right into the fleeing Film Star, who had shed all trace of his leading-man composure.

'Is there something wrong?'

'A bloody fire!' he yelled, as if projecting to the back stalls, and then vanished from view down the stairs to the safety of the street.

The inevitable had happened. A candle had fallen into the branches of the Christmas tree and started a blaze. The room had emptied and Ian, who had spent most of the night trying to corner Jackie, was throwing buckets of water over the tree in a vain attempt to quench the fire which, in fact, was not as threatening as the Film Star's actions had implied. I grabbed a glass soda-fountain and squirted it at the flames. It made little difference, but it was not long before they started to die down anyway. By the time the fire engine screeched to a halt out in the square, with bells ringing, the fire was over, as was the party.

Any further thought of sex that evening was clearly out, for when I looked for her, Margaret was crying inconsolably in the arms of her co-worker and fellow tree installer, Jackie. Their proud work had nearly caused the whole building to be burned down and they looked mortified. I left, wishing all a Happy Christmas, but everyone was distracted and my words fell on deaf ears. I walked away from Berkeley Square frustrated. Only minutes before I had been experiencing a surge of uncontrollable excitement. Now I felt all alone in the world, without a friend. I caught a taxi in Piccadilly and asked the driver to drop me at my home address.

'A good time?' asked the cabbie.

'Not particularly,' I answered. 'In truth, it was a little disappointing.'

'I wouldn't worry about that. It's what makes life interesting. The thrill is not knowing how everything will turn out.'

'How right you are,' I replied, gazing out of the blurred window at the falling sleet against the blackness of the night.

* * *

Christmas was over quickly; I had spent the week with Aunt Flo and cousin Rupert and their friends the Pilkingtons, a kind family who represented England at its best. My parents had decided to return to the sun and spend the holiday in the Caribbean. I was invited, but chose to remain in England and go to parties and get drunk. When they left, they gave me a generous cheque to buy something to 'keep me warm'. I missed them. My relationship with my father had continued to grow stronger throughout the year, and although our conversation remained stilted, there was undeniable warmth; things were better. I found a phone just after the stroke of midnight, and with a background commotion of bursting balloons and animated upper-class cheer, the three of us toasted in the New Year. 'To you, our darling boy!' screamed my mother down the phone, shrugging off her sadness and focusing on the present. They were coming to terms with their loss and that was the best Christmas present of all.

* * *

'The Kurzner Agency . . . just putting you through . . . thank you.'

The fire did not cause any lasting damage. Except for a

ruined sea-green carpet, all was as before. Mrs Kurzner juggled her stocks and clients and Mr Kurzner dealt with his long-drawn-out telephone conversations and weighty correspondence. Each day, a client would call and complain. I was learning that no one was satisfied and everyone was looking for a new agent – even the ones who were getting work. The New Year heralded a new beginning. For many of us, this means doing things like joining a health club to become fit – 'I am going to lose weight this year' – and actors are no different. The number of calls tripled that first week, with actors and playwrights all calling, full of optimism, to mark early January with a promising job interview. It was going to be their year, they believed. Often they brought a small gift of a bottle of wine or a box of chocolates, just to remind the Kurzners that they were still alive and that they needed work.

Margaret, with whom I had spent time in the script room on very intimate terms, was now distant and cold as the January temperature outside. I asked how she was, but she hurried away without making any reply.

Jackie was friendlier. During one lunch break she confessed that some months earlier she had slept with Ian Kurzner, the spindly son and creep. I was staggered, repulsed and interested, all at the same time. Whenever his name was mentioned, she had always maintained that he gave her the shivers and she found him repugnant.

'I was lonely, and had got chatting to him after a few drinks at the office summer party,' Jackie told me mournfully, 'and, well, one thing led to another.'

I pressed her for more gory details.

'Well, in all honesty, it was OK at the time. He was tender, generous and whispered undying love. I suppose I needed it.'

I was standing by the window, listening with rapt attention and eating my sandwich too fast.

'He's strange though and I'm unsettled. He calls every day now and sends flowers. I've seen his car parked over the road quite a few times in the evenings. Last night, he was waiting on my doorstep, playing me a Barry White song on a portable cassette player.'

'Which song?' I asked.

' "Never, Never Gonna Give You Up",' she replied. The poor girl was scared. She returned to her typing with a deep sigh.

'He sounds like a bloody lunatic. If he continues, I'd talk to Mrs Kurzner, if I were you,' I advised lamely.

* * *

Mrs Kurzner had noticed that since my return from the holiday break I was (as she put it) 'a little reserved'. I was sitting in their office talking to her about my Christmas; Mr Kurzner was getting some exercise by taking the short walk to the script room to fetch a copy of *Buck Rogers in the Twenty-Fifth Century* for an actress he had just signed. Their office seemed bigger since the carpet had overnight been replaced by a carpet of a pumpkin shade which gave everyone a West Coast glow.

Our chat was suddenly interrupted by the return of her husband. Hanging from his index finger was a pair of black knickers.

'I found these in the script room!' he said, twirling the lingerie around.

Margaret walked in and let out an involuntary scream as if she had just seen a mouse.

'They must belong to one of our actresses. Hanky-panky, I dare say, at the office party. Shall I send out a letter to see if anyone claims them?' Mr Kurzner licked his thin bluish lips.

'I don't think that will be necessary, Bernard. And Bernard . . . '

'Yes, my dear.'

'Put the knickers down and away from your face.'

* * *

I was becoming restless. It had been the same at school, after a dozen or so weeks I got itchy feet. I had done my job well and was respectful and always punctual. But my time in this establishment had run its course, and I was looking for an escape.

'Can I speak to Mr Kurzner?' an irritated voice barked from the other end of a transatlantic line.

I explained that both Mr and Mrs Kurzner were out of the office for the day. The irate caller ranted that he had been trying to reach Mr Kurzner for four 'fucking' weeks.

'Can I take a message, sir?'

'Listen, kid, back before Christmas I made a generous offer of a hundred thousand dollars for six weeks' work, and still no answer! He is a television star, for Christ's sake, and this is a movie, a lead role.' The producer remonstrated in an irritated mid-Atlantic drawl.

I could only apologise and promise that I would try my utmost to reach the agent.

'He has until six o'clock this evening, UK time. I will call at six on the dot. If you don't have an answer, the deal is off. There are plenty of other actors in this world who'd kill for a part like this!' He slammed down the phone.

If I'd learned anything during those few months on the job, it was that agents do not return phone calls, however important they might be.

* * *

Snow fell in London that day. Not the usual amount that powdered the car and thawed by breakfast, but a heavy fall. Berkeley Square Garden looked by lunchtime to have large balls of cotton wool as schoolchildren had been playing there all morning. I walked through, picking up some snow and shaping a snowball ready to throw at an unsuspecting victim. I had discovered a greasy-spoon cafe on the corner of Hanover Square, and whenever I needed a filling lunch, I made my way over there. Kathy, the owner, a middle-aged cockney, had from heavy smoking turned as grey as the pavement. Her hair was dyed red and her nails might have been filed in a pencil sharpener. If you looked closely enough she had five chins. 'Soup for you today?' she said as I walked in.

Comfortably alone, I sat sipping hot broth and gazing out of the broad window. The thaw had begun and the bare branches dripped water on to the heads of the passers-by. I had lost myself in contemplating the slushy grey puddles when from nowhere an idea struck me, an idea so crafty that I knew that I would be out of a job by the morning and still receive the allowance my father had promised since the summer. How liberating to be that brilliant naughty boy again.

I recognised that if I simply walked out of the agency, my father would not take that lightly. I would be unable to keep the news from him because he had called the office regularly ever since I started. I had also received a warning from mother that quitting 'would simply not do'. I would have to be fired and now I knew how that could be arranged.

I rushed the bill and gave Kathy an excited kiss on her cheek – and, believe me, I must have been excited.

'You look as if you've just won the pools, love.'

'Not exactly but nearly. Tomorrow morning, I will be in here at a quarter past ten. Have a hot chocolate ready for me, darling.'

'Why so flippin' early tomorrow?' she asked.

'Because I'm going to get fired by five past!'

* * *

Dead on six o'clock, the American producer called. The Atlantic delay on the line didn't help, nor did the echo, but I knew how the call was going to go.

'Can I speak to Mr Kurzner?'

'He isn't here, sir, but I do have a message for you,' I said in my newly acquired agent tone.

'And what is that?' His voice was sharp and aggressive.

'That the offer of a hundred thousand dollars is not acceptable, and he will not do it for less than two hundred thousand.' The producer, disbelieving his ears, asked me to repeat what I had just said. He followed his request with an outpouring of abuse.

'It's two hundred thousand dollars or nothing, sir.'

There was a pause before his final vehement message: 'Now you listen to me, you son of a bitch. First you can tell that actor to stuff the job up his ass, and second, as for the agency, I will never deal with you guys again. Do you hear? This is an absolute fucking bullshit disgrace – GOODBYE!'

He slammed down the phone.

My deed had been successfully carried out. By the morning, news would have filtered through that the incompetent telephonist had blown a big commission.

'How could someone be so stupid? I never liked him!' I could almost hear Mr Kurzner's voice.

* * *

The Embassy Club in Bond Street was packed. The dance floor upstairs was a scrum of bodies gyrating. I walked through to the balcony. There I was caught up in the music, people's smiles and the overdose of laughter. But then I noticed a figure standing at the other end of the balcony, half hidden, alone. Her back straight as a pikestaff, a look of self-assurance on her face, she had the arrogant air of a

Salian empress. Transfixed, I didn't feel my friend David's hand on my shoulder.

'She is way out of your league,' he joked.

I laughed, jumped out of my trance, and the two of us sauntered downstairs to get ourselves a drink. It was good to see my friend again. David had had his hair cropped, had a light Californian tan and had been using weights; he was changed since we shared our lives at public school. Shortly after our expulsion, his father (the third Earl of Amersham) had died in a riding accident. His horse had been frightened by a passing express train and the late earl fell headfirst and broke his neck. 'The last time we were together, he gave me a hard time for being a failure,' David said with lingering bitterness. To add to his sorrow, his childless older brother (the fourth Earl) had subsequently also died when his light aircraft crashed into the Amazonian forest. He adored his older brother, as I had mine; because of his death he inherited a title and estate that he never thought would be his. But although David and I were close and shared the horror of loss, we rarely talked about our innermost grief. There had always been hesitation in his manner so it was good to see, on the surface anyway, a burgeoning confidence.

Before I could say anything else to David, the figure on the balcony was making her way downstairs to buy herself a drink. We came face to face, and I offered her a glass of champagne, which she accepted; her name was Carolina. In her broken English, she spoke of her work as an actress. She had just finished filming a movie in Stockholm.

'What a pity,' I said. 'Until precisely six o'clock this evening I was in the movie business, but I decided it was time to move on. If only things had been different, I might have been able to help.'

Her empty champagne glass stood beside the full ashtray and as she added another stub to the pile she asked for my number. I scribbled it on the inside of an Embassy match-book. She then left without even a kiss.

'That was quick work!' David laughed.

Ravenously hungry, we ordered dinner from the restaurant to the side of the bar.

'And how is California?' I asked.

'Liberating! I'm having a ball. The women are amazing and so is the weather.'

He held his glass of malt whisky in a peculiar way – all fingers wrapped round it, whole hand like a bunch of bananas; he was the only other person I had ever met who held his glass in that way. I had always assumed the style was exclusively mine. Perhaps we were both holding on to something and couldn't let go?

'And what about the estate?'

'My estate manager runs it and I plan to visit at least three times a year. Things couldn't be better. In fact, I think they prefer me being away!'

He finished his whisky and made the gesture of tipping a glass towards his throat to the waiter.

The flavour of our pasta reminded us of summer and the delicious wine conjured up the vineyards of France. I longed for the hot weather. The winter still had us in its grip and I itched to get away.

'I'll be out of a job tomorrow so I'll have time on my hands.' I told him about my afternoon's work. 'So why don't I come and see you?'

'You will love it in Los Angeles. I bet you won't want to come home.'

Then David excused himself and went to the loo, while I stretched out my legs and took a long drink. He returned five minutes later, rubbing his nose and carrying a small silver box.

'Taken drugs?' I asked matter-of-factly.

'Yes, it's what I do these days. All in moderation, of course.' And as he spoke he took some small pills out of the silver tin. He gulped them down with another large whisky. 'TNT,' he said, half choking.

'Of course. Won't blow up, will you?'

* * *

I woke the following morning with no feeling of trepidation, only the certainty that I would be returning home in time for a siesta. I had a warm shower and brushed my teeth vigorously, humming at the same time 'One Of These Nights' by the Eagles; I was in a fine mood.

Billy was making a cup of coffee, and over breakfast we decided to miss the bus and share a taxi to Berkeley Square. Traces of snow could still be seen in gardens and on roof-tops, but the streets were now clear. It was a crisp bright morning, though the bitter chill remained; the heat of a taxi was a welcome alternative to the long wintry wait at the Fulham Road bus stop. The traffic edged slowly; bad weather generally paralyses London, but when it snows, the chaos is total. I glanced at my watch as Knightsbridge was at a standstill; I didn't want to be late on my final day; that would not do.

By the time we reached the office, I was thirty minutes late and irritated. The axe was about to fall and I was not at my post. I climbed the stairs, tapping on the banister, visualising Mrs Kurzner waiting at my desk with a face of disappointment and a lecture on how 'she had been let down'. The building smelled of something familiar, like burned toast. How odd I hadn't noticed that before. I opened the door and heard a murmur. I saw my desk had a huge bunch of flowers, red roses, lying on it. Strange, I reflected automatically, why hasn't anyone put them into a vase? I walked into the office and a spontaneous ripple of applause grew and built into a cheer, led from the front by a beaming Mr and Mrs Kurzner.

'In all my fifty years of business, I have never seen such initiative, such flare! You are an inspiration to us all and we are proud that you are part of our team.' Mr Kurzner was talking directly to *me*! 'We plan to take you off this desk and promote you to Head of Young Artists, with immediate effect.' I stood stunned and bewildered. My face still registering shock, I leaned my hand against the filing cabinet to get my balance. Holy shit, what had I done?

I would now be representing all the actors under the age of thirty and be given the office next to the owners and overlooking the square. Mr Kurzner shook my hand. 'I thought you were a bit of a waster, a fool, an imbecile, when you first came in, but I admit I was wrong.'

'Well, thank you, Mr Kurzner. I am glad I proved you right . . . I mean wrong.'

'We'd better put that advertisement back in the *Evening News*.'

The producer had called and reluctantly accepted the counter-offer of two hundred thousand dollars. The contract was being sent over later that day. Margaret, who had barely even said hello since Christmas, cosied up and gave me a full kiss on my mouth. 'You brilliant genius of a boy.' Jackie had run out and bought the flowers and Mrs Kurzner called me into her office and heaped praise on her protégé. Heck, this was much more fun than getting the sack!

My new office was small and welcoming. It had a throne-like chair that looked as if it had been pinched from the Palace of Versailles and an elegant desk with a dark-blue leather panel on the top. The tall window looked out on the topmost branches of Berkeley Square's trees. I closed the door, leaned back in my chair and placed my winter boots on the desk, my hands locked behind my head; this was my new home, my domain, and now it had come my way, I was going to enjoy it.

I hurriedly called my mother and father and broke the news of my promotion and they cooed; well my mother did. My father had suspicion in his voice. 'Tell me exactly what happened?' he demanded; no fool he. And eventually I spoke to Billy, who had been left waiting in the cafe for my grand 'unemployed' entrance. His booming laugh nearly shattered the phone.

'Maybe, Billy, I did it on purpose because I saw the opportunity to double the money for the actor. Perhaps I had vision?'

' "Because I saw the opportunity to double the money"? Don't be such a tosser!' Billy said, still bellowing.

Before my very eyes, I saw the birth of a monster, someone who believed his own hype, his own lies; I could be a great agent, I mused.

* * *

'You're wanted on the phone,' Billy called out, munching on yet another pizza.

'You must stop eating all that crap.' I castigated my friend.

On the line was a voice I didn't instantly recognise. It was Carolina from the other night.

'Shall we meet for dinner?' she asked.

'Absolutely,' I replied, although a sixth sense warned 'not so fast'. I chose to ignore the alarm bells and booked a table at the local fashionable Italian.

The window table at the San Frediano restaurant on the Fulham Road had an added advantage. It opened on to the cosmopolitan thoroughfare and therefore diners could be seen by the Chelsea locals. Social climbers blended with London's gossip-column names to fill the noisy space. They were an ambitious crowd, media types rather than intellectuals. The cooking was classic Italian and the clientele more likely to order spaghetti bolognese than the fish.

Carolina was running late, and by the time she arrived, I had read and reread the menu. She apologised, composed herself and gave me a puzzled smile. She wore a blue strapless dress and carried herself as if she were a ballerina. 'Do you mind if we change tables?' she asked; not the finest of starts. I grinned and called over Roberto, the friendly and affectionate owner, who clicked his fingers and rearranged the seating without a hint of irritation, although his restaurant was crowded. We were now in the far corner, surrounded by a coat rack, close to the men's cloakroom. '*Perfetto*,' she said.

I lit her cigarette and she took in a lungful of smoke. Her eyes remained fixed and she spoke softly but in an inflexible tone. Each time someone passed our table to go to the loo, cold air from the door reached my face. I asked about her career and it consisted of two semi-pornographic films and a commercial for a vacuum cleaner in her native Sweden. I nodded appreciatively. 'Sounds like you're doing well!' And then from nowhere she dropped a bomb into the conversation.

'My boyfriend said that he would kill anyone I was seen out with.'

I signalled my waiter for a whisky. 'You are joking, of course?'

She shook her head. 'I like you and I'm ready to risk my life and probably yours so that we can be together.'

I thought I was dreaming; my mouth went dry. It was her tone of voice when she used the word 'kill'. I knew she was being serious; she had that pathological intensity about her.

'His name is Stefano Santorini, you may have heard of him . . . no?' she said, as if sharing with me something evil.

It rang a disturbing bell. Now I was the one lighting a cigarette. Santorini, Stefano Santorini; the clean-shaven skull-like head popped into my memory extremely clearly. Hadn't he been splashed over the papers, having featured in a trial that had recently collapsed, the one involving gang warfare in the East End? The headline in the *Daily Mail* had been 'ARE THE ITALIAN MAFIA HERE IN OUR CITY?' My appetite was gone. I called the waiter over and asked for the bill, and quick.

'Are you crazy? You are the girlfriend of some Mafia boss?'

She shook her head when she should have been nodding. I didn't hesitate; resolutely, I threw the cash on to the table and hurried to the door.

Roberto and Carolina chased after me.

'Wasn't the food OK, Mr Alexander?' asked the concerned owner.

'Roberto, the food was fine ... it's the girl that's the problem. I have just found out that I'm having dinner with the girlfriend of Stefano Santorini.'

'Stefano Santorini?' he stuttered, crossing himself.

I stormed into the street in search of a cab. This was not the time to hang around. Carolina snatched at my arm but I pulled away, deaf to her cries of, 'Don't leave!' Her voice became shriller. By the time my taxi was hurtling down the Fulham Road, my nerves were jumping like needles on scratched vinyl. I double-locked the front door and, out of breath, I collapsed on to the sofa. Billy was away for a week's 'gay tour' of Marrakesh; I was alone. My bed was unmade and I thought of diving in for an early night; my mouth had a peculiar taste, it was called fear. The ringing phone broke the silence. I blinked and my eyes felt tired. I answered before the second ring.

'Sam, you don't understand. I have fallen for you. I have

never felt this way before.' It was Carolina squealing lies. Why was she doing this?

'Listen, we met for less than an hour. I did all the talking and you looked bored. I don't know you, I don't want to know you, and please don't ever fucking ring again!' I slammed down the phone and cursed the fact she had my number. Immediately, the phone rang again and I ignored it. But after the answering machine failed, I picked up to repeat what I had just said.

A man's roar came through with full force. 'I hear you have been playing around with my girlfriend – ' he started to cough and then cleared his throat. 'I know where you live, *pezzo di merda*, and I'm coming to get you!' The line went dead; my hand automatically went to my mouth like a baby's when he seeks his thumb for comfort. My flesh froze and I made a platitudinous remark out loud into the still room.

I called David Burford, but he was out carousing. I then rang my other co-desperado from school, Troubles Winter. After his expulsion he had gone to a reform school and had turned unnervingly straight. Early nights and a job in the city for a stockbroking house in Bishopsgate summed up his new way of life. I was not convinced he had reinvented himself and believed he was ready to leave the straight and narrow at any time. But I saw little of him in those days so my judgement might have been unfair.

Within the hour, I was sharing a coffee in his warm and thickly upholstered apartment and had taken up his offer of the spare bed. He lived in Lowndes Square, off Sloane Street. The owner spent most of her time in New York and he was 'looking after the place'; I sensed there was more to the story, but this was not the time to delve; I had enough on my tormented mind.

By morning, I had convinced myself that I was making a

drama out of a misunderstanding and went to work with porridge in my stomach and the worry pushed to the back of my mind. The day struggled by. I called casting directors in hope of getting an audition for one of my clients. There was nothing out there, only a car commercial requiring two midgets; I had none on my list. I returned home to spend a quiet and peaceful night in.

Lady Eliston was again trying to convey a message from her window, like someone calling out from a moving bus. I wasn't in the mood to play another game of charades, so I signalled her down.

'Three burly foreign men knocked on our door last night, asking if we knew where you were . . . most scary. You're not in some sort of trouble, are you? God, they were rather awful: they looked like escaped convicts . . . '

I gulped in the night air. My thoughts raced and I scrambled for my keys, which kept falling from my shaking hand. Once in, I slammed the door behind me and started to pace about, ordering myself to get it together. What to do, what to do? And then it came; there was one man who could come to my rescue.

Uncle Louis was not the property developer in the Home Counties that I had once imagined. He was in fact a *God-father* type, with a reputation so formidable that the mere mention of his name made hardened criminals cower. I had discovered this quite by accident when I'd knocked over a thug's beer in a pub in the Whitechapel Road. In anger, he'd picked up his snooker cue ready to wallop it across my head. The weapon was only inches from my skull when a stranger's hand grabbed it and threw it across the floorboards of the silent bar. When the thug was told that I was Louis Alexander's 'boy' the energy changed. He became indulgent, shaking his head incredulously, and apologetic drinks were offered all round.

I called my uncle, who answered his phone with suspicion in his voice.

'It is me, uncle. It's Sam. I need your help.' I told him my story.

'Don't let *anyone else* in except Don; he works at my office.' He was firm.

Don, tall and slim with protruding blue eyes, was ringing the buzzer within half an hour. He had with him his pal Chas, very ugly, like one of the fish in the Galapagos described by Charles Darwin. He was breathing heavily and looking like he needed sleep. It was as if they were on 24-hour emergency call.

'You remain in here, son, and we will be outside. You can rest easy now,' Don said, his voice having only a limited range of expression.

'Would you like a cup of tea?' I asked.

He shook his head. Chas nodded, but in doing so received a marble stare from his boss. Don stood squaring his toes to his smaller comrade, and with arms across his chest, hissed, 'Get a bloody move on.'

They left the apartment to pitch camp outside. One of them smelled of drink, the clear, bitter smell of Watney's, and the other was a red glow of cigarettes. They must have been in their late forties and had an inner menace that made me happy that they were on my side. It looked like dear Uncle Louis was on the case. When I got into bed, my eyes were wide open but not for long – I fell asleep feeling safe and did not stir until very early the following morning.

The men were still standing outside, cold but to attention, with crushed cigarettes beneath their black polished shoes. I asked them in for a cup of tea.

'You won't be bothered again, son,' Don said, with narrowed eyes.

'Thank you. I suppose you won't tell me what happened?'

'With respect, all you need to know is that it's sorted.'

They both drank their boiling tea in one and turned to leave.

'You owe your uncle a thank-you.' Don shook my hand and walked away.

'Don't I owe you the thank you?' I asked.

'No, we were just doing our job,' he called back, as Chas drew out yet another cigarette.

* * *

Uncle Louis was waiting in the lobby of the Churchill Hotel in Portman Square. I had called him from work and we had arranged to meet for tea. I told the Kurzners that I had a dental appointment.

Uncle wore a dark-grey chalk-striped suit, a blue shirt with white collar and an old school tie. He was inspecting his freshly manicured hands and humming a Frank Sinatra song ever so lightly. He grinned as I approached and gave me a hug and a pinch of the cheek.

'Let's get ourselves some tea,' my uncle said as he led me down to the restaurant. The room was large and airy with a scattering of guests. He examined the menu and ordered smoked-salmon sandwiches, toast and a large pot of tea.

Tea was laid on a white tablecloth. Uncle Louis swept off some imaginary crumbs. He crammed three sandwiches into his mouth at once, and then swallowed. Dragging off sideways the spectacles which he used very occasionally, he rested a hand on his chin and dropped an eyelid menacingly at me. 'I will never allow you to be in danger. Those Italian bastards won't bother you again. Please don't ask why. If anything like this happens in the future – which I hope it won't – call without hesitation . . . '

'I am sorry, Uncle Louis.'

'No need to say sorry, Sam; but don't let girls be your

downfall. You should try to find a special one and settle down. Don't be like your sad old Uncle Louis!'

Uncle Louis took hold of my hand and held it tight. 'You are family, my boy. When we lost Tom, for me it was like losing a son.'

As we were walking out of the hotel, a couple of strangers offered him their hands; he shook them warmly. He climbed into his blue Bentley, slipped a five-pound note into my top pocket and said, 'Be safe now, my boy.' And then my uncle slowly glided out of the hotel drive to live a life half hidden from those closest to him. I wonder if my father knew that he associated with men like Don? Aunt Flo would faint and mother would be disbelieving. I chose not to pry and to keep my uncle's contacts as a special insurance should I ever need it.

I walked through Hyde Park. It had begun to snow and the snowflakes collided as if in competition with one another. The cars nosed through the density of the fall cautiously. The park lights were dimmed by the uncompromising weather. I did not mind, as I was safe. I had felt mighty scared and now relief was tempered by awareness of my stupidity. For instinct had told me there was something 'not quite right' about Carolina, and yet I was too casual to hear what I was being told. I would never let such a thing happen again.

I turned into the dim light of my snow-shrouded street and bumped straight into someone who was wrapped in what looked like a dead tiger. It was Lady Eliston who jumped in fright but quickly composed herself. 'Now listen, I don't know what has been going on, Sam, but last night, before I retired to bed, I saw those ruffian fellows who were asking after you the other day.' She could scarcely contain her excitement. 'They were being shoved around and spoken to in a most unpleasant manner by two other toughs standing near your front door.' She paused for breath. 'The tall slim one caught me staring and mouthed an obscenity at me, telling me to mind my own business. Really, Sam, the sort of people you know!' With that, she returned to the warmth of her house and the sanctuary of her window.

* * *

The days merged into one another. I continued to be punctual and my reassurance to my actors that work was imminent was dispensed hourly with confidence. One morning, Mr Kurzner called me into his room and offered a single piece of advice: 'Agents are the last to be thanked and the first to blamed.'

The telephonist, I noticed, had changed three times in as many weeks. It seemed my shoes were difficult to fill.

The following day I booked an old film star for a role with the BBC. She was to play a vampire in an episode of *Dr Who*. She was full of thanks, however, and promised after the job was completed that she would treat me to lunch and 'suck the blood' from my neck. I chased the casting agents in desperation to make sure she had a follow-up job; I needed to keep her from having any spare time.

* * *

Jobs for clients were pretty limited. The Kurzners received information from a subscription service, listing the casting requirements for future productions, and these I scoured for a glimpse of an opportunity to launch one of my resting actors. The name of Elinor Spielman kept cropping up, always attached to the important productions. I *had* to arrange a meet with her, that I knew.

'She doesn't take kindly to cold calls,' advised Margaret, in one of her more haughty moods.

'Then how do you suggest I meet her?'

'Write, silly boy. If she likes one of your suggestions, *she* will call *you*.'

That felt like waiting to find a new girlfriend and not bothering ever to go out. The office cleared for lunch and I picked up the phone.

'Hello?'

'Is that Elinor Spielman? This is Sam Alexander. I'm calling from the Kurzner Agency.'

'Yup?' came back the mid-somewhere drawl.

'Listen, I'll come straight to the point . . . '

'Yes?'

' . . . I'm just starting in the business and need to meet you to try and find work for my clients. I hope I'm not being too pushy?'

'Come and see me at five this afternoon. We can have a cup of tea.'

'Do you really mean that?'

The receiver at the other end had already been hung up.

It was that easy. All the whispers that she was uncommunicative were rubbish. Although she hardly spoke ten words, she sounded a darling. I have an instinct, you see.

That afternoon I arrived at the entrance of her building like one of a pack of hounds slithering to a halt on hard ground. Talking of instinct, I knew something important was about to happen in my life, and covered the distance between offices at speed. The unwonted exertion left me short of breath; I made a note to get fit.

'Do come in.' She was not what I had expected. I suppose I thought from her reputation that she would be a small, surly woman, head in the air and supremely confident. I was right about her confidence, but she was humble and relaxed, dressed in a tailored suit the colour of oatmeal, and had thick long golden hair, drawn back tightly into a neat bun.

'I have some biscuits in a tin up in that cupboard.' We

were in the kitchen and she was directing me above the fridge. 'Hand them down,' she said, and added them to the tray she insisted on carrying herself.

The phone rang continuously, but she let the answering-machine pick up. 'My assistant has root-canal problems, poor thing, and had to make a dash to the dentist.'

'It's funny,' I said, 'you remind me of someone.'

'Someone nice, I hope?'

'Yes, someone very dear; but sadly no longer with us.'

I spoke of Mrs Wheeler, the old lady I had visited every Wednesday when I was at school. She had taken on a maternal role while I was away from home and I had grown to be very fond of her.

'It sounds as if you miss her.'

'I suppose I do, she was very kind to me when I felt lonely. She was reassuring and yet, like so many in my life, it seems, just as I was feeling settled in our friendship she died.' There was hesitation and a brief pause as my mind strayed back to sadnesses of the past.

Elinor was curious as to how I had reached this point in my life at so young an age. I spoke and Elinor listened: the fight for independence when I was sent away to school, the loss of my brother, the suffering that followed – 'I am terribly sorry!' – and the eagerness to be successful. 'It's like I'm on a crowded bus and can't find a seat,' I said.

Before I left, I passed over an envelope containing the photographs and the CVs of five actors. She was casting a John Landis movie being shot down in Twickenham and hoped that a face might trigger off an idea.

'You're a darling boy,' she said, 'and I wish you every success. I have no doubt you'll go far. But promise me, you won't let your head be turned by the false glamour that besets this industry. Those who follow the path of flattery and insincerity soon stumble and fall flat on their faces.'

I thanked her for the tea and made that promise.

Two days later one of my younger actors was called to an audition at Twickenham Studios and got the part of a doctor in the John Landis movie. Not a big role, but good enough. The satisfaction of creating that chance for the actor gave me a welcome boost after some recent knock-backs.

* * *

'Hey, Billy, do you want to join me at the Grill for lunch today?'

It was the beginning of the week and the weather was inching towards spring. The chill was less biting and everyone had a twinkle. I had shaken off a cold that had forced a bed-ridden few days. Billy had become a nurse so exemplary as to rival the professionals. He plied me with quantities of Lucozade and hot chicken soup; my rapid recovery was thanks to him and this was a chance to repay him.

Jackie typed and typed and only came up for air when the Kurzners went out for lunch. Margaret threw me the occasional flirt which I caught and tried to throw back, but she did not really want to play. We rarely saw each other after office hours but when we did, usually on a Friday night, we gossiped and laughed with companionable ease.

The Grill was going to be my special treat. I had received twenty pounds from Uncle Louis whom I had bumped into quite by accident on the corner of Pont Street and Sloane Street. I had just visited my doctor, and was still figuring out where to take my prescription, when I walked bang into my uncle. He was in an exceedingly happy mood, grinning from ear to ear. He was going to meet my father for lunch and was looking forward to it. As we said our goodbyes he slipped me some notes. When I took hold of the cash, there were two notes stuck together. I offered to return one of the crisp tenners but he would have none of it and sent me on my merry way; there was no mention of Don, violence or protection, and I thought it was best not to go there.

The Grill heaved with smoke and conversation and was full of rich men talking to powerful men who in turn were looking at seductive women scattered throughout the room. The walls were hung with a mixture of small figurative oils and big glossy black-and-white photographs of stars of today and from yesteryear. A well-built white-haired man with a goatee seemed to have the prominent pitch just by the front desk. I did not recognise him and wondered aloud to Billy who he was.

I had only been here once before, with my father and my uncle, but the greeting I got from Marco the owner gave the impression that I came here every day.

'For an Alexander, the best table in the house – bar that one,' he announced, as he jerked his thumb at the white-haired man's table. The man was now puffing on a well-chewed cigar with the confidence of someone who knew what he liked in life. His fat gut surged over the belt of his navy-blue suit and his breathing looked strained. Marco handed us our menus, and while he was doing so, I asked him for the man's name.

'That is Signor Jake Birkenfeld, probably the greatest actors' agent in the world. If Signor Birkenfeld says you are going to be a star, then that is exactly what you will be. He is a powerful man and our best customer.'

His words captivated my imagination. Oh, to be that powerful, to be at a point in your journey where a decision you make can change someone's life for ever! I longed to reach that point and had only admiration for this big man. I glimpsed my possible future and salivated at the vision. It was not something I had experienced before, this raw upsurge of ambition. I will be like that one day, I promised myself.

Billy was pouring himself a glass of red wine before I had opened my menu and was soon helping himself to another. He was always comfortable in a restaurant. His stomach was making high-octane rumblings and tonight he was drinking as if to drown a bad experience. Silly Billy, he seemed to fall in and out of love every night. His haggard eyes looked carefully at my face. 'Go for it, Sam,' he said. 'You can achieve anything you set your heart on. I know what you're thinking.' It was brotherly advice and I valued it. I felt a deep sense of peace that I was on the right track. Billy lit his cigarette before he had finished eating his soup, the flare of the match revealing how strained he looked, and I remember being concerned.

The talk in the restaurant was growing louder and louder when I felt a slight nudge on my shoulder.

'Hello there. I'm Jake Birkenfeld. I wanted to introduce myself. Would you join me for coffee? It looks as if you are having lunch alone anyway.'

I knew that there would be a connection, so his invitation seemed natural. I excused myself from Billy, who was gazing at a pretty boy at the next table. I moved to sit with Birkenfeld at the number-one spot. Without asking, Marco immediately brought over a coffee and I began to listen.

'Mr Alexander, or should I call you Sam?'

'Sam will do fine.' I was surprised he knew my name.

'I understand that you closed a deal recently that was both daring and inspired. I have also heard good things from Elinor Spielman.'

I sat stunned by the sheer audacity of the hype that had reconstructed my attempt to get the sack.

'Don't say anything,' he was chewing even harder on his mangled cigar. 'We need people like you, son, and I want to invite you to join the company . . . an offer you'll find difficult to refuse and an offer that'll change your life.'

Whatever the offer was, I would have accepted anything at that moment; the sensation of being needed was overwhelming. He wrote numbers down in biro on the white tablecloth: a good wage, a slice on the commission and a more generous holiday allowance.

'You'll get your own office, with your name on the door, and your very own secretary. Don't give me an answer now but call before the week is out.'

He shook my hand and left the restaurant. I returned to the table and poured some of Billy's wine.

He looked over his glass, 'Yeaahhhhhh?'

I smiled and told him that something strange had just happened. 'Let's get slaughtered, Billy.'

'I will drink to that!' he slurred.

We ordered another bottle and toasted my future. I pondered that only a few years after being expelled from my public school and convinced that I had no real future, I found myself wanted by the biggest talent agency in the world. Then I realised I didn't even know the name of his company. Marco filled me in. It was called, ISA – the International Star Agency.

'Hey, I know that guy. He buys his music from me,' Billy garbled.

'The International Star Agency. Yes, that sounds very good indeed.' I spoke my thoughts out loud.

* * *

My room at my parents' house had been stripped of its posters and the walls had been repainted a shade of sky blue. The house was having a makeover to distance itself from the past and embrace a new chapter. It was my mother's idea to lighten the atmosphere, and although I understood, I was doleful that rooms I had known since infancy were changing their character.

My father walked less ponderously than when we had taken the same narrow road to the pub the previous Christmas; his steps were easier and more comfortable. It was a lovely lazy day with the sun out and a hint of heat returning. There was really no need for overcoats, but the few others sitting with us in the pub's beer garden still retained their extra layer to be on the safe side.

The publican Ray was in a celebratory mood as he had just become a grandfather. All first orders were on the house. Polaroid pictures of the newborn were pinned over the bar and anyone who approached cooed and aahed at the mushroom head that stared back. The Union Jack hung limply from the flagpole by the side of the building and Stevie Wonder's 'Isn't She Lovely' played incessantly on the jukebox. We laughed in the atmosphere and it was a long time since I had seen my father's face quite so relaxed.

'I've been offered a job, father.' I spoke to him probably for the first time with real pride in my voice. I recounted the meeting in the restaurant and shared what I had discovered about the agency.

'That's excellent, Sam. You will do very well . . . ' After a pause, he went on to confide in me. 'Your mother and I have been having bereavement counselling. We go twice a week to a Jewish therapist in Oxford. It turns out he and I are distantly related on my mother's side. Anyway, he's a wise man who has some answers to our questions.'

I listened, too stunned to open my mouth – not because my parents were having therapy, but because my father was opening up to me in such a fashion.

'We're helping ourselves and learning to move on. Mum deals with her grief by keeping busy and looking after me; and I, well, I had given up. I didn't see a future.' He grasped my hand across the table and I wept with the poignancy of it all. 'I love you, Sam; I love you as a father loves his son. I will always be here for you, and if in the past I have been distant, I am sorry, so very sorry.' Our heads and hands met across the table, knocking over his empty beer bottle, and we knew that moment would remain with us for the rest of our lives.

We drank up and set off home in silence; all that needed to be said had passed between us back at the pub. As we came in sight of our house I glanced at my watch to see if we were late for lunch. I was happy now and confident about the future. Mother was waiting at the front door and hurried us to the newly painted dining room, where Harold served us with a delicious lunch.

* * *

Margaret was very upset; there were even tears in her exquisite eyes. I had just told her that I had accepted the job at ISA and she was genuinely distressed by the news. Her face fell like that of a child being deprived of its favourite plaything, and I wanted to kiss her tenderly and promise we would stay in touch.

'You've only just had promotion. You're not being fair, darling.'

I held her close, as I had during the Christmas party, but this was not the time for sex. I had more important things to do, like give in my notice. 'I wanted you to know before anyone else.' I stroked her hair and she grabbed my waist and pulled my body towards hers. 'Please don't go, we make such a good team,' and we started to kiss passionately; my mind raced between how sexy this was and whether I would be able to have a word with Mrs Kurzner before lunch. Eventually I pushed her away and straightened myself, checking my hair which I had had cut only the day before to look like David Bowie's on the *Low* album sleeve.

Mrs Kurzner was alone in her office doing *The Times*

crossword. From the beginning, she had been kind and generous with encouragement and advice; she was a fine person and I spoke with a heavy but resolute heart. She said that she was naturally disappointed, but there was little she could do. When I mentioned the pay I was being offered, she flinched and said, 'Without a guarantee of commission, you must have charmed the life out of them, Samuel.' The meeting was short and finished with Mrs Kurzner promising that she bore no grudge, just a little concern, and warning that I was moving on before the time was right.

'It feels like I've won the pools, Mrs Kurzner.'

* * *

I had arranged to visit the ISA offices during my lunch hour. The offices were on Upper Brook Street, close to Grosvenor Square. Former residents included Jimi Hendrix and George Frederic Handel. A street where once the rich and privileged lived, its grand houses were now the offices of affluent companies and the Agency was making a bold statement by leasing a five-floor red-brick building on the north side.

The receptionist seemed to know who I was. She was a chirpy little thing and chattered away, without a pause, until Mr Birkenfeld's secretary came to the rescue. 'Don't worry about Jenny, she has the sweetest of hearts,' she smiled, introducing herself with a firm handshake. 'Hello there, I'm Joyce and I'm going to show you around.' Her voice was cordial and deep. I was somewhat relieved that I was not attracted to her; it had been a problem over recent months that virtually every female I met became food for fantasy and I don't think a minute passed without my thinking about sex. I wondered whether this trait would follow me for the rest of my life.

On the first floor, the walls had been knocked through and the team of secretaries sat side by side. 'We're meant to discuss with each other the movies in production and exchange information on the roles that are available in theatre and television, thus working as a strong team. In reality, we keep the news to ourselves. I suppose I shouldn't been telling you this, but each agent is out for himself and his commission; frankly, it's dog eat dog!'

Everyone had left for lunch but there were five desks, some laden with papers, so I presumed there were five agents. Joyce pointed to the empty desk at the back with a plastic sheet covering its typewriter. 'That will be for your girl,' she said. 'I'm interviewing a selection this afternoon. Don't worry, we'll find a suitable one.'

On the second floor there were two offices, one of which was to be mine. It didn't have my name on the door yet, of course, but as we went in, a fresh wind blew through the open window as a sign of welcome. My eyes shot round the room like a lizard. 'This will do, and this is only the beginning,' I mused.

'Do you like it?' asked Joyce.

'It's just . . . right,' I answered, shrugging my shoulders with the nonchalance of a man trying to impress.

'I won't take you anywhere else for the moment as the other offices down here are not important. When Mr Birkenfeld wants to see you, you must climb to the top floor. *Always* knock, mind you. *Never* just barge in.' She clapped her hands as a way of saying her work was done, and I made my way down the stairs behind her.

'Oh yes, that blue door is the bathroom for agents only; you, of course, can use it.' She swung open the door for inspection. A gentle whiff of urine blew into my face.

'Thank you, Joyce,' I said half choking. 'I'm so pleased that I can start next week!'

Once more out in the street, I turned to look at the building and took a deep draught of fresh air; I smiled a self-congratulatory smile and returned to Berkeley Square.

* * *

Jackie's eyes were crossed as I came through the door. I wasn't sure whether she was drunk or giving me a signal. 'You'd better go in,' her finger was pointing to the Kurzners' office.

'Don't worry, Jackie,' I said, 'I have told Mrs Kurzner.'

'I think that is the problem,' came the reply.

I knocked gently on the Kurzners' door. I didn't hear an answer so I stepped inside. They were both drinking coffee and Mr Kurzner had the look of a hangman about him. I sensed Jackie peering through the crack in the door, like a priest covering a boxing match. This was not going to be a protracted bout and there would not be a sea of blood.

'My wife tells me that you have taken a job with a rival agency. I am most upset and feel very let down. I am disappointed at your lack of loyalty. I would like you to leave the office immediately without any papers or files. Also remember that all our clients have signed contracts and even if they want to leave to follow you, they will not be able to.'

I had no wish to argue but would simply like to have thanked them for the faith and warmth that they had shown me, yet it was not to be allowed. I left their room never to return. Mrs Kurzner had looked away while her husband spoke, which stung a bit, but the day was a celebration and nothing was going to stop that. Jackie gave me a hug, and said through a haze of cigarette smoke that she would call later; Margaret slipped me a note that read, 'Come for dinner tonight – eight o'clock, 6 Friston Street SW6. X'.

* * *

Margaret's apartment was small, lonely and rather dull. A stack of white unopened envelopes lay on the floor by the door. In the living room, an oversized television dominated the place, and copies of *Vogue,* some two years old, were piled on the coffee table. A small dining-table had been set with red napkins and two red candles were weakly burning; red was the colour of the day. The walls were painted a dull white and four dreary prints of horses were hanging too high above the blood-red two-seat sofa. A jasmine joss-stick filled the room with a haze of heavy incense, and Margaret gave me a joint as a welcome. I was offered whisky, which I accepted, and watched as a large glass was poured. The first taste relaxed me, and by the fourth gulp and the fifth drag, I was merry. I grabbed the half-empty bottle by its neck. My guts ignited as I finished the last drops and then quite suddenly I felt a wave of fear, a sense of foreboding. 'Pull yourself together,' I told myself.

The eating of the overcooked pasta steadied the room and I ate quickly, with a sudden acute hunger. She chuckled at my request for another plate, and as she walked back from the kitchen, I had only one thought. Her pale skin, her hair as black as a winter's night sky, the blue inquisitive eyes and thin languid body – all stirred the longing I had felt whenever she spoke to me or floated by; that night I wanted her urgently. I suggested we skip the cheese and biscuits. I took her hand and pulled her into the bedroom and on to the bed. I pushed her short skirt up, ran my hands over her stockings and touched her garter belt; I broke the garter straps with one hand and with the other I touched her breast and then whispered, 'I want you so . . . '

'Call me by my name, Sam. Call me by my name.' There was a tick of silence while I inhaled the jasmine in the night air.

'I want you, Margaret, I want you . . . '

I felt numb and anaesthetised; too much drink. Our sex was comfortable yet sad – the sort of sadness a lover feels when after a night of glorious love-making he awakes to find himself alone.

We shared a Camel cigarette and spoke little. I had no desire to run away and catch a cab. That was my usual practice when I had sex away from home, but this time I watched my smoke rings forming the shapes of different animals.

'Mrs Kurzner said that she would miss you,' Margaret told me, breaking the silence while her taste was still in my mouth.

'She hardly came to my defence when her husband started to have a go at me,' I said, with a sense of relief that I was sobering up.

'Pay no attention to that, darling, she allows Bernie to have his say and that is how she gets his money. You could learn from that.'

I turned over to put out her cigarette and said, 'That's enough of the word "darling", come here and stop being so posh.' I pulled her towards me and we started to kiss again and I trembled and grabbed her breasts and said, 'Do you know how many times I have dreamed of this?'

She shook her head and went down my body.

* * *

It was my first day and I wanted to create a good impression, so I was outside 25 Upper Brook Street by 9 o'clock. I was buoyant but a little apprehensive.

I pushed open the heavy black door and walked inside. The Filipino cleaner shyly continued dusting the banister as I climbed to the first floor. There, in front of my eyes, my name sparkled on the door of my new office: SAMUEL ALEXANDER. I took a step back and patted my heart and gave a quiet grunt. The office was just as I had found it the previous week. I touched the desk at its edges and slumped into my leather chair, propping my feet on the desk and as usual grasping my hands behind my head. The office hours were the same as for my previous job, ten o'clock until six o'clock, and so it was still early to be joined by anyone. Agents did not have a reputation for stirring before daybreak.

I strolled around, and trying to kill time, I visited the agents' bathroom. I opened the door and the room was a wreck. Someone had peed all over the seat and on much of the floor. It was a revolting sight. I nearly retched at the smell and quickly closed the door again. As I turned, I bumped straight into Mr Birkenfeld, already in the office and making his way to the lavatory.

'Welcome, welcome, my boy. You are most welcome and most punctual,' he beamed and continued to the door I had just closed. Oh no! He was going to think that I had peed all over the seat! I was humiliated. My optimistic mood had been ruined and I went to hide in the secretaries' room, wanting the ground to swallow me up.

'You look very pale.' Joyce had walked in and found me lurking by one of the desks.

I didn't bother to explain, just said hello and kept the embarrassment to myself. I was introduced to the secretaries one by one. I had trouble remembering their names but I noticed they all had a 'Stepford' aura.

Virginia was twenty-two, slim, blonde, spoke quickly, and had a degree in economics. She lived in a big house down a country lane in Surrey, with mummy and daddy, five sisters, an 'extremely big' swimming pool and 'a good deal of land'. She had a sunny smile and perfect teeth. She made me my first coffee but it was bitter and basically undrinkable. When I asked her to make me another, she said nothing but returned with a cappuccino from the local Italian cafe on the corner of Bond Street and Brook Street; it was frothy and delicious. She refused my money and said, 'Accept it as a gift this time.' Virginia was to be my assistant and I liked her instantly.

On Monday morning, the agents discussed the successes and failures of the previous week. My first Monday-morning meeting was more like a gathering of the living dead. The boardroom resembled an old-country-house dining room, with oil paintings of English landscapes on the Wedgwood-blue walls and a long Georgian dining-table with Chippendale chairs on either side. Joyce was perched in one corner, ready to take the minutes, and Birkenfeld sat at the head with the agenda in front of him and agents either side yawning openly. Mr Anderson, a warm friendly American, was so wrinkled he seemed to frown all over. He had a habit of leaning forward and dropping his voice into a minor key. Fumbling next to him was Mr Witherspoon, at least ten years older and fed up with the world, who had a way of moaning to himself and looking down his long nose at anything that was thrown in his direction. On the other side was Mr Bigby, a Texan, who seemed to be in a permanent state of despair. He was overheard by one of the secretaries screaming, 'I must get out of this god-damned place!' Mr Williams could easily have been mistaken for a rabbi, with his thick silver beard and curls flowing from his ears. He picked his nose constantly, always looking at his catch before popping it into his mouth. My stomach heaved at his performance. In this room sat the most powerful agents in Europe, and as I studied them my shoulders slumped and all my optimism and enthusiasm fell away like soft flakes of ash from a cigar.

Birkenfeld gave a short and flattering welcome speech

about 'new blood' and 'a wonderful find in our midst', while the other agents continued to pick their nails and their noses. Mr Witherspoon kept looking at his watch and huffing and puffing, until he lost patience and exploded: 'I have business to do.' As he stormed out, I think he said, 'God, I hate actors!' but I must have misheard.

Bigby sighed and Anderson whispered to pay no attention and that it didn't mean anything. 'He behaves like that every week.' The meeting was hastily disbanded. I had been warned that I would be the youngest by at least forty years but until that morning I had not quite believed it. I returned to my office dismayed by what I had seen. Had I made a terrible mistake? On my way, deep in thought, I bumped into an agitated gentleman wearing a tweed suit. He trotted on without acknowledging my apology.

'That's Kenneth Williams, isn't it?' I gasped.

'Lesson one,' Joyce said as we met on the stairs, '*Never* stare or shout at anyone you might recognise in this building. They are stars, not aliens. Lesson two: for the first few weeks, keep your mouth shut. Never make jokes. Never discuss a problem, expecting fellow agents to help. Once they smell blood – even if they're heading for retirement – they will move in for the kill. And three: only talk about your success not your near miss. They don't want to know that an actress lost out on a lead by a hair's breadth.' She put her finger to my mouth, 'Keep it shut.' All this advice seemed to suggest I was in for a perplexing time. Life couldn't be this difficult, surely?

For the first few weeks, I heeded Joyce and said nothing in the meetings, just listened. I had also been given this advice at school but I chose to ignore it then, which led to trouble. This time was different and after I'd been silent for ages, Mr Birkenfeld sidled up after one long day at work to congratulate me on my contribution. 'Fantastic input, young man, you are an asset to the company.' I don't know if he was being sincere, but the warmth of his words made me feel good.

*   *   *

There are stars, and then there are Stars.

'Mr Birkenfeld would like to see you, Sam,' a sprightly Virginia said.

His door was always closed so, as cautioned to do, I knocked. I was unsure whether what I heard was a cough or a 'Come on in'. I knocked again.

'Bloody well come in!'

Birkenfeld's office was large and white; it was the size of an expensive apartment. His desk was piled with scripts, loose papers and scattered pens. Just over his shoulder there was a family photograph – his wife and two sons taken on holiday in Israel, standing arm in arm in front of the Western Wall. His wife was at least twenty years younger and a former Miss Israel. 'She was once a Bond girl,' he had told me. On the walls there were black-and-white photographs of the stars, all personally signed 'with thanks' to Birkenfeld: Yul Brynner in a Western costume – 'Mister Ten per Cent, one of the good guys', an assortment of Peter Sellers – 'crazy son of a bitch but a fucking genius', Ava Gardner – 'the most beautiful creature in the universe', Frank Sinatra outside The Sands in Las Vegas – 'my friend Frank', and Sammy Davis Junior in a New York bar – 'one of the most talented'. His life was on show and it radiated success. The carpet was beige and deep and the suede sofa was where he would take his half-hour siesta after lunch. Two colossal televisions were on with the volume turned down and piles of VHS tapes were stacked beside them. He was chomping on his cigar and finishing a call to someone.

'Now listen, young man,' Birkenfeld said, putting the phone down, 'we have Telly Savalas visiting this week from New York. I thought it would be good experience for you to take him to lunch. I have to be out of town tomorrow and so you can go to the Grill, sit at my table and sign it off on my account.'

'Do you mean Kojak – "Who loves ya, baby?" and the lollipop?'

'Yes, exactly. He will be here just before one tomorrow. Sam, I know you'll be your charming self.'

As I was leaving, he picked up a call from Chuck in Hollywood – Charlton Heston for those not in the know. I was learning fast.

* * *

The following day after the consumption of too many coffees, and a lot of nervous office small talk, Virginia led Mr Savalas in. He was warm, relaxed and looked just like Kojak in real life; he was at that time one of the biggest stars in the world. We shook hands and I was afraid he would recognise me from just a few months before when he called me a prick for shouting out, 'Who loves ya, baby?'

'Sam, I want to go to HMV to buy some music. Let's go there first and then we can have our lunch.'

We walked along Upper Brook Street to Bond Street and turned left towards Oxford Street. Irritatingly, a celebrity-hungry pack had started to follow us. Telly was so recognisable that the procession rapidly grew to uncomfortable proportions.

'I think, Mr Savalas, you will need to sign some autographs.'

'No, Sam, the key to fame is to keep moving. Stop for a second and it's all over.'

By the time we reached the corner of South Molton

Street, at least fifty fans were on our trail, calling out, 'Who loves ya, baby?' and, 'Want a lollipop?'; a moron in a purple pork-pie hat was attempting to sing his number-one hit 'If' – worse than Telly ever did.

'The assholes that call out "Who loves ya, baby?" all the time must drive you mad.'

'You can say that again.'

'The assholes that call out . . . '

'I was kidding, Sam.'

HMV was becoming a bad idea; there were no taxis and we were practically cornered. I pointed to the Bond Street Underground as our only way of escape; Telly followed enthusiastically.

'Never been down here. What an adventure!' He was like an excited child. We had lost the baying mob. They had abandoned their chase and not followed us into the depths of the Underground. Telly was my responsibility and I did not want to lose him. I observed as we walked down the escalator that the public paid little attention; no one expected to see the great Kojak travelling on the Jubilee Line.

The platform was deserted, apart from a distant figure disco-dancing at the far end. I stood like a bodyguard as Telly walked about reading the peeling posters and studying the tube map. Our sole 'entertainer' was now heard singing Anita Ward's 'You Can Ring My Bell', like a loud drunken angel, waving his umbrella as if it were a conductor's baton. I narrowed my eyes and looked more closely. He had a skirt on, green hair and a short tartan jacket. I wasn't sure he was in fact male, and while trying to work it out, it dawned on me that I knew him. It was Valentine, a lover of Billy's whom I had met on many occasions at the breakfast table, usually hungover on a Sunday morning. My heart stopped and I hastily turned away. 'Please, please, let the train arrive.' I was praying with my hands clenched, panicked by helplessness.

'Samuel, hello! Samuel! Is that you?' shrieked Valentine; the game was up.

I led Telly towards the edge of the platform as the train sped into the station. Should I push him over? 'Star murdered to save minder embarrassment. Judge sentences ex-public-school boy to life . . . before the killer was sent down, the judge said, "Humiliation is simply part of life, learn to live with it." '

The doors opened and I struggled to pull Telly after me into the carriage. 'Come on, Telly,' I urged.

Valentine was running with legs askew, hair tangled and arms flailing down the platform. We stood facing the doors, waiting for them to close: Telly was waiting, I was praying.

The doors started to shut, and just as they were about to meet, Valentine's umbrella poked between them; encountering an obstruction, they sprang back. Valentine, make-up running, was looking directly into my eyes. I gulped as he shrieked at the top of his panting voice, 'Sam, are you going to Billy's orgy on Saturday night?'

A deafening silence followed. Life can be so unfair. The doors shut and the tube train picked up speed as it plunged into the gloom of the tunnel. I felt I was watching the scene from above, detached from the appalling shame inflicted by this stranger. The lights flickered, and in the fluorescent flashes, Telly must have seen me dying. My legs wobbled, my hands felt clammy. Telly finally broke the silence. 'Well, Sam, are you?'

* * *

Posh girls all shrieking to be heard over one another and a bar full of Dunhill cigarette smoke. The Phoenix pub was overflowing into the cold February night. Bella ignored me as she stayed in her corner, working on an unsuspecting Etonian. 'Be careful,' I wanted to warn him, 'there is madness there.' As she spoke to her catch, her cigarette wagged up and down and she gestured like an over-exuberant tour guide. We had hardly spoken since our one night together, and if we caught each other's eye, she would just hiss, 'Sssssnake,' and move on.

Billy was holding court by the bar, surrounded by a sea of adoring faces; he was everyone's friend and everybody loved him. He rarely accompanied me to this toffs' pub but tonight was different. He complained we had not seen enough of each other and said that it had been my fault. I think he wanted to confide to me that he was falling in love.

'Valentine is such a disgrace!' he chuckled, while telling the assembled company about a visit to the travelling funfair over the river in Battersea Park. 'There were six of us, including Sam,' he patted my head, 'and before going to the fair we decided to have some Indian food nearby. The fair was heaving with Ferris wheels, dodgems and useless stands, but I was desperate to win a tortoise. God knows why! Anyway, before I spent a fortune trying to throw a fucking ping-pong ball into a small fish-bowl, we all decided to go on this contraption called Planet Spin. It was like a spinning tube that made you stick to the wall while the floor descended. Fun really, except when the ride finished I noticed that everyone leaving the ride was splattered with curry sauce. Valentine, the silly ass, had taken his Indian takeaway in with him and the ride had made it spin all over everybody!' Billy's audience collapsed into laughter. Valentine this and Valentine that. Billy's conversation was about one thing at that time. He was gloriously happy though.

'Sam, will you come outside for a moment.' It was Margaret, whom I had seen little of since our one-night stand. I had dreamed of being with her virtually every day up until that time, but when it finally happened my passion waned; I was still avoiding commitment. Margaret had an anxious face and a flustered voice. I had never seen her in the pub before, but this was no social outing. The night had grown uncomfortably, painfully, cold. Half bent under a street lamp was a bedraggled figure clearly in pain. I moved closer and discovered it was Jackie. The blaze of light illuminated half her face, and I could see immediately that it was bruised under the eye and marked to the side of the mouth. I turned her to face me full on, but she hid in her arms, not wanting to reveal the evidence of physical abuse. She looked virtually unrecognisable, as if her face were wrapped in Sellotape, distorted, without expression. I bit my knuckle with sheer shock and revulsion.

We could not remain outside as it had begun to rain heavily. We returned home in Billy's car, through the deserted London streets, not saying a single word.

Jackie sipped her tea slowly, not because of its heat, but because everything in her life had gone into slow motion. The tension had been building for ages, ever since she had spent her first night with Ian. The brief affair that followed was in no way proportionate to his subsequent obsessive behaviour. He parked his car most nights outside her Fulham home, looking up at her first-floor apartment until he saw the lights go off and then driving away, tormented by his infatuation. The incessant phone calls and persistent questions followed, but he never contacted her at work. She spoke about this to no one because she was scared that she would lose her job. Ian threatened to tell his parents that she had used him and then discarded him like a 'chewing-gum wrapper'. As she told her dreadful story, the three of us shrank at the terror of it all.

Earlier in the evening she had shared a drink with a male family friend and they had kissed as they said their early good-nights. Jackie was opening her door when Ian appeared from the shadows and invited himself in for a drink. Once inside, he became violent and laid into her with his fists. She fell to the floor and he started to sob and beg for forgiveness. Once he had left, she called Margaret, and together they came in search of advice.

'We have to call the police and lock this son of a bitch away,' said Billy, and I agreed.

But Jackie was reluctant and wailed at the suggestion. 'Please don't, he will get off and I will lose my job and he will still be out there. I know he will . . . I know . . . and I love my job,' and her voice trailed off into desolate tears.

'You can't love it that much!'

She didn't answer and Margaret took her hand.

I was firm. 'Jackie, you must stay here tonight. Take my bed,' I insisted, 'and I will sleep on the sofa.'

Billy was changing the sheets before I had finished my sentence. She was now our patient and would be cared for until she regained her strength. I left her with Margaret in my room, having found her a clean pair of pyjamas; Billy had tucked his hot-water bottle into her bed for extra comfort.

'I'm going out for ten minutes, I need to make a call.' I was talking to Billy in the kitchen.

'What are you going to do?'

'I need to make a call, Billy.' I left the apartment and walked along thoughtfully. I had had a decision to make and it had not been made lightly. I found a phone box on the corner of Limerston Street and the Fulham Road, by St Stephen's Hospital. It had the usual splintered glass on the floor and I methodically crushed the scattered pieces with my shoe, expressing my anger. His number was written in red felt-tip in my small black-leather address book. I dialled carefully and with resolution. He picked up the receiver and I skipped the formalities. I explained what had happened and he listened without interrupting. I described the brutality that Jackie had been subjected to.

'Whatever it costs, please deal with it. I am not sure how far you should go, but just teach him a lesson. I don't want him killed, you hear, but I want him never to be able to mark a woman again. I have an address – '

'Don't worry, son, have this one on the house and, believe me, by the time we are finished, he will understand.'

Don replaced the phone and I walked away – in truth, without a twinge of guilt. I believed that I had done the right thing.

* * *

Jackie had a sound night's sleep and Margaret explained the following day to the Kurzners that she had flu and would not be in. Billy, the darling he was, took the day off, just to care for her. Jackie's face started to heal almost immediately; her mind, however, was another matter. I spent the day wondering if my phone call the previous evening had triggered anything, but I was not going to check and only spoke to Billy to hear how our patient was doing. Virginia remarked that she had never seen me so distracted, but I gave a 'family' excuse and the day drifted by without further comment.

I walked up to Bond Street to catch the bus home and as I passed near HMV I bought an *Evening Standard* from the paper-seller to read on the journey. Page 4 had a small story that caught my eye:

CRAZED KNIFE ASSAULT IN ISLINGTON

Ian Kurzner, a 29-year-old bookseller from Islington, suffered multiple injuries in a frenzied attack outside his shop in Upper Street last night. Detective Inspector Kenneth Simpson said, 'It was a horrific attack and Mr Kurzner is lucky to be alive. We believe the thieves were probably taken by surprise and made their escape before they could complete their robbery, as there was minimal loss to property. It was a senseless assault. Certainly it's one of the nastiest that I've ever had to deal with.'

I folded the paper impassively.

Jackie was asleep on my return and Margaret was in conversation with Billy. She described how news of the attack on Ian had been received with horror at the office, He had sustained a broken arm, a number of knife wounds and severe bruising. 'I shouldn't tell you this, but those bloody yobbo animals even slashed at his genitals.'

'I call it payback! Perhaps there is justice after all.' They both looked shocked at my reaction, in spite of how they felt about him. There had been an edge to my voice that even surprised me; I had discovered a side of myself that I didn't know existed. I enjoyed the power of making the phone call and seeing a result. We kept the news from Jackie, who already looked far better than only hours before. She was regaining her strength and seemed grateful for everything. She would stay another few days until her face recovered its soft lines and bore less trace of bruising. When we did tell her of Ian's injuries, her response was muted; she didn't seem to care and who could blame her?

* * *

David Wingate, Margaret's father, was a stiff, upwardly mobile type who ruled his home as a captain rules his frigate. When his business rivals both went bust within a few short weeks of each other and he became the area's leading poultry distributor, he promised himself two things: that he would buy a new, sensible, charcoal-grey Vanden Plas Princess and that his only child from now on would socialise with 'only the best'. Margaret subsequently attended nearby Cheltenham Ladies' College, where she enjoyed every second of every day.

There would be no university for Margaret, rather to the disappointment of her parents. Instead, she got a job in London and her father bought her a dreary ground-floor apartment off the Wandsworth Bridge Road; she was living there the evening Sam Alexander went over for dinner. It seemed that God did not answer her youthful prayers, perhaps because she was not asking them in the right way, or more likely because she had yet to find what was right for her – in her own estimation and not that of her parents.

* * *

Margaret had called that afternoon and asked whether she could take me to dinner. She needed to talk to me about something.

'Of course,' I had replied. 'But it's my treat.'

We met in Verbanella on the corner of Beauchamp Place. The usual prompt and accommodating Italian service coped easily with the two crowded floors and it was not long before we were tucking into our *prosciutto melone*. Margaret had let her hair grow and it made her face softer and more sympathetic. As she embarked slowly upon her melon, I thought of our 'night' and decided that it was time to apologise for not calling.

'Don't be silly, I'm sort of used to it,' and a whiff of loneliness wafted across our table. 'Anyway I need to talk about that.' I called over the waiter and asked for a bottle of the house red. We had ordered by the glass and mine had already been demolished.

'Yes, about that night . . . ' There was a terrible pause, 'I'm afraid I'm pregnant . . . ' Her voice had changed, her tone had become less brittle, her fingers clenched round one of the folds in her dress

'Shit . . . I'm very sorry!' – probably not the right words to utter at that precise moment in our lives.

Her lip trembled and all of sudden she looked weary. I tried to be wise; I tried to find the right turn of phrase. I felt like a blind man groping his way around a busy town.

'I want to have a child with someone ready to share his or her life. I understand that we don't have a relationship to build on . . . we have both been foolish.' Margaret stared at her plate with her blue, blue eyes. She wept and, after a long pause in which she seemed to have been to a different world, told me that she had arranged for us to go and see someone; the rest of the dinner was silent.

* * *

We had an appointment with the Pregnancy Advisory Service off Tottenham Court Road at eleven o'clock. Margaret had decided to walk, although it was raining yet again. It was constantly wet in London that month. I, meanwhile, had taken a taxi and, being early, was left waiting for her arrival out on the street. I took cover under the awning of the next-door newsagent. Dolly Parton's forthcoming tour was being advertised and Spain was still in a state of political turmoil after a failed right-wing coup. The rain for a moment was so fierce that it seemed to be assuming a pattern as the spikes of water hit the ground. It started to remind me of hundreds of crucifixes washing away the sentiment of the day, and soon I became mesmerised by the rhythmic pounding of the water. Then, it suddenly ceased and Margaret appeared, straight and purposeful. She was glancing at her watch as she came towards me along the pavement. The Rolex was a Christmas present from her father, which she would later tell me had made her sad. She arrived firmly in office mode; she was in charge and direct. All that vulnerability, which I glimpsed at the table the other night, had been washed away with the rain.

We did not have to wait long before we were called into a gloomy office. The overweight ginger-haired woman with vast bosom who interviewed us was friendly but businesslike; there was no formal introduction. I did not know what to expect so I went with the flow. Margaret and I both answered the mundane questions as to address, age and phone number before she finally came to the point and asked us what we planned to do. Margaret, in a clear and precise manner, said that we had decided on a termination.

'We hardly know each other, and bringing up a baby on my own is not something I want to do.'

The affected 'darling this' and 'darling that' had long gone. Her voice was soft and carefully modulated. She looked at me to elicit my support.

'I feel I'm too young and, as Margaret says, we don't have a relationship. I believe it would be unfair to the child.'

'OK. In that case, there is an appointment available tomorrow at midday. You,' she was pointing at Margaret, 'will now go next door for an examination, and if the doctor confirms your pregnancy, you must report to this Twickenham address at half-past eleven.'

And that was it. No questions about whether we understood that making this decision could haunt us for the rest of our lives, no warning that there would be occasions in the future when we might wonder what our child would be doing if alive on that particular day. No, there had been no depth to the questions, just a bland formality. But these weren't observations I had on that day. No, I was only too happy with the ease of it all.

Margaret did not want me to wait; instead, I arranged to pick her up at eleven o'clock from her home next day. As I was leaving we shared a moment of tenderness when I held her hands and said that I was sorry. She squeezed my hands back and gave a half smile. The damn waste resulting from that day still swirls in my head like a sand storm in a cold desert.

* * *

I had forgotten the drear of Margaret's flat. In the cold light of morning, it looked even more depressing. The pungent smell of last night's discarded Indian gusted out from the interior. I sat on the red sofa and flicked through an old edition of *Vogue*. Margaret went to her bedroom to fetch her overnight bag. She might have to stay the night so she was advised to bring a change of clothes 'just in case'. Just in case of what? I dreaded even to inquire, I did not want to ask myself many questions that day.

She looked pale as I carried her bag out to the waiting taxi. I wanted to make conversation as the silence was agonising, but I could not find the right words. We spent most of the journey gazing out of the windows at the busy traffic getting up speed on the A4. I didn't like the silence in the cab. I longed for something to lighten the atmosphere but we were both oppressed by the reality of what lay ahead. The weather was kind for once: there was no rain, just a still clear blue sky with a freshness in the air.

It was like booking a table. I half expected the woman at the front desk to ask whether we wanted a sea view. But 'we' was only briefly on our lips; soon Margaret would be alone. I said my goodbye without a kiss and she was led upstairs, case in hand and shoulders slumped. I had promised that I would call in the afternoon to see how things were, but as I walked back to the taxi, the detachment that had become natural to me so early in my life reasserted itself and I felt no responsibility as the cab hurried back into central London.

Margaret spoke little of what happened that day. Probably as I was having lunch alone at a sandwich bar in Dover Street, she was being operated on. The scheme of things seemed out of kilter: I walked through the London streets as I usually did, while Margaret lay on a table facing the realities of life and death in a room of strangers.

Her lonely figure stood waiting when I arrived to fetch her on the dot of six. I picked up her overnight bag and carried it to the car. As I did so, she fleetingly touched my back, but then withdrew her hand as if she'd been scorched.

'I'd like to spend the night and look after you, if that's OK?' I ventured, as we approached her front door.

Her reply was a simple, 'Thank you.'

While she switched on the lights and took in her things, I dashed around the corner to buy some food. In the unflattering neon light of the supermarket, I bought some wine, Lucozade, cans of Coke and wine gums. Next door there was an empty pizza restaurant and the cook, eager to gain some customers, cooked two oversized pizzas.

'We're new in the area. I hope to see you again.'

I replied that was unlikely, but thanked him anyway.

Margaret, by the time I returned, had retreated to her bed. The phone didn't ring; she had no friends to comfort her; she wasn't in the mood for pizza either.

'Why don't you call Jackie?' I asked.

'I don't want anyone to know,' she said, her voice trembling. There was always a sense of disappointment about her, but that day disappointment seemed to overwhelm her.

'I am so sorry, Margaret.'

'May I have some Lucozade?' was her reply.

I left her to make up a bed on the sofa and find an extra blanket, and when I looked into her bedroom again she had fallen asleep. I peered at her so-English face and thought how fragile it was. She was alone with her tattered dreams. I stood by her side, convinced that this episode would be forgotten and would never return. We had done the right thing, of that I was sure. I gave her a gentle peck on the forehead, and switching off her bedside light, went to my makeshift bed. The flat still had a musty smell and was far too warm. How the British hate to open the windows to let the air in. The room was spotless though and that made the heat more bearable. I turned on my side and not for one moment did it cross my mind that I had murdered someone that day. I believed we had done what we had to do to ensure life would work out for us both in the future. Remorse and shame were keeping well out of sight; I even congratulated myself on being a gentleman and standing by Margaret in her hour of need. The fucking selfishness of it all!

PART TWO

It was my nanny, Miss Wales, who inadvertently introduced me to California.

'Don't be in such a hurry!' she hissed as I ran and fell on the gravel outside our house.

The small stones drank up the blood that gushed from my knee. The sight of the open wound made my eyes fill with tears.

'Don't be so silly! You must learn to be brave.'

Too young to know that 'silly' was a silly word to use, I got up and gingerly took slow footsteps into the warmth of our house. Miss Wales was unlike the foreign girls who care for their charges with sympathetic kisses and badly broken English. No, Miss Wales regarded it as her life's work to equip those in her care with the right values and proper good manners.

The gash was long but not particularly deep. The blue-veined hand of the elderly spinster wiped away the blood, smeared the wound with a slick of Savlon and covered it up with a heavy plaster. How I wished my mother was home to perform the minor operation.

'Where is mummy?' I demanded, sounding not only hurt but spoilt.

'Your mother is in London and won't be back until later. If you don't stop making a fuss, you can go upstairs and think about it.'

'Think about what, stupid?' I snapped, my tears miraculously dispelled.

'Right upstairs you go to the nursery . . . for a six-year-old you can be very cheeky.'

I turned my back, and with shoulders slumped, marched to the top of the house.

'I'll fetch you when it's time for dinner.'

I sat in the centre of the playroom, arms folded, squeezing in my stomach and spasmodically kicking my legs into the air. How unfair life could be! I remained in a bored sulk until I recognised my salvation on top of the large chest of drawers. I went to the door and placed my ear close to it; there was no sound of Miss Wales. With a smile of triumph, I climbed up to switch on the television.

The black-and-white grainy pictures were of a place bathed in sunshine. Large numbers of cars, enormous houses and the flash of cameras. Where is this paradise, I wondered? I turned up the volume to hear what was being said. 'Hollywood, the city where they pay a thousand dollars for a kiss.' I have never forgotten those startlingly provocative words. I wanted to dive into the television and magically be in the city; this was the place to escape to, and from that afternoon I was planning to do just that.

* * *

I was setting off for lunch when Mr Birkenfeld summoned me. His large depressing figure was pacing the well-trodden and protesting floorboards. I still dreaded being called to his office. It smacked of reporting to the headmaster; I always thought that I was in trouble.

'I want you to travel with the Knight and me to Los Angeles for the Oscars. We'll be leaving on Monday. Not only will you be of help to the Knight, but it will give you the opportunity to connect with some of your associates from the ISA offices in Hollywood.'

I left Birkenfeld's office speckled with his spittle. I wondered whether his oafish behaviour indicated disrespect for himself, but it was little more than a fleeting speculation for I was agog with excitement. I would be travelling with one of the most famous actors in the world: a man knighted for his work over six decades on stage and screen.

The call could not have come at a better time. I needed a change, a boost from the despondency of recent weeks. Margaret had already started to drift off my radar. She had made it clear, when I called to check, that she wanted to put the trauma behind her, and hearing my voice was not going to help. I respected her plea and kept my distance.

The lugubrious Mr Witherspoon was the first person I bumped into after hearing the news. 'I'm off to the Oscars next week,' I told him exultantly.

'How dull! It really is the most ghastly occasion; dreadful ceremony, attended by sycophants and morons.'

'Come on, it can't be that bad, can it?' I didn't want to hear the downside.

'Don't be seduced by it. It's all fake, fake and more fake,' and he wagged his finger to drive home the warning.

I was already growing tired of the parade of old age that plagued my working day. The care-worn attitude was demoralising and I deplored the negative effect it had on the rest of the staff. Once again I felt the loneliness of youth.

* * *

'Oh, hello,' I said to a handsome fellow passenger as we walked towards the first-class British Airways desk at Heathrow Airport. I thought I recognised him as a friend of my father's from the City who had visited us when I was still struggling at school. He seemed surprised by the approach, but he nodded politely.

'We are going to be flying together,' I said pulling out my 'golden' ticket. This was my maiden first-class flight but I was already behaving as if it were the way I always flew.

'So it seems, doesn't it. And you are . . . ?' he queried, his tone authoritative and aloof.

'Sam Alexander,' I smiled and offered my hand, which he shook.

'I'm Terence Stamp.'

'What, the actor Terence Stamp?'

He nodded and the ghastly realisation dawned – he *was* the actor and not an old family friend. I had watched *Billy Budd* on television the previous month, which explained why he seemed familiar.

'I am sorry, I thought you were someone else.' I backed away embarrassed and deflated.

After he had checked in, as a way of apology I called out, 'Loved you in *Clockwork Orange*!' but, agitated, he hurried away.

* * *

The Knight was punctual and walked into the terminal unnoticed, wearing a mackintosh and carrying a green Marks & Spencer plastic bag; a porter by his side wheeled in his two suitcases. The Louis Vuitton luggage was the only clue that there was wealth, otherwise he could have been mistaken for a scruffy tour guide. He wore round metal-framed glasses and the ordinariness of it all made my expectations for the coming days take a nosedive. He's tired, I thought, remembering he was over eighty years old; 'seventy-nine' he would correct me later.

'Sir, my name is Samuel Alexander and I will be travelling with you.'

He said nothing, instead went for his pocket and pulled out his pen ready to give me his autograph.

'No, sir, I work with your agency. ISA.'

Instantly, the mist lifted from his rheumy eyes. He took his hand from his pocket and shook mine vigorously,

'Hello, hello, hello.' In a trice, the film star from the black-and-white movies emerged from under his hat and the prospect became considerably brighter.

'I see you have met. Excellent!' Birkenfeld had arrived, with his five cases, fat stomach and two porters; suddenly everything changed gear.

We were escorted to the VIP lounge but the Knight insisted that we move to join the rest in the first-class waiting area. Even among the rich, the Knight quickly drew the attention of a gaggle of admirers, paying their respects and asking for autographs. He treated all with the same generosity and magnanimous smile. He signed anything that was shoved under his nose, whether it was a strip of paper or a human limb. I fetched a drink of water and he drank it with small quick sips. He did look old at times, and I wondered whether it was a good idea that he was still being exposed to the scrutiny of the world. I scolded myself for having an opinion. I was too young and not experienced enough to know about these things. If Birkenfeld said it was all right then it must be.

Birkenfeld spent his time profitably, first talking to Terence Stamp and then moving on to an American actor who was extremely familiar but whose name escaped me.

'I will sign his Yankee arse before we cross the Atlantic,' boasted my boss, working up a sweat in all the excitement. The Knight was offered a ride to the gate in a wheelchair; it would have been a fifteen-minute hike otherwise. He accepted with grace and I walked beside him; everyone we passed either bowed or smiled. It was surreal, like escorting a beloved member of the Royal Family, and the warmth that beamed from strangers' faces was moving. 'Good luck at the Oscars!' someone called out.

* * *

I was wearing Tom's cherished three-buttoned charcoal-grey suit. We as a family debated whether he should be buried in it, but I did not like the idea and promised that one day I would wear it myself. The time had arrived, and the Saturday before I left, I visited Angelo our family tailor. The Italian remembered when he had first seen it; he had an encyclopedic memory for his alterations and recalled when my brother had first brought it in. He was an emotional Italian from Naples, and, seeing me in the suit, he said, 'You look important, you look rich and you look as if you are about to win something.'

'Thank you, I am none of the above but I am very flattered.'

His sweet talk did no harm to the business – this charming small man, with neat pencil-moustache and a laugh like an old lift climbing a high building. 'It fitted your brother,' he checked the back, 'but he needed the legs to be altered. Yes, a 32-inch inside leg . . . Such a handsome man he was! Do you remember he always wore that Eau Sauvage – ' and he stopped, overcome with emotion. He lowered his head. 'I loved your brother. He was so special. This suit will fit you with not a crease from before, I promise.' He started to pin the material. 'You are slightly bigger than him. The arms need extending here, but the shoulders fit perfectly.'

The mention of Tom's physical body upset me profoundly and I turned away and felt my eyes stab.

* * *

Birkenfeld had left me to sit beside the Knight, and was two rows in front, reading a bagful of scripts and popping Valium. Bored, I decided to stretch and walk around the cabin. He was checking the pages with red pen, as if correcting an examination paper.

'I find writers more difficult to represent than actors.' I listened and knelt beside him; he reeked of a sweet-smelling cologne. 'They are most important, though, and don't get enough respect. Heck, if you are an actress coming to town, you don't go sleeping with writers ... now do you?' He returned to his script.

'What are you reading?' I asked

'Oh, some piece of crap!'

'What's it called?'

'*Ghostbusters*.'

* * *

The Knight had recently completed two movies back to back and the talk was that Birkenfeld was overworking the legend. The first was an African adventure with a touch of *King Solomon's Mines* and the second a Jewish love story, shot in Boston, in which he played an Orthodox rabbi.

During our lunch, his conversation drifted from the 1930s to the present day. He spoke in three languages, Swahili, Hebrew and Shakespeare's English – an evident hangover from his last two film roles combined with the dominant thread of his career. How strange the human brain is. I was now the one giving the performance, for I smiled and conversed and gulped down another brandy even though I had little idea what he was talking about.

When the in-flight film began, we put on the uncomfortable headphones, and settled to watch *Ordinary People*. It was probably the most difficult film I could have seen at that time. The movie depicts the loss in a family of an older son. I watched with my eyes full of tears and my hand covering my mouth to muffle my sobs. By the time the end credits ran, I was reduced to a shadow of the boy that had boarded the plane. My shoulders drooped and my chin trembled. Could I never rid myself of this pain? The Knight, who I was beginning to think should not be travelling, clasped my hand and squeezed it.

'I lost my brother and I found that movie very difficult. I am sorry to have made such a fool of myself,' I mumbled.

'I lost my son, twenty-five years ago, in a boating accident. I understand your grief. There is not one day I don't think of him.' And he took my hand again and his words restored my baleful spirits.

The flight was coming to an end, and as the plane began to make its approach, the captain revealed that we had a legend on board and announced the Knight's name to all the passengers. Applause rippled like falling dominoes through the cabins and soon the whole 747 was cheering.

He looked bemused. 'What's happening?'

'They're welcoming you to America, sir,' I replied.

From his seat, he gave his familiar wave. No one at the back could have seen, but all on board sensed his appreciation.

* * *

It was my first view of Los Angeles and the prodigious size of the place stunned me. The plane descended over houses; a refracted sun skimmed over the disparate swimming pools and freeways packed with cars looking from above like flies hovering over a corpse.

The Knight pointed to a vast collection of hangars. 'Those are the studios,' he said, and I marvelled that what I saw below was the epicentre of the movie industry. The wheels screeched on to the tarmac and the sun blazed through the small Boeing windows, lighting my face like a single spotlight on a darkened stage; destiny was calling and I believed it was pointing straight at me. 'I am in Los Angeles,' I whispered.

Solicitous staff cleared the route to the customs, and again, as in London, people clapped and cheered as the star walked by. Birkenfeld urged the procession to keep moving and grew impatient when the customs officers started to want photographs.

'This would not happen to Kenny Rogers!' Birkenfeld ranted. Our luggage was picked up from the carousel immediately, the nobodies being pushed out of the way by airport officials.

'You shouldn't behave like that. Really, it just won't do,' complained an ancient and offended aristocrat, witnessing the brutality.

'We have the biggest star in the world right here and nothing is going to get in our way. We aim to make his time at this terminal a most pleasurable one!' came the curt reply from one of the officers.

'Huh! I thought he had retired years ago,' she huffed.

Holding his hat in his hand, the Knight walked with humility into the strong sunlight, where the heat gave the impression that invisible fires were being stoked specially for the occasion. The applause continued as the Knight gave a final wave and bent over to enter the waiting car. This was going to be my first ride in a monster limousine and a bigger one could not have been found. It was as long as a cricket pitch and our feet sank into the plush carpet inside.

A structure resembling a flying saucer about to land on its four legs hung over us as we motored out of the airport. 'It's a restaurant,' said a gentle voice; the voice belonged to a girl who'd been sent to greet him by the film company behind the Knight's latest movie.

* * *

February Long had woken that morning at first light, as usual. She looked lovelier than ever after her peaceful sleep. As she brushed her teeth she avoided her reflection in the tarnished mirror and thought about the poem 'A Martian Sends a Postcard Home' that she had read before falling asleep. The line 'Only the young are allowed to suffer openly' made her muse on her childhood and her freedom to share her misgivings openly with her parents. 'How lucky I am,' she thought.

As the kettle boiled on an old-fashioned gas-ring, she wandered out into her little garden and breathed in the crisp air of Mount Olympus in the Hollywood Hills. February and her actress friend had rented the slightly dilapidated house for a year now; although in need of a good lick of paint, the house had positive vibes and the two were happy. She never felt lonely, even now that much of her time was spent alone as her friend had been in New York for the previous four months. She had a job off Broadway and the play's run had been extended. February had promised that she would go and visit, but her job at Twentieth Century Fox had restricted her travel and indeed her freedom. But she needed to pay her rent and was fastidious in everything she did. As she sat outside, the heat began to rise; she sipped her coffee, contemplating her morning.

Today she had been asked by the head of marketing to 'look after' an actor who was arriving in town to attend the Oscars. 'As we have made his last two movies, it's our responsibility to take care of him,' she was told. 'Meet him off his plane and be there for him right until he leaves town. It seems he will be arriving with his agent and one other.' It was not the sort of thing she had done before, but it sounded easy enough and she looked forward to the change in her day. She knew of the Knight, mainly because he had appeared in one of her favourite movies, but meeting stars did not impress her. Her father was a respected cinematographer and was friends with many of the legends that lived in the town.

The plane was not due to arrive until early afternoon and so she decided to drive down to Farmers Market off

Fairfax with her pad and do some sketching. Painting and drawing were her first love, and whenever she had time, she would work at her art. She had unquestionable talent but it was a lonely pastime. 'Thank God,' she had thought, 'I have a job, else I would get pretty withdrawn.'

* * *

'I love your name. I've met a January, but never a February,' I said.

'I am a child of the sixties and my parents embodied the spirit of the decade. I sometimes wish my name was Jane though,' she replied with more than a hint of playfulness.

Why was she so familiar? What is it about someone that puts one at one's ease within seconds of meeting? Then I realised her colouring was similar to Lana's and she had a smile that I recognised as Lana's. Her arms and whole body were golden too, and so slender that her bones were softly defined.

I turned away, eager to find a distraction before she caught me staring. Down the 405 we drove, the yellow smog that everyone warned about invisible to my eyes; it did not exist. A stream of battered, oversized cars with dented hubcaps played a game of dodgems in a race to reach their destination. The pace of the freeway was frenetic and the sound of hooting and the moving mass of metal had me spellbound.

'First time here?' asked February.

'Yes and everything I have seen so far blows me away,' and I gazed into her eyes, green as emeralds, as grass after rain.

'Don't exaggerate,' she said, laughing in a way that made you want to share the laugh with her. 'We haven't gone anywhere yet.'

'That's enough, young man. Cut the crap,' interrupted

my boss. 'We have a busy schedule ahead and I want you focused on the job.'

Scolded, I withdrew and stared out of the window like a little boy told off for eating too many sweets. The Knight caught my mood and gave me a wink.

The wide red carpet was out for our arrival at the Beverly Hills Hotel; the manager, the assistant manager, head of security and the concierge were all in a row to greet us. The Knight emerged into the sunlight and the manager presented him with a blue box wrapped in red ribbon. He immediately handed it to me and I handed it to February. We were then escorted into the pink birthday cake of a building and led in different directions depending on rank. The Knight was taken to the Presidential Bungalow, Birkenfeld to the Garden Bungalow and I was off to an over-decorated, garishly appointed suite. As soon as the porter disappeared with his generous tip, I dived on to my king-size bed with its plump pillows, squealing with delight and jumping up and down like a deranged kid. I opened the mini bar, checked out the bathroom and switched on the television. This was America and I wanted to sample everything. My room overlooked Sunset Boulevard, and after a shower, I put on a snowy white robe and looked out at the passing traffic; it was still warm, still light. No wonder, the British move out to California; just by being here, I felt a success.

Birkenfeld rang the room to say that the Knight was retiring early to combat the jet lag and he himself was off to meet with the Chief Executive of ISA in the United States. 'Do what you like, young man, we will see you in the morning.'

* * *

There was a message waiting on my arrival from David Burford, Earl of Amersham. 'Call immediately.' But even as I was dialling his number there was a tentative knock on my door and the strained voice of my school friend.

David looked terrible, a change from when I had last seen him in London. His breath was sour, his hair was greasy and his eyes were bloodshot as ice cream streaked with strawberry sauce. As he stretched for a drink from the mini bar, a stain of sweat was visible under the arm of his sky-blue shirt. He drank the miniature bottle of whiskey without pouring it into a glass and shuddered like a child who had just swallowed medicine.

He had decided to spend more time in California and was renting a house out on Mulholland Drive. The death of his father had left him with a huge inheritance, which he was running through at a rate of knots. He was living life to excess and who could blame him? He had the money and the looks to do it, but only for a limited period. That afternoon he seemed rapidly to be losing both. David unfolded a small packet of cocaine, and tapping the drug from the outside, poured a small heap into a tiny spoon. He placed the powder under my nose and I sniffed it up without hesitation. I was eager for pleasure and had no qualms about indulging in a drug that had contributed to my brother's downfall.

'I need to ask the concierge to give a script to some actor,' David told me. 'I'll be back in a moment, then we're going off to a friend's party.' As he was leaving, February was passing the door. I called out and invited her in for a drink; David lifted his eyebrow as they passed each other. 'Invite her!' he signalled to me with his eyes.

'You look settled,' February said, seeing my clothes strewn across the room. She picked up a shirt and draped it on the back of a chair. Outside the window a dog was barking in the lane below the hotel. She looked down and laughed and my spirits soared at the sound of that laugh.

'Silly dog,' she said quietly. She turned and we stood staring at one another, silent above the glow and hum of the pulsating city. It was absurd, even farcical.

'I'm a bit tired, but I feel very happy,' I said, looking to break the sudden stillness.

'You say "happy" as if it's a relief.'

'It is. I haven't been happy for a while.' I checked myself for being too open.

'Well, if you need someone to talk to, I'm a good listener.'

Her words again triggered a memory of Lana, when she had said on the night that I met her, 'I'll listen, I will always listen.' There was nothing casual in the resemblance; it was so exact that for a second I couldn't remember who this was; this over-familiar face.

Yes, it was her hair, the colour of light honey, and the pretty, small nose. I looked down at her hands and they were delicate, the fingers long. I wanted to say, 'Haven't we met before somewhere?' but I knew she would think me crazy, so I said nothing and laughed at the silliness of it all.

* * *

The Earl of Amersham drove his black Porsche with roof down along Sunset Boulevard like a boy vexed by confiscation of a bag of sweets. His driving made me regret that I had invited February to join us but she was less alarmed than I was. We were heading towards a house on the top of Beachwood Canyon, overlooking the Hollywood sign. This was my first time on Sunset Boulevard and I tried to ignore my errant friend and take in the legendary sights passing before my eyes. Giant billboards towered over the strip, and seeing the Whiskey A Go-Go club (where the Doors played in their early days) provoked a memory of when I got high listening to 'Riders on the Storm' one lonely

Sunday at school. The pine-scented air rushed towards my face and my friend's negativity ceased to affect me.

En route, David turned left on to Laurel Canyon through a maze of twisting bends and glorious turns to pick up a script from a friend.

'These are the Hollywood Hills, near to where I'm renting. Few survive the treacherous corners if they've had a drink too many.' He spoke this line as if he were stealing it from a classic movie, and at the same time negotiated a tight fork in the road. David announced to anyone who cared to listen that he was a producer looking for the right project.

'Heck,' he said, 'I have enough money to back it myself.'

'Bad idea,' was my murmured response, but I let it drift away on the cool Californian breeze.

He parked competently enough outside a house on Lookout Mountain, and February and I waited in the car. Silence prevailed. I sat in front fearful of turning round, scared that if I did I would try to kiss her. Far too soon for that. I switched on the radio and 'Lollipops and Roses', sung by Jack Jones, was being played. And I knew as we listened to the 1950s' lyrics – 'Tell her you care, each time you speak, make it her birthday each day of the week . . . ' – that should we have a future and grow old together, then this would be our song, special to no one but us. I knew it that night in the dark of the Hollywood Hills. I did, I promise I did.

* * *

The party being thrown was at the summit of Beachwood Canyon. The house resembled a Norman castle, and in the garden were fishponds, waterfalls and a folly. The pool was heart-shaped and surrounded by a group still looking sober but grabbing for the drinks served by flushed barmen. There was an air of importance about those at the crowded poolside and I felt insignificant, and even more so when I looked up at a canopy of stars that made one's own mortality seem so trifling. The jet lag was beginning to get to me, but I would not allow it to spoil my night, and I continued to work my way around the pool, drifting through conversations rising in volume and crashing like waves into raucous laughter.

It became clear that agents were not high up on the totem pole of respect and honour. This struck me as an injustice as I understood that agents were the ones who really made the town tick, but each time I introduced myself as one, there was a stutter, a gesture of revulsion, an instant retreat. I promised myself that I would ask Birkenfeld what this meant.

Then I let it drop in conversation that I had that afternoon flown in with the Knight to escort him to the Oscars. The news swept like a tornado into the rambling house and out again. Within minutes, strangers' hands were clasping my arm and in alcoholic whispers strangers' voices were inviting me to dinner 'at the beach'. It was a crash course in how to get on in this town: rule one, either be a big star or represent one. I had acquired some charisma; they wanted to believe in what I had said and my being enigmatic added to the intrigue. I planted this information safely in my top pocket with my brand new collection of contacts.

* * *

February and David were nowhere to be found. I stepped down to the guesthouse where a separate party was in full swing; revellers lay on the floor laughing at tall tales, and actresses never tired of being told that they were the next big thing. I was becoming increasingly tired and had reached a point where I imagined my name was being called.

'I know I don't look Jewish, but honestly I am.' A creature seeking a quarry like a pointer cornered me, thinking I might be interested in conversation. 'When I was younger I wanted to join the Hitler Youth. You know, be violent towards

Jews and daub swastikas all over town. I was brought up in Europe, you see.' His accent was suburban English. 'Just in time, my father told me I had picked the wrong cause as I was Jewish myself.' And he guffawed at the irony.

'Strange thing – my close friend recently found that he had Jewish blood . . . which reminds me I have to find him.'

'Listen, before you go, take my card, just in case you need anything.'

The Jewish Eichmann turned out to be an agent at the William Morris Agency.

'Oh dear,' I thought, 'I hope they're not all like that. If so, I'll be a producer by morning.'

Underneath the elaborate gatehouse, I had been told that there was a hidden door leading to a 1920s' speakeasy. I found the door and, down some stairs, a narrow room decorated in South Seas style, with a bamboo bar and piano at the far end. It was dimly lit by pink lights and at first it was hard to make out who or what was there. I approached the bar and saw David with February. My school friend was busy snorting drugs from the mirrored counter. The gantry had a line of exotic bottles lit from behind by a green light which fell eerily on their faces. Heavy cigarette smoke and the sound of Cleo Laine singing Johnny Dankworth's 'All Gone' floated in the air. On the long sofa lay a movie star gazing into the void; on the floor beside the sofa, a fabulously seductive woman in the act of taking a drag from a large joint was silhouetted by a wedge of light. February smiled and beckoned me over. Her index finger moved slowly and seductively in the direction of her mouth. Her full lips pecked mine slowly and in the the semi-darkness we started to kiss passionately, with my best friend taking his drugs from the bar at our side.

* * *

The bright sun shone down on our breakfast. It was so bright one felt permanently caught in the flash from a camera. The Knight was quiet, lost in thought, while Birkenfeld was talkative and I was away in a daze of time zones. The morning was set aside for an interview with the *Los Angeles Times* and an exclusive interview with the leading anchor from CBS. Birkenfeld again made an early exit and left me in charge. 'If they ask too many tough questions, stop the interview.' He then bit off and spat out the top of his cigar and left the bungalow. I wanted to ask what was considered a 'tough' question, but hoped my common sense would tell me. He clearly trusted my ability.

The Knight was unfailingly charming, kind and distant. The flight had taken its toll and he was still somewhat disorientated. The *Los Angeles Times* was the first through the door in the person of Mrs Doris Pullman, an enthusiastic movie critic in her sixties with too much black eyeliner. She spoke hurriedly, without drawing breath, about the Knight's career. She had arrived with a bright-eyed February, whom I had last seen being driven away by my intoxicated friend. She showed no hint of a hangover from the night before. I had been concerned about leaving her with my drug-fuelled chum, but she'd assured me that she would be fine and by that time I was too weary to argue.

I disappeared into the adjoining room to fetch the Knight. He was sound asleep with his shoes on, flat out on the bed. He was snoring loudly and I considered leaving him, but I decided that he would want to work. I shook his arm and he started up with a grunt. He adjusted his eyes to the sunlight and could now make out it was me leaning over him. With a spark of humour, he started to recite the words of Iago from *Othello*:

'And what's he then that says I play the villain,
When this advice is free I give, and honest,
Probal to thinking, and indeed the course
To win the Moor again?'

'Oh good,' I thought, 'he's all right then!'

* * *

Mrs Pullman curtseyed so low that I ran to pick her up as I was sure she had fallen. The Knight had changed from Shakespeare's most sinister villain to Henry V, and as he accepted her hand, he took a step back and recited:

'This day is called the feast of Crispian:
He that outlives this day, and comes safe home,
Will stand a-tiptoe when the day is named,
And rouse him at the name of Crispian.
He that shall live this day, and see old age,
Will yearly on the vigil feast his neighbours,
And say, "Tomorrow is Saint Crispian." '

Madness, it seemed to me, was in the room, but after the histrionics there followed a faultless interview and everything he said was taken down with reverence. After a good hour, I moved from my seat and told her time was up. She backed out reluctantly, still thanking the Knight.

'I don't know how you do it, sir!' I felt slightly bewildered by the stream of consciousness that had emerged from the Knight's mouth.

'Years of practice, my dear boy. The key is not to tell them anything.'

'I understand now,' I replied, relieved by his answer.

The Knight remained in his chair, staring languorously into the middle distance and sipping a cup of tea. He was already exhausted; his performance with the journalist, had siphoned the strength out of him. He seemed to want to be alone, and, unsure what to do next, I called February to join us.

'Are you all right, sir? Can I fetch you anything?' I mouthed my words slowly, as if I were communicating with a four-year-old child. 'Would you like some fruit?' I began to peel off a banana skin.

He shook his head, said nothing and started to dribble slightly. February disappeared into the bathroom and brought back a tissue with which to dab his mouth. He gave another one of his grunts, switched on the television and fell to surfing the countless channels. He stopped suddenly when he found one of his movies. It looked like it was made well before the war. It had that grainy hesitation that grows over the years like moss on the branch of a tree. He had drifted away down the long path of memories and for the time being it was difficult to follow and bring him back.

I made a decision. 'We're going to cancel the network interview,' I was looking steadily at February. 'He's not in a state to eat a grape now, let alone talk to a stranger about his life.'

'Do you think that's a good idea?' February asked, not convinced I was making the right decision.

'I see no alternative. I'm not prepared to let him become an embarrassment.'

We left the Knight watching his old movie, absorbed and unaware of the change to his schedule.

* * *

The network anchor, wearing expensive brown brogues beneath his navy-blue Park Avenue suit, remained surprisingly sanguine at the postponement. Perhaps that was why he was so highly paid . . . good under pressure. I had cleared my throat as a way of announcing bad news and explained that tiredness had taken its toll on the old man; he was suffering from jet lag. He needed rest before tonight's Oscar rehearsal, which would come hard on the heels of the British Academy lunch where he was to be the guest of honour. 'We may be able to rearrange for tomorrow afternoon.'

'That needs to happen,' said the anchor. 'I'd better call New York and tell them it's off for today. They won't be too happy.'

Birkenfeld was walking in as the anchor was walking out. He looked at me, with face and shoulders asking the question. I told him straight that I hadn't thought the Knight was up to it and he was resting in his room. He said nothing and went to see his client.

February walked over and touched my hand reassuringly. 'You're very good,' she said.

'Do you think so, truly?' and we stole a kiss before my boss returned.

Birkenfeld closed the bedroom door behind him and came over to me. 'You showed initiative and courage in making that decision. To cancel a network interview was one hell of a step and for that I congratulate you. Get them on the phone; I'll reschedule for tomorrow before the awards. You're a good lad. I knew I could trust you.' He turned his back and slumped on to the sofa, chewing an unlit cigar. The inches around his girth seemed to have increased over the last twenty-four hours and he released his belt and let out a sigh of pleasure. I brought the phone over and he rearranged the day, hung up and flicked off his shoes. 'We'll try again tomorrow afternoon. I am going to have an hour's sleep before the lunch. You guys take a hike.'

Birkenfeld's belief in me had banished my feeling of insecurity and boosted my confidence. We headed from the suite in search of a soft drink.

February sipped on her extravagant strawberry milk-shake, her lips smacking around the straw. Her offer of support in the first hours of our friendship had made a profound impression; I appreciated her concern. We sat on green barstools, made with no regard for comfort, at a curved soda-fountain counter. The banana-leaf wallpaper lent a tropical air to the narrow room.

February was drawing in pencil on a piece of pink hotel paper as I spoke of my life back in England. The quick strokes formed a shape before my eyes, like thick cream being poured from a silver jug. My longing for her was growing with each minute of the day. Yes, she was exquisite, but it was her originality and self-containment that were even more seductive. What is it about some people that makes them so magnetic?

'I want to be able to draw and paint for a living, that's my ambition.' And I watched as she concentrated, the tip of her tongue poking from her mouth a sign of the effort she was making.

'Here we are.' February handed me her drawing and I glanced down. It was certainly my face but I didn't recognise the hurt etched around the finely drawn eyes. It reminded me of when I was a small boy of about five, waiting for my mother to pick me up after school. I would be standing alone in the playground behind high black railings, always the last to be collected.

She saw my reaction. 'It's only a sketch, Samuel. Don't look so worried.'

'I don't want you to see me as a wounded child.'

'But that is what you are; your fragility is plainly visible.'

I shook my head, firmly in denial, and she kissed my cheek as we left to join the others for lunch.

* * *

Stewart Granger looked remarkably well; he was every inch the Hollywood star, and though he was now well into his sixties, he had the suppleness of a man far younger. The British Academy lunch was conveniently held downstairs in the hotel. It was an opportunity for ex-pats and Hollywood to celebrate. Granger's very 'English' welcoming remarks were amusing and frivolous.

Orson Welles followed and gave a speech revolving around Winston Churchill. Once when Welles walked into a restaurant in Venice with a potential Russian investor, a mere nod from the great man's bald pate had garnered him a million-dollar advance. On sitting down, the Russian had said, 'You know Winston Churchill? I am mighty impressed.'

The following morning, Welles bumped into Churchill. 'Sir, thank you for acknowledging me yesterday; your mere nod helped me raise half the budget for my next movie.'

At lunch later that next day, Welles returned to the dining room with the same Russian. This time, on seeing Welles, Churchill slowly rose from his table and gave an exaggerated bow. The Russian wrote another cheque.

This was a lunch of many more speeches, many more anecdotes and much innuendo, but the invited were there to hail the Knight. I sat between Oliver Reed and Deborah Kerr, not as young as I had imagined (I was still thinking of *An Affair to Remember*) but still lovely, and now with a charming air of wistful melancholy. She occasionally spoke and politely listened to the obtuse conversation I was having with Olly.

'Call me Olly,' he had said, his tongue sticking to the roof of his mouth. 'Hell, I need something for this hangover!'

He snapped his fingers and ordered a brandy. When it was placed in front of him, he popped in an Alka-Seltzer.

It was his second brandy of the day. 'It's the second one that counts,' he explained. 'Anyone can down one drink first thing the morning after, but it's the second one that sends many a man to the nearest bathroom.'

We spoke about public school and he loved my story about a close friend who had been head boy at St Edward's in Oxford, one of whose famous old boys was the war hero Sir Douglas Bader. When, after a drunken final year, my friend went to say goodbye to the headmaster, he was told, 'We have had two legless head boys here at "Teddy's", you and Sir Douglas Bader.'

Olly roared with laughter. He spoke of *If* as being one of his favourite films and grinned at the memory of the final scene – the scene of the revolution.

'How strange that it is now accepted by the Establishment! Just before I was expelled, it was shown to the whole school as the "film of the summer",' I said.

'Very English,' Deborah Kerr remarked. 'When something is threatening, the English Establishment borrows it and introduces it into society as theirs.'

'How right you are,' I agreed. 'By the way, Miss Kerr, I adored *Born Free*. I thought it was so moving, and when you saw Elsa with her cubs . . . I cried and cried.'

She signalled the waiter for some more water.

Olly ordered another brandy. 'Do you play golf?' he asked, changing the subject and rocking in his chair to the throbbing in his head.

'Of course I do,' I lied.

'Good, let's meet at the Brentwood Country Club on Wednesday; say, eleven o'clock.'

We shook on it. Champagne flowed and glasses clinked. Loud memories of the theatre, a yearning for London and the gossip of Wardour Street filled the room. And if you'd closed your eyes, you would have sworn that you were sitting in Simpson's in the Strand rather than a stone's throw from Sunset Boulevard.

The Knight made a stirring speech and joked about his years in repertory. He swung from being funny and alert to gazing round like a lost child. He sat down to a standing ovation. He caught sight of me on my feet applauding and threw me an exaggerated wink; I was beginning to feel mighty special.

* * *

The towering columns of the Dorothy Chandler Pavilion rose before us like some latter-day Parthenon. Hundreds of workers were hurriedly preparing for the movie industry's big night. Our limousine passed through barriers, and out of the car's darkened windows we saw faces peering in, trying to guess who was inside. The weather was bright with not a cloud; complaints about the consistency of the fine weather were beyond my understanding – I was delighted that I had left the incessant rain back on the London streets.

We had arrived at the venue for the rehearsal. This was ultimately a live television show and so the run-through had to be precise. Names of the winners were guessed at and an extra would walk up and pretend to receive his award. All presenters were summoned and our Knight was no different. Our entourage was growing, with a photographer and make-up and hair team now joining the crew. The dressing-room door had the Knight's name printed on it within a golden star and we trooped in to find flowers and more flowers heaped on every surface. 'Did someone die?' the Knight joked.

Birkenfeld beckoned me over. 'I want you to stick to him – like glue you hear? I have to be out there in the auditorium tomorrow night, working the room, and it will be for you to escort him to the stage.' He was looking at his client, 'Out with the old and in with the new.' I was not too sure if he was joking, but the grey head of our host Johnny Carson broke my train of thought, appearing round the door like that of an ostrich in search of food. The two stars' warm embrace was captured by the eager photographer; in seconds Birkenfeld had muscled himself between them, his heavy arms clumped over their shoulders. 'Best friends,' he squealed. I was beginning see how the intimate photos of Birkenfeld with the famous had come about.

The Knight was going to make two walks on to the stage. He was to receive a special award for his life's work, and was later to make the 'Best Picture' presentation. 'This way, this way,' an over-officious stage manager led us through the jungle of wires and a backstage area looking more like Billy Smart's Circus. There were two elephants preparing a dance with Mickey Rooney and a troupe of horses ready to do their shoe shuffle with Cyd Charisse and Ginger Rogers.

The first part of the rehearsal was uncomplicated; the Knight was to be introduced by Cary Grant and a montage of his work would then be shown. Cary Grant was unavailable for the night's rehearsal and had a stand in – Ralph, the uppity, gay security guard, who was scolded for overacting his role. 'Henry Fonda would not fucking behave like that!' bleated the director from his booth in the auditorium as Ralph performed a little Highland jig prior to his introduction.

The presentation for Best Picture seemed easy enough. The Knight had to read out the five nominations written on the outside of the envelope. After each name a short excerpt would be shown, and at the end, the envelope would be opened and the winner revealed. The Knight listened to the instructions carefully, then he strolled to centre stage and in one take performed his duty. 'Now that's a star,' beamed Ralph, who had been somewhat subdued since the director's shout from the auditorium. 'I'm not that bothered,' he moaned, 'he's a lousy director and his last movie was a disaster with a capital D.'

In the limousine back to the hotel, Birkenfeld said we must meet in the morning for the Knight's Armani fitting.

'Does that mean we are free for the rest of the evening?' I asked.

He nodded, so I nodded at February and February nodded back.

'You be a good boy now,' said the Knight, patting my knee gently and then giving my chin a pinch.

* * *

The Polo Lounge at the Beverly Hills Hotel was packed with celebrities from the film world. Being the night before the Oscars, the buzz of speculation, talk of business and pervasive air of self-congratulation were rife. The tables were reserved and the food and drink inexhaustible.

February and I had decided to sneak in for a drink, but hearing the braying laughter and seeing the haze of smoke, I suggested we go elsewhere.

'No,' she replied, 'this is where you should be and this is where we are going,' and she whispered to the man at the door and in we walked to an outer table which seemed to be waiting for our arrival.

I ordered myself a Ricard and February asked for a soda. Her beauty was effortless and encircling her dress she wore a belt like a snake coiled round a jungle tree. By merely looking at her, I felt possessed; 'Make conversation,' I kept saying to myself, 'make conversation.'

Cary Grant took the table next to us and I pointed him out. 'He's my favourite,' I whispered. His white shirt was open inside a navy-blue suit jacket and his deep tan looked as natural as if he had been born with it. We caught a snatch of his table's conversation. Cary Grant was saying that a man could only love someone he knew well, and that it was the quality of the love that mattered, not the glamorous trappings. February and I gave each other a smile and toasted his words – and him as a fine human being.

'Tell me about your family,' I asked and she pulled out a black-and-white photograph of her parents drifting in a boat along a river winding into a tree-lined backdrop.

* * *

Edward and Helen Long had brought up their child February in La Honda, fifteen miles from Palo Alto – a back-to-nature pastoral idyll surrounded by soaring redwoods and moss-grown woods. The house was reached by a wooden bridge over a meandering stream. It attracted the intellectuals, and those that lived permanently on the edges of society. A community formed and kids played in the woods where the redwood trees were streaked with fluorescent paint and fantastic metal sculptures of outlandish creatures competed with the wildlife. A revolution was happening and February and her family tasted the zeitgeist. Her measured conversation and pauses for thought as an adult were in direct contrast to the community's stream-of-consciousness way of life. Her parents remained with their child in La Honda when Ken Kesey, the author of One Flew over the Cuckoo's Nest, took a group from there to go on his Merry Pranksters bus ride across the States.

'I remember waving off the bus. It's my first clear memory. It was painted with cryptic hieroglyphs and mystical symbols in bright colours.'

My mouth fell open. I was tripping just listening.

'I spent many nights under the stars, learning to live close to nature. It was like a long holiday, my kindergarten of life.' February tossed her honey waterfall lascivious hair back from her forehead and lit a cigarette, taking a deep drag and blowing the smoke like a bruise of fog above my head.

'How did you end up here?' I asked, now distracted by her eyes, green as eucalyptus leaves. I leaned over without warning and kissed her on the mouth.

She ignored my lunge and replied, 'All I remember is we left suddenly. No goodbyes.'

'You are driving me crazy.' My interruptions were being ignored.

'The next I knew, we were unpacking in a farmhouse in Topanga, where my parents still live today.'

'Will you kiss me?'

'I've asked my parents why we left so suddenly, but they are deliberately vague. I suppose one day it will all come out in therapy.' And she gave an infectious giggle.

'Well, what do you think happened?' I tried to focus on the conversation.

'Too many drugs? My father wanting to return to Los Angeles? He is a cinematographer by profession and I think he wanted to get on with his career. I once overheard dad say to mom something like, "The more they talked about love, the more badly they needed it." '

'Strange you don't want to know the truth . . . ' Again I lost track of the conversation. 'If I became your slave, would you set me free?' I asked.

'Never. I would keep you for ever.'

I leaned forward and started to nibble her earlobe.

'You have to behave in a place like this,' she purred, and teasingly pushed me away.

Out of the bustle of waiters and table-hoppers, Mr Birkenfeld suddenly appeared at our table and introduced his American equivalent, Marvin Cowen, the number-one man in the talent-agency business. Mr Cowen's list of clients was impressive by even the most cynical standards. I stumbled to my feet, but remembered the stiffening in my trousers so immediately sat down again.

Mr Cowen exuded power. No easy feat for someone let down by an ill-fitting suit. 'I am hearing good things about you, Sammy. Come and see me at our offices on Wednesday morning, let's say eleven o'clock.'

I paused. 'I'm sorry, Mr Cowen, I have a meeting with Oliver Reed at the same time. Would you like me to cancel?'

'I love this guy – Sammy is in town for two minutes and already he's setting up meetings. Come and see me at three.' And then he pinched my cheek like my grandfather used to do, with no thought of the pain he was causing. With that, the busy pair waved their farewells and with fixed smiles moved on to the next table to join Jack Lemmon.

'No one has ever called me Sammy before. I'm not sure I like it.'

'He's probably the most powerful man in the movie industry.'

'The most powerful man in the industry? Well, if that's the case, he can call me what he likes.'

* * *

'Let's get out of here. I have a surprise for you.' February took my hand and I followed. As we were leaving she stopped to kiss a leading man.

'Sam, may I introduce you to Fred Astaire.'

We shook hands and he gave me a generous smile. 'You be good to her now,' he said.

'Of course I will . . . but we are not together, we are just friends!'

The star looked at me with obvious sympathy.

As we passed the reception desk, I was called over to

pick up a waiting message. It was David asking me to join him at a party in a bungalow at the Chateau.

'I think we should forget that, don't you?' And she plucked the paper and tore it in half. Who was I to argue?

Her blue Alfa Romeo sports car was waiting outside and we drove along Sunset in the direction we had taken the night before. The roof was down and a slight breeze ruffled our hair. As we reached the 'stop' at Vine, February kissed my cheek and whispered, 'You have to trust me now. I'm going to tie a scarf around your eyes and then we're going to drive for fifteen minutes, park and then take a short walk. You OK with that?'

Was I OK? We were at that stage at which, if she asked for anything, I would have readily agreed. The chemistry between us and the balmy Californian night were leading us to only one perfect conclusion. She firmly tied a silk lemon-scented scarf over my eyes. The evening wind picked up and caressed my face and the sound of automobiles sang in my ears: I was happy and I was liberated.

The car came to an unexpected halt after a succession of tight bends. February said nothing but instead took my hand and led me over a stretch of uneven hard ground. I had total faith in her and felt no fear. I was not particularly inquisitive; I enjoyed the element of mystery. We reached a low wooden fence. I had a sense we were way out in open country, and took comfort from the scent of animals and the scent of pine. On the other side of the fence the ground sloped down steeply and I felt uneven grass underfoot and heard the whisper of a distant town. She grabbed my chest from behind and told me to stop. 'I'm going to take off the scarf now.' Slowly she removed my silk blindfold. In front of my eyes there was a huge white towering letter, supported by scaffolding, and, beyond, a vast city aflame with pulsating lights.

'Hollywood!' I gasped.

I had been led to the Hollywood sign and was looking from behind the tall letters down on the City of Angels. She clasped my waist, and now it was her turn to close her eyes. I gazed at her, and like a light scattering of rain, the lovely things about her gently fell into my heart. We started to kiss passionately. Our bodies entwined themselves around each other. And when our shadows met, I half expected the man in the moon to smile and to cry out, 'Don't ever let her go!'

* * *

30 March 1981

I looked into the mirror and yawned. I felt I had been dreaming that I was dreaming. I filled the sink and the soap slipped from my hand into the hot water, flopping and bouncing like a burlesque dancer. The mirror steamed over and I drew a love heart and pierced it with an arrow. I quickly rubbed the drawing away; February could have walked in at any time. The smell of pine still lingered on my skin and I allowed myself a contented chuckle. The overhead glare in the strip-lit bathroom, instead of highlighting the vulnerability of my face, created the pleasing impression that my skin was blemish free; I looked alive and marvelled at the vibrancy of my eyes. It must be the expensive quality of the lighting in the Beverly Hills Hotel bathroom; they think of everything in this place. I contemplated grooming my hair with the special French hairbrush that mother had bought me for my birthday, but I decided against it and let my hair remain tousled. It was the morning of the Oscars and I was excited not only by the prospect of the evening's show but also by the fact that I would be going with one of the greatest actors of the twentieth century. I knew I had to savour these experiences;

too often in the past I had squandered opportunities that had come my way.

February was in bed. She looked like a bird, her body spiralling towards me like a condor in the sky. I leant over and pulled away the sheet. She smiled her peaceful smile and I hugged her harder, closer, until suddenly our mood was shattered by a muffled explosion coming from outside.

I pulled away from February's arms and crossed to the door. I could hear footsteps scurrying in all directions. I peered out cautiously and was immediately accosted by a woman who was half made-up for the afternoon's ceremony, but whose hair looked as if it had been buffeted by an angry wind.

'Have you heard?' she said, her tone verging on the hysterical, 'the President has been shot!'

'Jesus Christ!' I slammed the door in her face.

'What's wrong?' February asked.

'Some crazy woman says that the President's been shot!'

February, without a word, hurried over to the television and switched it on. A self-important anchor was announcing the grave news. It was her big break to be working at this precise moment in history and she was not about to let the side down: 'President Ronald Reagan has been shot and wounded after a lone gunman opened fire in Washington. He is currently undergoing emergency surgery at George Washington University Hospital.'

An unreasoning terror seized my mind at the thought of the consequences of this attempt on the President's life. I turned to February, whose expression defined the moment with a shocked intensity of incomprehension. I automatically took her hand, and together we left our suite and hurried off in search of Birkenfeld.

His bungalow was littered with scripts and had the unpleasant stench of half-smoked cigars. He was having a quiet lunch with the Knight, who was eating slowly and prodding at his salad like an opening batsman testing the pace of the wicket. Birkenfeld had his tomato-and-lettuce sandwich halfway into his mouth.

'Have you heard about the shooting?' I asked.

'Anyone we know?'

'Just the President of the United States.'

' "We are but as the instruments of heaven. Our work is not design but destiny." ' The Knight had spoken.

'Put on the bloody television!' commanded Birkenfeld.

The anchor was still in full flow: 'The President had appeared from the hotel smiling and walked towards his limousine, turning momentarily to acknowledge calls from the waiting press. A burst of gunfire was then heard and immediately afterwards the President was bundled into a bullet-proof limousine and whisked away . . . First Lady, Nancy Reagan, is understood to be on her way to the hospital to visit her seventy-year-old husband. . . . The attacker is described as being in his twenties and blond . . . The Vice-President, George Bush, is currently on his way to Washington from Texas. . . . The American Stock Exchange has suspended trading and tonight's scheduled Academy Awards have been postponed until tomorrow night.'

'Shit!' Birkenfeld stormed and at that very moment the phone rang. The Academy was relaying the already 'old' news. 'Yeah, yeah, yeah,' he replaced the phone and let out an anxious and unattractive burp. 'It's postponed for sure.' Birkenfeld's head made a circular movement and his eyes flittered towards his client with concern. The Knight may well have made it that evening, but he was increasingly out of touch with reality. February was glued to the television news and would from time to time relay an update. Birkenfeld wandered around the suite making pellets from a bread roll and flicking them at random targets, while the

Knight stretched himself out in his chair. How drowsily content he looked.

'Sounds like some lefty liberal faggot.'

'How did you reach that conclusion?' I asked, getting more than ever irritated by my boss's behaviour.

'Listen to the news!' he was jabbing at his ear with a fat index finger, insinuating that I wasn't that bright. 'In his twenties, blond . . . probably has hair down to his shoulders and can't even spell Reagan.'

I started to spell the name silently: R–E–G–A–N. Shit, I didn't think I could spell it either.

'I used to represent that son of a bitch,' announced Birkenfeld.

'Who?' I asked.

'Ronald Reagan. He was one of my first clients. He should've stayed in the movies. If he had no one would have taken a pot shot at him . . . but then again . . . '

The phone rang and February picked it up. 'It's Gregory Peck.'

Birkenfeld went to grab the phone.

'No, it's for the Knight,' and she withdrew the receiver from his grasping hand.

The whole room pretended not to listen, but of course we did. Unfortunately there was little to hear as the caller was doing all the talking. It looked as if the Knight was having difficulty getting his tongue to work. He hung up.

'Well?' his agent asked.

'He wanted to know if we could have dinner tonight.'

'And what did you say?' Birkenfeld snapped, obviously eager to be part of the soirée.

The Knight fell to pondering the framework of his recent conversation, and at last, as if waking from a dream, said, 'I'm not sure. I'm a little confused.'

The room went silent and alarm spread from face to face.

February escaped to go home and flee Birkenfeld's exasperating presence. I walked the Knight out for some fresh air. It seemed a good idea for him to feel the benefit of the California sun. As usual, the customary bows greeted him as we passed through the hotel into the sunlight. As we strode lightly along the drive towards the bustle of Sunset Boulevard, a paparazzo asked whether he could take a photograph.

'Only with my friend,' the Knight replied, and grabbing my shoulder, he pulled me beside his frail body. The pap's face dropped, but he snapped anyway.

'Thank you, your lordship,' salivated the pap, backing away sycophantically and in so doing nearly stepping in front of a passing limousine.

We continued our walk, and once on the Boulevard, we paused and I asked with a dry mouth, 'Are you all right, sir? I mean are you going to be fine picking up your Oscar?'

'I am in good health, Sam.' It was the first time he had called me by my first name and I felt a wave of pleasure. 'Don't worry, when I have to perform, I always do a first-rate job; I have *never* let anyone down.'

And I believed him.

* * *

31 March 1981

'How do I look?' I asked, straightening my bow tie.

'You look very handsome.' February was stroking my hair and looking over my shoulder into the mirror. My skin smelled of February's jasmine scent and my mind was alert. All traces of jet lag had disappeared. The wounded President was going to make it: he'd apparently even joked with his wife Nancy, 'Honey, I forgot to duck.' The Oscar machinery was up and running again.

It was an odd sensation: here I was dressing up in black

tie with the strong afternoon sun shining and a warm wind drifting through the open window. The Oscars started at six o'clock and all over town everyone was preparing for Hollywood's big night, either getting kitted out in their best bib and tucker or buying in a pizza to watch it live on the television.

The hotel staff gathered to give the Knight a generous send off, forming a line of honour. Their soft applause carried him and his wooden cane to his waiting limousine. 'Thank you,' he said modestly and shook hands with anyone who chose to come forward. He played his part with dignity and exuded his usual generosity and benevolence. His life was reaching its culmination and he carried himself exactly as a star of his stature should.

The drive across town was clear at first, but traffic clogged the approaches to the venue. We had the radio on and Birkenfeld gave a running commentary on who was favourite to win.

'It's Scorsese's year, make no mistake about that. Best damn film I or any Member of the Academy has ever seen. Bob de Niro will win the Actor and Mary Tyler Moore will get Best Actress. There's a buzz about *Ordinary People* and they'll throw it some sort of recognition. We all love a bit of misery!'

'Yeah, yeah,' I thought, and smiled and listened as he lectured; he was his own best audience and it was getting to the point where I wanted to slap him in the face. How quickly you can go off someone.

The Knight was not listening. Serene as ever, he rested his chin on the top of his cane. 'A gift from Ralph Richardson. He said that I would one day find it useful – "a day not too distant in the future" – and he was not wrong now, was he?'

February looked breathtaking in a blood-red tight-fitting

dress revealing every ravishing curve. She had long pearl drops in her ears and a Russian wedding ring on her middle finger. Her nails were as red as her dress and I noticed, not for the first time, how delicate her hands were. Her hair had a sweet smell not unlike the lemon sherbets that I used to consume by the bagful when I was young.

But even with this beauty in front of me, the journey was beginning to drag as we crawled our way to the Dorothy Chandler Pavilion. At last the door was wrenched open, the sunshine flooded in and a security guard in an Alcatraz-type warder's uniform peered into the car. I had the tickets and passes in my hand, so I clambered out. Silence followed by a roar. Mouths open, faces magnified in hysterics as the stars appeared. 'This way, this way,' PR girls yelled and the Knight gave each network a short interview. This was a celebration; the veil of celebrity lowered for the world to glimpse and marvel at. The red carpet full of half-conversation, half-laughter, a semiquaver of sound.

The dressing room was even more crowded with flowers and congratulatory cards than before. The Knight was one of the few who did not have to share a room. Backstage was a line-up of every act one could imagine: vaudeville, burlesque and even the circus.

After making sure the Knight was comfortable, Birkenfeld left pretty sharpish. 'Look after him. It should be fine. If anything goes seriously awry, come and fetch me during one of the commercial breaks.' And then he disappeared.

February had left to find her parents, who were also sitting out front. The room was still, the Knight was at peace humming and whistling the sort of tune one usually hears from a military-sounding marching band. He tapped his cane, and could have gone on for hours, but was interrupted by the make-up and hair. He sat without a word in front of the mirror while a ton of blusher was piled on to his famous features. The thick marble-white hair was combed soothingly, and the Knight closed his eyes, already physically tired and in need of sleep.

'Pardon my intrusion, gentlemen,' a deep, resonant voice roused him. It was the director of the show, a pale stubbly man, carrying a sheaf of papers. He had a long black jacket on and a pair of striped trousers that made him look like a registrar. 'I must repeat what I said yesterday – that this is an absolute honour . . . ' he was talking to the Knight but looking directly at me. 'Mr Cary Grant will introduce you for your special award. Then, as the other night, a short montage of your films will be shown, and afterwards you will be handed your Oscar and will make your speech.' He then turned directly to the Knight, 'You will have three minutes, tops, to say your thank-you.' The director began to pace about. 'Forty-five minutes later you will return to the stage and call out the nominations for Best Picture. Again as rehearsed, you will call out each film listed on the back of the envelope, a small excerpt from each will follow and when you have repeated the five nominations, you will open the envelope and announce the winner.' The director spoke precisely and acted out the opening of the envelope.

'I am not a moron!' objected the Knight.

And I laughed and the director laughed and retreated in a hurry.

'You told him, sir!'

Rising with the help of his cane, he huffed and said, 'I cannot stand being treated like an imbecile.'

* * *

Cary Grant made a humble and generous introduction to the hushed gathering. The smell of lilies and lilac rose from low-cut dresses. The men in tuxedos were ranged motionless on the red-velvet seats.

After receiving his Oscar and holding it like the handle of a sword, the Knight's three-minute speech ranged from the absurd to the languid. And to conclude, he quoted part of his favourite speech from *The Merchant of Venice*: ' "Hath not a Jew eyes? Hath not a Jew hands, organs, dimensions, senses, affections, passions? Fed with the same food, hurt with the same weapons, subject to the same diseases, healed by the same means, warmed and cooled by the same winter and summer as a Christian is?" ' A strange choice, as he was neither Jewish nor had he ever played the character of Shylock on stage. His final words were, 'I thank each and every one of you for your support, your care and your love for this fragile Englishman.'

The audience cheered and cheered the old boy off the stage. Tears ran down the cheeks of many and the unflagging clapping and stomping had to be curtailed by a commercial break. As he walked off, he took me to one side and said, 'Was it all right? I always wanted to say those words on stage and I wasn't going to blow this opportunity.'

'You were magnificent, sir,' I fawned.

* * *

Quite suddenly I felt very alone. The Knight was pacing the floor of his dressing room. He was my responsibility and I was reaching the point where I thought his appearance in front of a worldwide audience was not a good idea. February was sitting with her parents and Birkenfeld was busy ingratiating himself with potential clients. No wonder I felt a weight on my shoulders.

A knock summoned the Knight for his second appearance. Straight on to the stage he walked, with me leading him by the hand until the final moment.

'The nominations are . . . ' the Knight glanced at the outside of the envelope, '*Ordinary People*, Ronald L. Schwary, producer;' a short clip was then shown. '*Raging Bull*, Irwin Winkler and Robert Chartoff, producer;' an extract was shown. It was running perfectly and I began to calm down. After the nominations were over, the Knight scanned the envelope and said, 'And the winner is . . . ' Everyone backstage froze, my heart lurched; it was if someone had pressed a switch and everything went into slow motion; a stage hand hissed, 'He hasn't opened the envelope!'

'And the winner is *Ordinary People*, producer Ronald L. Schwary.' Wild cheers followed, with an admix of shocked surprise as many believed it was *Raging Bull*'s year. Schwary was off his seat and running up the steps to accept his Oscar from the bemused Knight, who was holding the still-sealed envelope.

While the acceptance speech was being made, I beckoned the Knight. He walked gently backwards until out of the sight of the cameras and the audience. From the wings, I snatched the evidence. A scrum-like crowd peered over my shoulders, 'Open it, for God's sake open it!' they cried. I ripped it asunder and snatched the card from inside – and there in thick black capital letters read: '*ORDINARY PEOPLE*.' A cheer of relief rippled around the Knight.

'Did I do anything wrong?' he asked.

'No, sir,' I replied, 'you were perfect!'

* * *

Oliver Reed was waiting with his golf bag on the first tee at the agreed time.

'Does it ever rain here? I asked, as yet again, after the day's fierce sun and blazing heat, I had found it hard to sleep.

'Rarely,' he replied. 'For the English, it's a slice of paradise and should be respected as such.'

'My boss is impressed that we're meeting today. He

thinks I'm trying to sign you – not simply having a round of golf.'

'Well there is no reason why we can't combine the two, most people do in this town. Anyway, let's not think too much. It's not healthy to think too much early in the morning – could lead to a brain tumour. My friend's wife died of a brain tumour caused by thinking too much in the early morning.'

I smiled in a noncommittal sort of way.

As we bashed our way round the course, Olly took the occasional slurp of brandy from a hip flask. If he was suffering from a hangover, he had decided to override it with some singing – out of tune and not very inspiring. But I didn't grumble; it was better than a friend of my mother's who used to visit when we were very young. She would practise her scales from dawn to dusk, her top notes quavering like lines of washing in the wind, and my love of opera died before I was six. Her name was Sarah Cray and she married a rich man from Canton Graubünden in Switzerland. He proposed to her in the middle of one of her impromptu recitals – anything to stop her singing – but made it a condition that she would never sing again. She thought of her voice, she thought of his money – she retired that afternoon.

'You have a go,' Olly said throwing me a putter on the eighteenth green. 'Get it near, and we'll have a birdie. Hole it, and we'll have a magnificent eagle.' It was an uphill putt of at least forty feet with a slight bump on the way. I stood over the ball and tried to concentrate on hitting it with confidence and the right amount of strength. The only putting practice I'd had was on a crazy-golf course in Margate. As I drew my club back, I promised myself that if I holed the putt I would come out to California and make it my home. It was similar to when I was young and made secret promises to myself that if I held my breath from the lamp-post to the corner of the street, a wish would be granted.

I glanced at the flag, eased the putter back and struck the ball. I watched it move purposefully and fast over the immaculate green. It rolled straight, without deviation, and 'bang' into the hole it fell.

Olly strode over and shook my hand. 'That was fantastic. You've done this before.'

'I haven't,' I replied, 'I'm a quick learner.'

We walked chortling into the clubhouse to find a cool drink. He ordered a large whiskey and I thought, What the hell! and joined him. It was eleven-thirty and that early drink on an empty stomach in the morning heat went straight to my head. I felt dizzy and sick and the most natural thing would have been to lie down. Instead I went to the bathroom and cupped cold water on to my face with my hands.

Olly knocked on the door and asked if I was all right. 'I've mixed some Alka-Seltzer for you – with water.' He came in and handed it to me and I downed it in one. 'You're not there yet, are you? Still young!'

I nodded my head in vigorous agreement and began to sober up.

*   *   *

The buzz of activity permeated the whole building. People rushing, the phones rarely silent. I was waiting to be summoned by the most powerful agent in Hollywood. Movie posters featuring famous clients covered the walls and on the coffee table a copy of *Variety* lay open at the calendar section trumpeting the previous night's successes. A photograph of the Knight holding his Oscar was on the front page, alongside Timothy Hutton, the new young 'hope', looking wide-eyed and phlegmatic. There was no reference to the envelope incident, to my relief, and I shuddered again at the thought that *Raging Bull* might have been the name printed on the card instead of *Ordinary People*. I presumed the Knight had simply read out the name at the top of the list of nominations.

'Well, did you sign him?'

'I will, but today we were simply getting to know each other. He was deciding whether he could trust me – and I suppose vice versa.'

I was in good confident form and not overawed by being in the presence of Marvin Cowen. He had ordered his secretary not to put through any calls, except from Oscar winners. The office was predictably oversized and dominated by two stretches of window that overlooked Beverly Hills. Just like Birkenfeld, Cowan smoked a cigar, but his build was the opposite, slight and trim. You could tell by his clothes that he cared about the way he looked and had a degree in vanity. He sat in a swivel chair not unlike mine in London and swung gently from side to side as we conversed, which made me feel quite dizzy. The photos of his stars and friends littered the shelves, among a prodigious collection of books, and on his desk lay an open trade paper and a pile of notes. I noticed Ayn Rand's *The Fountainhead* among the books, and although I was not aware he had followed the direction of my eyes, he rose, walked to the shelf and pulled out that exact book. 'Take it. I think everyone should read this,' he said, draining his cup of coffee.

I thanked him in a discombobulated manner and held the book awkwardly on my knee.

'I will get straight to it. I want to offer you a job. I want you to join us in Los Angeles. We need a young English voice to represent the agency. We have another English agent, Charles Boeye, Commander Charles Boeye no less, but he's an old timer with old ideas. He's only still here because he represents a couple of actors who still bring in the bucks, but let's keep that to ourselves, shall we? There's a new wave of English talent emerging and we require someone who speaks the same language, someone who understands how English men and women tick.' He imitated a jolly Dickensian manner. 'So what do you think? We will pay your rent for a year, double your salary and give you every opportunity to be the success I'm sure you have it in you to become. I've talked with Birkenfeld and he's given the idea his blessing. So tell me, does it excite you?'

I thought immediately of February, of her warmth and the love that was growing between us. I thought of the golf shot I had buried earlier in the day. How strange life can be; ever since I stumbled on that advertisement in the London coffee bar I had felt a hand on my shoulder guiding me. I was becoming a success without any real effort on my part. Life cannot be this simple. Nothing can be free. How am I going to pay for this good fortune? Did I have to lose my brother for my career to run as smoothly as it has? I loathed even thinking that way. I must rid myself of such thoughts. At school, I felt I was cursed. Now it seemed I was blessed. My life had turned around and the possibilities were invigorating and bewildering at the same time.

'I'm very flattered, sir, but it could be difficult. You see, my parents . . . they lost their other son. My elder brother died in the US a couple of years ago and I think it would be hard to leave them right now.'

Cowan leant forward in quiet resignation. He put the cigar he was smoking – or rather puffing frantically – in the ashtray. This was not a man who took no for an answer. But his mood had changed, and not in reaction to my saying that I might not be able to accept his job offer. He raised his shoulders up to his ears with a weary mournful smile. He had lost his sister two months before to a virulent strain of cancer, he told me. As he spoke of the days that led up to her death, he glanced at a photograph he kept beside him; she wore a black beaded evening dress and smiled radiantly at the camera. His tortured expression brought back the pain I knew so well of looking at a picture of someone you held dear. Your heart relives the past, but not for long enough, and the jolt back to reality is always excruciating.

'You think about the future, kid. Ask your parents and listen to what they have to say. I am only hearing good things about you.' He spoke kindly.

We shook hands and I carried out of his office a copy of *The Fountainhead* and a job offer. I closed the door behind me, overhearing him order his secretary to get Walter Matthau on the line. His commanding voice had returned and once again he was at the helm of his talent business.

* * *

I had not been able to reach David for more than twenty-four hours. We had missed calls and when I had tried to phone him after the Oscars there had been no answer. When I finally got through, he answered with a desert-dry mouth and the impression he might be sick at any moment. The throbbing of his head could be felt at my end of the line. I was convinced I heard him down his first drink of the day.

'I have been offered a job,' I said.

'Hold on,' he replied. 'I'm just going to get myself a smoke.' There was total silence for a moment, then the sound of him lighting a match and taking a deep drag. 'I'd love you to be here. I can't tell you what it's meant to have you close.' His words were followed by the sound of uncontrollable sobbing.

I had a vision of David stretched out on his bed, a blanket wrapped round his wasted body, surrounded by filth and vomit, but I was powerless to help him; the memory of my brother's death in similar circumstances was all too fresh in my mind.

'I will be back soon, David. Take good care, you hear?' Distressed by the tenor of the phone call, I gave him February's number and asked him to look after her – a miscalculation if ever there was one!

* * *

I was tempted to take the sleeping pill that February had slipped into my hand at the airport. She stood in front of me. Her hair tumbled to one side and the golden light was reflected in her green eyes. Our parting was restrained, and although I could see I was falling in love as plainly as I could have seen a fox on a field of snow, I preferred to follow the public protocol of a kiss on the cheek. Reticence triumphed over desire, and I denied myself an honest farewell. 'Goodbye, my angel.' I had a strange feeling I had known her all my life, and was convinced I was going to see her again soon.

'Why didn't you tell that beautiful girl that you loved her?' asked Birkenfeld with irritating joviality as we were making our way to our flight; I half listened, and, trying to act composed and not looking ahead, I walked straight into the automatic doors, which had not opened.

The Knight ignored my obvious injury. 'You should have taken her by the hand and said:

> "If I profane with my unworthiest hand
> This holy shrine, the gentle sin is this:
> My lips, two blushing pilgrims, ready stand
> To smooth that rough touch with a tender kiss." '

'I would have done just that, if only I had your voice, sir,' I replied, blood trickling from my nose.

* * *

The entire first-class cabin was asleep, enfolded in dreams and harsh blankets. We were over the Atlantic and I was alone with my thoughts about the offer I had received earlier that day. I had wanted to call my parents immediately I left Mr Cowen's office, but I knew it would be better to debate it face to face at home surrounded by everything that was familiar. I wanted to grasp the opportunity, but knew it would be difficult to leave England. Perhaps in a couple of years' time, then it would work, but I concluded that everything was still too raw and I was needed at home.

I drummed my fingers in frustration and buzzed the steward to bring a brandy which I swallowed in one. No problem there then. I peered into the infinite darkness beyond my window and cursed the tragedy that had wrenched the guts out of our family. 'Damn Thomas. Damn him for his foolishness and damn him for his weakness!' I stormed inwardly, torn between anger and tears. Fuck it. I buzzed the steward again and asked for a pen and a sheet of paper.

Dear Sir – I have been offered a job in Los Angeles. I think I want to go. I think I want to test myself in an arena that will challenge my ambition. What shall I do? You have shown such wisdom over the last few days, I want to be like you when I grow older; I want to take my final steps in life with the same grace and humility. How did you find the peace that we all search for? Has all the adulation added to your sense of fulfilment?

Am I too young to move away and make a life on foreign soil? Am I too young to be asking these questions? Are there times when decisions become easier and the struggle to find answers less tortuous? Questions, questions, questions.

My school life was marred by loneliness and confusion. At last the clouds have begun to clear and I am finding life to be welcoming and rewarding. Perhaps I am frightened that if I take the wrong turn, everything will be lost and I will return to my former parlous state. Why do I worry so?

I think I am falling in love again. February is not like the month that bears her name. She is warm and generous and I miss her already as I write these words, 30,000 feet above the Atlantic. I had been told it was difficult to meet one's soul mate, but I think I have. Am I deceiving myself? Am I just desperate for a close relationship after the loss of my beloved brother?

I am not sure I can leave my parents at this time – the selfishness of such a decision would be difficult to live with. They are good people, but they are still shattered by what happened to my brother. I think leaving would cause too much pain. Should I just forget it and wait for another offer once I have made my name in England?

I am sorry to burden you, but watching you at such close proximity over the last few days has been an inspiration. I see you as someone who exudes kindness and wisdom in equal measure, and I admire that as much as your undoubted success on the screen.

Yours faithfully,

Sam

I had planned to hand the letter over to the Knight when we landed, but it remained folded in my pocket. I decided to try to answer the questions myself.

* * *

The first call I made when I returned was to Margaret.

'How are you?' I asked.

'I'm fine.'

'Good . . . ' I replied. 'Well . . . ' I ploughed on, 'the Oscars were fun and Los Angeles is fantastic. The sheer size of the place is overwhelming and the weather is sublime. The light is so bright, it's like a flash bulb going off . . . How is Jackie, by the way?'

'She's well . . . thank you.'

'Good . . . Listen, I just wanted to know how you were. I hope you didn't mind me calling.'

'I don't mind, Samuel, but I want to be left alone for the time being, everything is still very raw. Do you understand?'

'Of course, I do,' I lied. 'Whatever you say.'

'Goodbye, Samuel.'

'Goodbye, Margaret.' The phone went dead. ' . . . I am so sorry.'

* * *

At lunch, Harold was as attentive as ever and my father had carved the meat in the way I had grown accustomed to, with precision and concentration. I entertained the table with stories of my Los Angeles trip. They were all eager to hear tales of the Knight. I had not realised my mother was such a big fan; she could reel off the names of all his movies. 'If I had known, mum, I would have got his autograph.'

Aunt Flo was in her usual chair, and my parents had invited Uncle Louis, with his new friend Mandy: big hair, big breasts and as vivacious as if she had swallowed helium. She was far too young for my uncle, meaning that she was in her mid-twenties, but she was indeed very cute in a Barbie sort of way and my admiration for my uncle grew further.

'How do you do it, uncle?' I'd asked him earlier. I had in recent months become far more open with my uncle. In answer, he stuck his hand into his jacket and pulled out a wad of twenty-pound notes. He riffled through them with a naughty laugh. 'That's how!' Before he repocketed the cash, he handed me a couple off the top.

'Thanks, uncle, you're the greatest!'

'No, Muhammad Ali is the greatest; I am just your Uncle Louis!' How different from my father he is, I thought, more relaxed in his body and freer in conversation. We did not mention my latest call to Don, but I knew he knew, and he knew that I knew that he knew.

Aunt Flo talked at lunch about her son Rupert having a 'special' girl. I had always presumed that Rupert was gay, but had remained firmly in the closet to spare his mother's feelings. The girl was described as being serious, the only daughter of a solicitor in St Albans and a student of law at London University.

'Yes, but what does she look like, auntie?'

'Don't be shallow, Sam,' mother interrupted, 'looks are not important; are they, Louis?' For one moment I thought my mum was being funny.

'She looks like Angela Rippon!' my aunt answered.

'Hope she has her legs!' interrupted Uncle Louis. Angela Rippon, England's famous BBC news anchor, had cameoed a few years before on *The Morecambe and Wise Show*. Seen before that appearance as a rather dull newsreader, she performed a dance routine on the show that had revealed a most sensational pair of 'pins'.

'That's quite enough, Louis. She's adorable and Rupert seems to be very happy. I think that they might even get married.' And with that the conversation moved on.

Lunch was like it used to be and it was a relief to hear the banter return and feel the long silences were at last a thing of the past. Violet had cooked the most delicious apple crumble and I smothered my pudding in thick hot custard. The old peaceful atmosphere prevailed in the house; it promised to make what I planned to say later a little easier. Harold poured coffee and my father talked about the possibility of buying a house in the South of

France. 'We've seen something that could be fine for us.' He went on to describe the villa, and the swimming pool which overlooked the sea. 'It lies between Cannes and Juan-les-Pins, up in the hills. You will be able to join us for your holidays, Samuel.' My heart sank again; any talk of future plans which involved me made my 'chat' more difficult. I was consumed with nerves.

* * *

I had spent the afternoon discovering a little more about the alluring Mandy. Her looks belied an intelligent girl who clearly had a deep affection for my uncle. She'd got a first at Oxford and since leaving had worked in an art gallery in central London. 'That's where I met your uncle; under a Francis Bacon.'

'Did he buy it?'

'No, he thought it was too expensive, but he bought me!' and with a naughty giggle she pirouetted to show off to me her shapely form.

She had moved into my uncle's St John's Wood house and was planning to stay. The house in Hamilton Terrace had been dedicated to his bachelor life. An oversized television was in every room and there was no sign of a feminine touch. Gianni lived in and trebled as his driver, butler and cook. Born in Sicily, he spoke like Marlon Brando in *The Godfather*. My mental picture of my uncle was becoming even more fantastic. Gianni must once have been a member of the Mafia, and when in the past I had joked that he should have been an extra in gangster movies, I was unaware that I might well have hit the nail on the head.

'I don't mean to sound a downer, but he tends to go through his girls,' I said tactlessly.

'That's not a problem. He has not come across someone like me before. I think he has met his match.'

I noticed as we spoke that her eyes were blue and also that they weren't quite straight.

By the time we sat for an early dinner, everyone else had left and I knew that this was the time to discuss Mr Cowen's generous and tempting offer. Even before I began to tackle the issue, my heart was heavy. There was a part of me that didn't want to bring it up. I still felt confused and struggled to be decisive. Although I tried to act like a man, I knew I was still a boy and at times such as these felt very young indeed.

We were served shepherd's pie and as I poured out the ketchup and piled on the peas, I broke the silence. 'I saw David – you know, Lord Amersham – in California. He's trying to break into the movie business out there.'

'As long as that's all he's trying to break into,' my father instantly replied. They had never approved of David and my father always suspected that it was he who encouraged me in the bad behaviour at school that led to my eventual expulsion. Absolute rubbish of course. I was somewhat impressed by the 'bad boy' in my friend, but David was so out of sync with the normality of life that he was hardly a Pied Piper figure. This was not the best starting point for the conversation. It was my mother who sensed that something was on my mind and as my father poured the wine, she asked me what was troubling me.

'I have been offered a job in Los Angeles working for the same agency for much more money. I don't know what to do. I want to face the challenge but at the same time I don't want to leave you . . . now that I'm your only son.' I didn't want to, but I started to cry.

My mother left her chair and put her arm around my shoulders, wiping the tears from my face. 'You know that we love you very much and our love is unconditional. We want the best for you and for your happiness. We would not be good parents if we felt otherwise. Do what you have to do to be happy. If you want to go, then go, Samuel! Your home will always be here – as will we.'

She kissed the top of my head and for an instant I closed my eyes. It couldn't have been easy for my mother to say those words. I turned to my father, who sat five feet away, tears glistening in his eyes. I got up, went over and gave him a firm hug. His body was rigid and he remained silent as I knew he would; my mother spoke for both of them now; I could see the change and knew that it would stay that way for the rest of their lives. However hard my father tried, part of his spirit had been broken.

The day had tired me and by nine o'clock I was in bed. Just as I was dozing off, I noticed that my clothes, thrown on the chair, had assumed the shape of a figure, and as I looked closer, I was sure that I could see Tom.

'Tom is that you?' I whispered. 'Tom, I think I want to move to California. I've met this divine girl and fallen in love. You would like her, Tom, I know you would. She's gentle and beautiful in every way. Oh God, I wish you were here to meet her! You may know this, but a friend of mine – Margaret – had an abortion recently. I was the father, Tom, and I haven't come to terms with what we did. To be honest, I know it was wrong and I'm trying not to think about it too deeply. It's a painful subject and I have had enough pain for the time being. And now I've been offered a job that is well paid and appeals to me no end. Oh Tom, you would be so proud of me. I am trying to be a good brother, but I miss you every second of every day. Please keep an eye on me, I need that, and I know mummy and daddy do too. How they miss you, my darling brother!'

And then quite suddenly I shut my eyes and fell asleep.

* * *

I was sitting in the Grill, the restaurant where we'd first shaken hands. I may have been hard on him recently, losing patience with his overbearing manner and his oafish behaviour. Yes, he was a hard-hitting, no-nonsense, straight-talking son-of-a-bitch schmoozer, who could bore for England, but whoever employed Birkenfeld for guidance could rest assured that they were in the best possible hands. He was the consummate agent and he was taking time out to have a pep talk with me before I caught my flight to the West Coast.

I ordered the fish with chips and side of spinach, my favourite. Birkenfeld had the steak tartare and sank three large vodkas. 'You are going to be loved, loathed, and when you have power, feared.' He was now taking deep, satisfying draws on his full-bodied Cuban Bolivar cigar. The aroma wafted over the entire restaurant. He was oblivious, and when he offered me one, I took it without hesitation.

'There is no such thing in Hollywood as an overnight success. Listen to me here – ' he leaned forward, pretty much drunk. 'Nothing in that town happens overnight. Anyone who reaches the pinnacle of success has worked their guts out to get to that point. They have seduced, manoeuvred and cajoled. Don't ever let a client believe that they can just walk along the red carpet to the premiere – they can't. They'll have to work damned hard to get there.'

I wasn't getting a word in edgeways.

He ordered a cognac and asked if I would like one.

'What the hell,' I replied.

'Good, the drinks are on me!' Birkenfeld snapped his fingers at the waiter. 'Make it two doubles in those big balloon glasses . . . You have it, Samuel!'

'Have what, sir?'

'You have unflappable charm and a level head on your shoulders, you're always punctual and you have a good instinct about people. The Knight thought you were "fantastic" and so do I.' He was undoubtedly now sloshed. Our expensive Russian cognac had arrived and my nose dived into the over-sized glass; I closed my eyes and floated into the Romanov court in St Petersburg. Legend had it that during the Revolution the Bolsheviks paused for a week and imbibed the entire store of cognac from the imperial cellar.

I drank the brandy. I felt it sink to my stomach, then immediately come right up again and tickle my larynx. I made a gesture like a seasick man too deep in his deckchair to get to the rail to throw up. Then the wave of liquor fell back and warmed my stomach and made me feel better. I listened to advice that was becoming increasingly slurred: 'Remember all agents hate actors. Yup, we hate them – and they're not too keen on us either. Very early on you will join the hit-lists of actors you have rejected. Retribution will be unleashed when one of them gets a starring role. He will pass your name round the town and soil your reputation. But don't be fearful of this; it will be very natural for you to recognise the ones that belong on the big screen rather than selling real estate.' He offered another brandy and I blithely accepted; he re-lit his cigar, burped and leaned over the table. 'Once you sign the Big One, remember that everyone in town will be trying to steal him. Trust no one, not even your closest friends. They will smile and take your hospitality, but in the end will be trying to snatch your meal ticket. They don't have to be fellow agents. They can be a friend of a friend – or a friend of an agent – but if they can shaft you and in return get a bonus point, then – believe me – in that town, they will; loyalty is as scarce as a square meal in Africa. Actors are easily seduced, especially by an agent who has an excellent client list. Don't forget that when their agency contract is coming to an end you must drive over to their house and get them to re-sign, well before it expires.'

'How long before?' I asked.

'Six months latest.'

* * *

We left the restaurant sozzled at four o'clock. We were not the last to leave. We decided to walk back through Berkeley Square. Everywhere an atmosphere of briskness suggested many were late finishing their lunch and were hurriedly returning to their work. As I looked up to my old office, I thought of Margaret and her reluctance to talk and also my unwillingness to confront what we had been through. I pictured Jackie with her bruised face and felt an inner satisfaction at having been able to stop any further violence; I sensed that something was pulling me away from it all. My step grew quicker until Birkenfeld called out to me to slow the pace down. I saw then I was leaving for America not only for love and ambition, but to escape the dark forces that disconcertingly seemed to be dogging my steps in this town.

Virginia had arranged for clients to come into the office to hear the news that I was heading west. The agency had decided to keep just the two who had steady work in a television series; the rest were thrown back on to 'Narrow Street'. They all took the news well; surprisingly well, except for one who snarled, 'Bastard,' into my face before he stormed out. I'd never liked him and had only taken him on because he was married to a friend of a friend. There is no place for sentimentality in my line of work. To soften the blow, I had promised the rest that if they made it out to Hollywood, I would be 'there' to help in any way I possibly could. They were hardly going to turn nasty if they had an offer like that, now were they?

The elderly and crusty Mr Witherspoon had taken on

Virginia, she of the ready smile and unfailing good nature. He had remained aloof ever since my arrival and would only pass the occasional comment about what I was wearing or about the insolence of youth. His secretary had found a husband on holiday in Cuba and had left without a backward glance. 'No bloody loyalty there,' he grumbled as he climbed the stairs to his office. He had not asked whether it was all right to approach Virginia, which might have the 'proper' way to behave, but as I was leaving anyway I buried my irritation.

* * *

My exit from the London office was quick and without fanfare. I was not really leaving, I was just moving six thousand miles away. 'But surely you would like to share a goodbye drink with everyone?' asked a slightly confused Virginia.

'No, my dear. From my background, we don't say goodbyes. It reminds us of too many painful partings.'

* * *

Billy was genuinely upset that he was losing his flatmate. He treated me to dinner at the Caprice on Arlington Street and we got through quantities of champagne and toasted the new chapter. We spoke of the good times we'd shared and drank to more of the same in the future.

Billy had always been the outsider, even though his heart was warm and generous. He was the one irritated on returning through the school gates to hear the majority raise the cheer of salutation. He'd dreaded the tyranny of routine as much as an old lag returning to prison. Perhaps that was why we got on so well; I had thought exactly the same.

He seized the bottle in a stranglehold and squeezed out the last drops of the expensive champagne to toast my future success. He was proud of the way that my life had developed and although he was only four years my senior he spoke like someone far more mature. Promises were made that he would visit very soon. 'I need to find someone to move in to help me with the rent, but before letting your room, I'll make it clear that it's only theirs for as long as you stay out in California. If you decide to come back, the room will be yours.'

I grinned as he spoke, but knew that we would not be flatmates again. If my adventure didn't work out, I would return and start afresh and that would mean a new career and a new home. I kept these thoughts to myself and lifted my glass and thanked him for his friendship and his love.

'You are a big softy really,' he said in a camp accent.

I was silent for an instant, but my eyes spoke for me in the hum and glow of the restaurant. 'No, I'm not,' I replied at last, 'I'm as hard as nails.'

We didn't catch a taxi, instead we walked along Piccadilly and across Hyde Park Corner towards home. Billy was eager for fresh air and I wanted to say my goodbyes to the familiar streets. The city was still and there was hardly anyone on the pavements. As we strolled past the terraced houses with lights burning in their rooms, I thought of what I was leaving behind. I stopped outside Scotch House and looked under Bowater House, and my heart lurched at the memory of the interview that had set me on this path, and of the waitress in Dino's who had mouthed, 'Good luck.' Strange the things that stick in the mind.

Billy pointed out a half-torn concert poster for Adam and the Ants and laughed, 'Ooh, look what you're going to miss!'

Before turning each corner, I looked behind, whispering a sad farewell. To the casual observer, my behaviour must have seemed bizarre.

'This will probably be my last walk on a street for some

time. In Los Angeles, if you walk anywhere people think you're mad.'

'That's true,' Billy replied. 'Sounds awful. Are you sure you want to live in a city like that?'

'Yes, I'm absolutely sure,' I said, with unmistakable doubt in my voice.

* * *

'You look as if you're only going for two weeks,' my father observed as two compact cases were lifted on to the weighing machine.

My mother remained strong throughout our goodbyes, but I could sense that she was finding it difficult. They had picked me up early for my eleven o'clock flight and the drive to the airport was like one of those journeys back to my boarding school after the holidays: a stillness and hardly a word being said. My father was at the wheel, my mother sat beside him. Then it struck me it was my parents who had driven my brother to the airport for his move to New York. That would have been the last time they had touched him or seen his handsome face. The pain must have been acute for them now – retracing the road with their younger son. I rebuked myself for my insensitivity as the Lucozade billboard signalled the M4. I was on the point of asking my parents to turn the car around. What should have been the most exhilarating of days was in truth a sort of re-enactment of the last rites.

The coffee was awful, but I drank it slowly and deliberately. My father was talkative and demanding of the waitress. 'I wanted my eggs fried!' he said, although he had ordered them scrambled. We were sitting in a restaurant above the passport desk waiting until the last minute before my flight was called. I had wanted to run out of the car and fling my arms around my parents and vanish but they insisted on walking in with me and waiting for the plane to be called.

'We'll let you settle and then be out to see you in September,' said my father.

That would be in twelve weeks, which didn't seem particularly long, and I found my father's words reassuring. Distress at leaving a parent was an emotion familiar to me from my early life. Those distant waves as I left to go to my prep school and the departing train's slow pull away from Liverpool Street Station were part of a recurring pattern. One minute you were safely protected from the outside world, next you were handed over to officious schoolmasters who ordered you to do this and do that with not a grain of compassion for your youthful vulnerability.

My father had arranged for a 'business' friend to provide a room until I found a more permanent place to rent. Douglas Sinclair had recently completed a deal that my father described as 'being good enough to buy half a country'. Other than that I knew little of the man. 'Now call us when you reach Douglas's house.'

I held father firmly and kissed my mother. She noticed a flake of cream on my neck, which she wiped off with her index finger. 'Sam, my darling, you are a big boy now. Wipe your face properly after shaving.' And she smiled brightly and kissed me tenderly on the cheek.

With a bag over my shoulder, I walked into passport control, turned my head and waved my parents goodbye and, eyes filled with tears, turned again and headed to another land.

* * *

February stood among an excited throng waiting for the passengers to emerge from the immigration gate. I wanted to run into her arms and give her the most passionate kiss, but I was pushing a trolley and had to swerve to avoid an old man who was picking up a cigarette butt from the dirty ground. My bags went flying and my grand entrance was spoiled. Quickly, I gathered them up, took those few steps into her arms and gave her a long, lingering kiss. The relief of feeling her skin again so close washed over me as palpably as if I had been drenched by a bucket of water. I mused that this woman was not of this earth.

'Welcome home, my darling,' she said.

The sun beat down on the Californian freeway and the Hollywood Hills hazed in the heat. Beneath the open-topped car, the road sizzled and seemed to scorch my face. The sky was a pale washed-out blue and the shock of the high temperature made any tiredness instantly disappear. The summer was here and the world was full of possibilities. It was ninety in the shade and the jumper that I had worn on and off for the previous six months was taken off to reveal my white shirt, drenched in sweat. I cared not, for I felt liberated and rid of the grey gloom that had followed me to my British Airways seat. I had swallowed two sleeping pills on the flight and fell into a deep, deep dream which was long and grotesquely complicated; I remembered little of it. When the captain announced that we had started our descent, the stewardess came over to make sure I had my seat belt fastened: 'It looked as if you could have slept all the way to Australia.'

* * *

Douglas Sinclair, originally from Edinburgh, lived among the well-manicured lawns of Holmby Hills, east of Beverly Hills. The house was on Carolwood Drive, a sharp right off Sunset. Star Maps were sold at a corner store to help tourists find the addresses of their favourite film stars, and the store helped us to identify our turning. 'Star Maps

Sold Here' was written badly in pink ink on a piece of shoddily torn cardboard. Business was brisk; the two who ran the store opened at eight in the morning, and even late at night, they were still tempting the tourists to seek out the wrought-iron gates to the homes of Jimmy Stewart and others.

'He's not here. He won't be back for a week,' a Scottish voice informed us when we rang the bell from the street.

'My name is Samuel Alexander and I was told that Mr Sinclair was expecting me ... Hello ... Hello ... ' The buzzer sounded and we both scurried back into the car and drove up the steep drive to a 'mid-century modern' house designed by Raphael Soriano. By an extraordinary coincidence, I had a postcard of one of his designs on my side table back at my parents' home in Oxfordshire; this was surely another sign that things would work out. The house was built principally of steel and blended faithfully into the soft grass mounds and curves that surrounded its wide structure. It was sublime but endangered; others like it were disappearing from the landscape due to southern California's earthquakes and wildfires.

Without a word, Fey – a small red-headed dynamo of a woman – led us to the far end of the house. My room was sparse, with a television, large double bed shrouded in mosquito netting and a deep white comfortable armchair. There was a single film poster on the wall above the bed – Robert de Niro in *Taxi Driver*; a plump beetle skittered across the star's face. The bathroom looked as if it belonged in a fine hotel. Clad in white marble, it boasted two basins and a shower that could fit five.

'I'm here every day until after lunch. Let me find you a spare set of keys and show you how the security works. The fridge will be kept full and you must help yourself. As I said, Mr Sinclair will be back in a week. The far end of the house, the west wing as we call it, is closed; those are Douglas's private rooms. Other than that feel free to go where you like.'

The white saltire hung from a pole to the side of the driveway. 'The Pride of Scotland,' she said dourly in her Glaswegian accent. 'Is this your girlfriend?' she asked, giving February a curious look.

'Yes, I am,' February answered, offering her hand, which was ignored.

A shimmering swimming pool directly behind the house looked more like an extension of the main building than a separate entity. I brushed the cool water with my hand and had the urge to strip off my clothes and dive in; instead, I splashed water over my face. February stretched herself out on the lawn in her Wimbledon-white summer dress. We were now in shadow, as the sun was so low in the sky that it caught only the roof of the house. I gazed at her, with water dripping from my face, admired her long brown slender legs against the green of the manicured lawn and felt deeply content.

* * *

'I will be over very soon . . . I need to visit someone first.' David had rung and was planning to come over and visit my new pad.

Jet lag had caught up with me. I had collapsed on the sofa with the networks spurting out their game shows and prizes. I slept soundly and sweetly until an irritating sound, like noisy birds in eucalyptus trees at dawn, began to nag the inside of my ear. I groaned and pulled a pillow over my head. Then suddenly I sat up and shook myself awake. It was David and February buzzing from the street.

'Let us in – we've been calling for thirty fucking minutes,' complained his lordship.

David had lost weight since my last visit and a slick of sweat mantled his face. His hair was cropped closer than ever and his eyes were hazy and unfocused. He was swigging vodka from a bottle – igniting his guts, titillating his liver. A smell oozed from under his arms, the smell of a decaying human being; I had smelt it before.

'One hundred dollars a gram,' he boasted as he pulled a small bundle from his white Levis.

He unfolded a brown packet and revealed a dune of cocaine. He emptied it all out on to the table and started rhythmically to tap the powder into lines. He measured the lines with a meticulous concentration that I had not believed him capable of in all the years I had known him. Very smart and always near the top of the form, he tackled his work shambolically, in a gear well below his potential. He was lazy, but clearly not where his drug use was concerned; in this he was dedicated.

He snorted two lines and then passed me the note. As I leaned on to the table he spoke of his father with unusual candour. He took a deep pull on his cigarette, tobacco stains showing on his fingers. 'I'm not afraid to say I didn't like him. He never had a direct conversation with me . . . never.' He rubbed his nose. 'He was lazy and hoarded his inheritance. It was a tragedy because he was a gifted artist. He drew beautifully. I have a drawing of his that I carry around.' He then fished in his pocket and brought out a sketch. It was in dark pencil and showed the face of a young Tahitian girl of quite exquisite beauty. Each line conveyed character and spirit. I looked at the drawing and then passed it to February, who sighed at its flawlessness.

'See, I told you he was good,' and he took back the paper and tucked his sensitivity away with it, safely back in his pocket.

'You should have it framed,' I said.

'Yes, I suppose I should,' and although now shaking, and with sweat beginning to fall from his hairline, he prepared more lines to numb the pain and keep his fears at bay.

'I only take this shit in the evening. I don't need it at any other time. Just for fun really.'

'That's strange. That's what my dead brother said,' I replied pointedly.

But he wasn't listening; he was savouring his drug, meeting it like an old acquaintance and beginning to find out what it was really like. He was a junkie, I had seen it before, yet even with everything I had been through, I was still unable to say those words directly to his face. 'You are a fucking junkie and you need HELP!'

'What the hell do you see in him?' February asked me after he had left.

The rising sun was sparking on the pool. I was exhausted, but the question intrigued me. It was a question I had never been able to answer. What *did* I see in him?

'I was very lonely at school and he was my friend. We shared those days and supported each other. He was my first true friend, and although we share little now, we will always have that bond . . . '

'But he's out of control.'

'Out of control . . . ' I repeated, as if struck by a whip.

* * *

I had seen little of Mr Cowen since I arrived. But yes, he was there when I first walked into the building and he shook my hand and personally showed me my new office. It was light, open and a good size.

'It's your choice. Display whatever you like here,' the CEO said, tapping on the plain white walls.

'And if it isn't suitable, do you come round with a big red marker pen?' I asked.

He didn't answer, not understanding my quip. It was a memory from my schooldays. When we put up a poster which the housemaster found unsuitable, he drew a heavy red cross over the offending artwork and we were ordered to take it down immediately. Strictures like this had blighted my 'privileged' teenage life.

'This is Gregory and he will be your personal assistant. I'll leave you to get to know each other.'

'Very rare for Marvin to show someone their office! You must be the new "great hope".' Gregory was tall, slim, and as white as a shroud. He had the sort of face which triggered the question, 'Are you sure you're all right?' But he was strong in build and stood up with the same forced ease with which he sat down. As I looked out of my window I saw the yellow smog hanging over the city like an unwelcome guest.

'It's always there and it's getting worse. I'm from the East Coast, and as soon as I landed, I started to retch.' Two fingers disappeared into Gregory's mouth. He had in his other hand a diary already filling, even before I had taken a call.

'Staff meeting at eleven, free for lunch at the moment (but I think the Commander wants to take you out), half-past two head of television, four o'clock your personal stationery will be delivered. Believe me, this will not last, so enjoy the freedom when you can. And tonight you are going to a screening. You need to sign and you need to sign immediately. At a screening, actors are particularly vulnerable – especially if it's a turkey.'

'How long have you been here?' I asked, assuming his efficient voice to be that of experience.

'Seven years, four months and three days.'

'And you've never gone on to be an agent?' I was not hanging in with niceties.

'No, I'm a fully fledged assistant. When a new agent

arrives from out of town, I am appointed as their PA to show them the ropes and guide them through the agency commandments.'

'And how many agents have you assisted?'

'Twelve – and few make the cut.'

'And how many do you mean by few.'

'Two!'

That was very reassuring.

* * *

'It's very good to be English around these parts,' Commander Charles Boeye confided, as we shared a lunch at Ma Maison on my first day at work. This was *the* restaurant to be seen in.

There was something odd about my fellow English agent Commander Boeye. Something just didn't seem to fit. The accent sounded posh and he wore the same Vetiver cologne as my father. There was not a hint of America about him.

'Where were you at school?' I asked.

'Harrow, during the war. Harrow on the Hill, North London, near to Wembley of all places. Damn too young to fight I was, blast it . . . miss the old place though, I had a damn good time. The school refused to evacuate when the bombing started. So impressed was Winston Churchill that he returned to the place for the first time in forty years; a bit like the old school song, what?'

He was clearly a phoney; the sort of slick con you were more likely to meet in the Old Kent Road than in a Beverly Hills restaurant. He represented two highly paid actors and this alone covered his salary and a high percentage of profit for the agency. He was a director of the company; had a spread on Mulholland Drive, only blocks away from Jack Nicholson; and sported the regulation tan with a precisely trimmed airforce grey moustache. Studio executives and fellow agents paused at our table and paid their respects.

'Pudding?' the Commander asked.

'Yes, rice pudding if they have it . . . with some jam . . . Very good of you to take the time to treat me like this.'

'No problem, old boy, my absolute pleasure. You already have a reputation. That was some deal you pulled off from behind the telephone desk. Fantastic, if you ask me.' He lifted his glass of white wine clinking with ice and proposed a short toast.

'Nothing really!' I'd gone slightly red.

'You see that's what the English have.'

'And what's that?' I asked.

'Modesty, old boy . . . modesty. By the way, rice pudding is rarely available. Go for the strawberries, if I were you.' The Commander rolled his eyes wearily.

He paid the bill with his gleaming American Express card and as he wrote out the total he said, 'Always add fifteen per cent, old chap. Very different from England here – these kids live on their tips.' He finished off lunch with a semi-amusing anecdote about one of his dogs trying to fuck Elizabeth Taylor. 'No, not like that, old boy – you know, when they cling round the leg.' I remember he pontificated a little about British politics, but thought Jim Callaghan still led the Labour Party. That again was strange; Callaghan had resigned the previous year. I chose not to correct him as I was trying to be kind. Perhaps charades such as this shape the town – you act out a character and few dare to challenge you.

The valet rushed off in his fitted red jacket to collect the Commander's racing-green Jaguar. The Commander slipped two bucks into his young hand, revved the engine and strapped on his belt. 'Make sure you get yourself a fine car, old boy, it marks you in society. I'd make it a black "beamer".

Who cares if you live in a shit hole, no one need see that, but your car represents your standing. Here take this.' The Commander opened his glove compartment and pulled out a business card: 'Santa Monica Classic Rental'.

'Mention my name, you should get a good rate.'

'Thank you, Commander.'

'Forget the Commander bit, old boy. You can just call me sir.'

'Thank you, sir.'

* * *

Twenty film agents were seated around the circular table – it was like a scene from an Agatha Christie movie where the characters are going to get killed off one by one. There was a high level of anxiety as each agent spoke and described how the previous week had gone. Marvin introduced me to the gathering in a short welcoming speech. They were generous words but in the room's response there was no sense of geniality – more a sigh of 'good luck'. Strong viscous coffee was served and if anyone had had a hangover it would have been swept away with one drop. I sat with eighteen men and one woman; they controlled the town. Ambitious and determined to win at all costs, they ran the most powerful agency in the world and would expect me to measure up to their own uncompromising standards. There was to be no rest.

Gregory had become grim faced on the subject of survival 'When your number is up, it becomes shamingly obvious. Mr Cowen delivers the blow without fuss; he always says that "there is no easy way to let people know that they have no future with the agency". Last year he fired his closest friend, a guy who was godfather to his children and best man at his wedding. Why? Because he didn't reach the minimum target. Right now, look out for the smallish brown-haired man with a mock-mournful expression on his face and big tortoise-shell glasses. His name is Greene and he's on a life-support machine.'

'How long does my honeymoon period last?'

'Four weeks,' Gregory answered, without a hint of irony.

David Greene had a reputation for being a good listener with a quiet and unassuming manner. This appeals to a certain type of actor or director, but they were evidently in short supply in town. He had not signed anyone new for six months and he was moving into the last act of his personal drama. When the final curtain falls, your office files are confiscated, locks changed and security told not to let you in. There is no fond farewell, just a hefty boot into the street. It's a charmless, unmerciful end.

'Mr Greene, please?' Cowen asked for his week's report. The headmaster wanted to hear some good news. I felt uneasy watching the torture. Poor Mr Greene was clearly sensitive, his voice gentle.

There was silence round the table and the merciless audience waited. He spoke hesitantly. 'I have a call set with Roman Polanski on Monday. It sounds like he wants to join us. And after *Tess* that would be a good signing, wouldn't it?' He was unsure, the confidence leaking from his frame. I wasn't sure either.

There was not a rapturous response. To the trained ear, the dissenting murmur meant the guillotine was being prepared. Sure, Polanski had received an Oscar nomination for *Tess*, and it had won three other Oscars, but it was barely commercial at three hours long. To cap it all, Polanski's damaged reputation meant he couldn't even enter the United States without arrest. Polanski had his own sword of Damocles suspended over his head.

'Hope the call goes well,' encouraged the boss. Mr Greene did not respond. He kept his head down and a droplet of perspiration plopped on to the table. He lit a cigarette as if he were about to be blindfolded and led before a firing squad.

'Jesus,' I murmured, 'can it be this much of a strain?'

The next agent to speak was a different breed altogether. Susan Gralstein was forty, two chins overweight, and notorious for spouting profanities and being 'more powerful than her famous clients'. She was wearing what looked like a purple tent, and chain-smoking. 'When you have a meeting with Susan, you never come away laughing,' I was told; 'the "lesbian in a kaftan" does not crack jokes: she cracks the balls of the men she is negotiating with.'

She had enemies waiting at every turn for her to slip up, but her boots were so thick that it was unlikely. She had her critics, but her clients, in contrast, defended her 'as so honest it's painful'. She took a deep drag on her Marlboro cigarette, held her breath for a long time and then let a thick billow of smoke out to drift over the room. She addressed the gathered with a croaky sexy voice. Within her first minute she announced that three new clients had been signed.

'These actors may be stars, but they were all out of work. That means emotionally insecure and in need of a boost. I called them and reunited them with that "bitch", confidence. They will soon be making the kind of money that they fuckin' deserve.'

Shit, this monster is good.

'The fields are fertile, gentlemen. There are many more out there to be signed. Go fuckin' get 'em! I can't do it all myself and not everyone wants a loud-mouth vulgarian New Yorker like me.' And she gave a patronising sideways glance at Mr Greene, who unlike the rest of the company was not boosted by her wrath but backed away like a retreating army.

The meeting wrapped up with 'whom to steal in the

coming week'. After Susan's speech about vulnerability in an actor's life, the nets were cast and set to catch fresh fish. Harrison Ford, Cher and Tom Cruise were high on the list. Tom Cruise was fast becoming the hottest young name in the business, and Harrison Ford was currently sizzling due to the buzz surrounding the release of his *Raiders* film. The actor had earned a living as a carpenter when work had dried up in the 1970s.

'For God's sake, someone must have employed him to build a desk or something?' Marvin Cowen demanded.

Commander Boeye piped up. 'He did a small job for my Malibu house but I think I was slow in paying. Don't think he has ever forgiven that one. Sorry, old boy.'

'*You fool!*' yelled Cowen impatiently.

'He made a sun-deck for Sally Kellerman . . . ' Susan Gralstein remembered.

'Who is Sally Kellerman?' I asked.

'She played Hot Lips in *M*A*S*H*. Before your time, kid.' Susan stubbed out her tenth cigarette.

'OK, anyone who knows Kellerman call and say we want her to sign to the agency. Set up the meeting and in the conversation ask casually if she paid on time for Harrison's work on her sun-deck and also whether they still talk. If they do – and have remained friends – set up a dinner party with Harrison Ford . . . Does everyone understand?' The boss was in full flow.

Everyone nodded except Susan, who was distracted, unable to find another cigarette. For an awkward moment she glanced at Greene for one. He slowly pulled one out and grudgingly handed her the fix she needed.

'You did good, young Samuel . . . ' Commander Boeye winked at me as we left the room.

'But I hardly said a word.'

'That's what I mean. Silence is key at the beginning.'

I believed that was not the first time I had heard that. I walked away trying to remember who said, 'I am a stranger in a strange land.'

*   *   *

The 'private' screening was on the Warner Brothers lot in Burbank. It was a high-profile release so the room that late afternoon was packed with actors, studio executives and a few chosen agents. The screening process reflected the 'Upstairs Downstairs' of the industry; this was definitely Upstairs. Downstairs generally attend the test screenings. The majority are assistants who ask other assistants who then ask a potential starlet who asks waiters who ask the valet. Sounded like fun, and as some who attend were undoubtedly the future, I saw that it was too soon to allow myself to be locked away in the privileged upper sector.

Mr Cowen had submitted his list and my name was ticked off. I drove by security and the main gates on to the land originally bought with the takings of the first talkie, *The Jazz Singer*, back in 1928. I found my seat in the small theatre, shyly waiting alone to be joined by the others; the rest remained outside until the last possible moment before the movie began. They vacuumed up the free snacks, smoked their cigarettes and swigged the drinks from the open bar. Eventually everyone had taken their seats in the intimate brown-carpeted screening room. Sitting on my right was an elderly slight man, bald head and black oversized glasses. It was super-agent Irving 'Swifty' Lazar, so nicknamed for closing three major deals for Humphrey Bogart in a single day. 'Hmmm,' I thought, 'perhaps I should conjure up a nickname for my public profile?' I resolved to find something suitable.

As the first frame appeared, I felt eyes seeming to pierce the back of my head. I turned and found Susan Gralstein looking right through me; I smiled but she blanked me, eyes fixed on the screen. How strange a reaction, but I was beginning to deduce the whole town was slightly peculiar. The movie started slowly and then crawled throughout. I had overheard the director say that his hope was the audience would leave with a smile on its face; I left with a grimace on mine. I had spent the second half wanting desperately to have a pee but would have disturbed eight people in getting out of my row. I kept busy by thinking of February, and as soon as the lights were switched on, I pushed poor Swifty Lazar out of the way and ran to the restroom. I stood humming while I relieved myself and wondering whether I should approach the lead actor. He must be anxious after that showing; I would step in and offer my support, just like I had been advised to do earlier in the day. Yes, he was going to be vulnerable. This was a dog-eat-dog town (or, as Woody Allen once said, it's worse than that: it's a dog-doesn't-return-another-dog's-phone-call town).

The actor was standing alone at the bar. No one was talking to him. You are a star, I thought, a big star; but you are only as good as your last movie. But really, it can't be that bad, can it?

'I would like to buy you a drink,' I said looking at the Movie Star. His eyes did not meet mine.

'What did you think of the movie?'

'To tell you the truth it was appalling; you have been badly let down by your director.' He took the drink I was offering. 'The whole thing is a mess and your career could suffer because of this. My name is Samuel Alexander, I am an agent at ISA and I want to help.' I was forthright and honest; perhaps too honest?

He had pulled away as I was talking and downed two glasses of studio white wine, but as he took on board what

I had said, his face lit up. 'This is what I have been waiting for my entire career; someone who tells it from the gut.' He asked the barman for paper and pen and wrote down his number. 'You call me! I am going to creep out of here and hope no one notices.' And with that, he melted like a ghost through the throng and was gone.

Honesty may well be the best policy, I mused, and had my glass refilled. As I leaned over the bar, radiating confidence from every pore, I felt a nudge in my ribs; it was Miss Susan Gralstein.

'That was virtually pornographic. You screwed him just right.' The beaming agent had admiration written all over her pudgy face. 'You will go a long, long way in this business. You have the instinct; the taste for the kill.' She licked her lips.

'Thank you,' I replied not sure if she was being that serious. Before I could discover more, she was pursuing the director. Surely, she didn't want to sign him after that disaster? But the lady was insatiable and everyone was fair game.

I decided to celebrate the night's new-found confidence and called February.

'I'll be at yours in an hour,' she said.

'Then I'll be back there in fifty minutes,' I replied and sped out of Burbank with smugness painted from ear to ear. I thought I had found the secret, the secret of signing stars . . . doubt well sort of.

* * *

Douglas was expected back in the morning. I switched on his expensive sound system and the strains of jazz drifted like smoke through the rooms. From the deckchair by the pool I stared at February pouring a drink; there was still heat in the air and the light from the house filtered into the night sky as if the house were breathing. The track moved to 'Flamenco Sketches' and I walked and pulled the magnificent creature to my body. We kissed, a little drunkenly, but so what? We took our clothes off and dived into the pool. I was excited and my heart pumped so loudly that I thought it would wake the neighbourhood. I bit her wet earlobe, 'Have I told you that you are the most beautiful girl in the world?'

She shook her head as a tease and we swam together to the edge of the pool. We kissed again and interlocked our fingers. She bit me on the shoulder with such ferocity that she drew blood. The sting of pain goaded me to bite back and soon we were attacking each other like wild animals, but now back in the chair from where I had been watching her. As we made love, I thought I had died and was in a casket being carried from the hearse into the church. Crowds were watching from the road and nudging each other as the coffin passed. It was a London street and the rain was torrential. It streamed down the walls, running in a torrent into the drains, which started to overflow, with exotic fish flapping for joy and the water a mess of colour. I shook my head and tried to rid myself of the hallucinations. I looked down and stared into February's piercing eyes: they were open and staring back.

'Make me forget. Help me, please!' I begged, grieving at my recent past.

'Forget about what, my darling?'

'About everything; everything.'

* * *

The sheets were on the floor, a pillow covered my face. February had left a note stuck to the alarm clock: 'I have gone for a hike with friends. Did not want to wake you – will call later. X'.

I panicked – the bedside clock flashed it was past eleven

o'clock. I was going to be late for work, and so early in my career! It was not good enough. I leapt out of bed like a man late for his own wedding and stood under the hot shower trying to sober up. I looked in the mirror and decided not to shave. What a sight, I thought, and I glimpsed my mother's disapproving look; it reminded me to call my parents later that afternoon.

Fey was waiting with a cup of coffee and a bowl of All-Bran. She was far kinder than I'd at first thought; she had shed her hard exterior and a sweeter nature had emerged. She reminisced about Scotland as if the country were a cruel lost lover. Her tough upbringing in the Gorbals district of Glasgow was painful to relive.

'Do you know what "Gorbals" means, Samuel?'

'I would love to know, Fey, but I am mighty late for work. In fact, I'd better call my assistant Gregory to make an excuse.'

'You'd better relax, young Englishman. It Saturday and unless you work weekends you can take it easy today.'

My body slumped back into my chair. I was so relieved that I forgot to be angry at my forgetfulness. I looked at Fey and she looked back. She smelled of baby shampoo and sweet tobacco.

'Gorbals comes from the Gaelic *gort a' bhaile* "field of the town".' Fey continued where she had left off. 'But it was not a field of green grass. It was a field of grime and sewage. I was born in a wee tenement room, as were my two brothers and two sisters . . . and – '

She seemed about to recount an ugly chapter from her life when a stranger's voice interrupted. It belonged to a tall man of about sixty, broad-shouldered with thick tawny hair and narrow brown eyes. His army fatigues were tucked into canvas mosquito boots, and his white T-shirt read 'Float like a butterfly and sting like bee'. He stared at me, and, squinting his eyes and jutting out his big jaw, he recited, to my surprise, a long poem by Muhammad Ali.

'Ali composed that before his Rumble in the Jungle in 1974 with George Foreman. I'm Douglas Sinclair, your absentee host.' He offered his hand and we shook firmly; he spoke with a Scottish burr. 'Bring two coffees to my quarters, dear Fey, and I will have eggs with a healthy portion of potatoes.'

Douglas led as we went to 'his' side of the house. A glass door opened on to a narrow staircase that climbed to a huge open drawing room, with an unlit log fire in the centre; music played loudly in the background. 'I will eat my breakfast unaccompanied,' he said, switching off the stereo. Countless pictures hung on the pale walls, a collection of contemporary American paintings from Jackson Pollock to Norman Rockwell, enriching the room with a wealth of colour and genius. He noticed that I was struck by the art and enjoyed watching my reaction to each discovery. I believe it was at that moment that I fell in love with contemporary art. Feeding into the vast room was the murmur of a television. I followed the noise that travelled the room, lit up the room, then disappeared into diphthongs. It was coming from a colossal television playing a pornographic film. Clumsily shot characters falling over each other and mouths shutting and opening like the mouths of dying fish. A thousand thoughts raced through my mind like cattle in stampede. I turned to Douglas and apologised for snooping. I stood ready to make an exit. 'Do you mind if I use your phone? I need to reach my girlfriend. I will of course be paying for all my calls.'

'Do you mean that cute blonde girl?' he asked.

'Yes, February,' I replied. 'How do you know she has blonde hair?' I presumed he had met her earlier in the morning.

'Well, I have been in my house over these last two

weeks – hiding, if that's the word, in my quarters. Isn't that true, Fey?'

Fey had stepped into the room to collect the breakfast tray. 'Yes, that's absolutely true, Douglas. You've been here in your private rooms all the time. Would you like some more eggs?'

I gulped and turned paler. What had he seen? Why hadn't he introduced himself? The music must have made sleep impossible last night and, hell, there was a view from his drawing-room window of the entire swimming pool. I shuddered at the thought of it and reverted to apologetic schoolboy.

'Please forgive me, Douglas. I'm so sorry for the noise and for inviting strangers to your house when I am one myself. I will immediately pack my bags and hope that you will come to understand that I was just letting off steam and being a fool.'

Douglas looked at his housekeeper and asked, 'Shall we forgive him, Fey? Of course we shall, you silly boy. I would have been disappointed if you'd sat alone and not taken advantage of your new home. I insist you stay as my guest as long as you like. There's just one more thing – never trust a man of almost the same age who calls you sir.'

I nodded, not really understanding what he was on about. His conversation was strangely unsettling. Listening to him was like listening to a mediocre military band playing the National Anthem full of bum notes.

* * *

I met the actor in the Polo Lounge at the table by the door leading to the terrace. He had taken my call and was anxious to meet. The movie was opening nationwide on the Friday and these were going to be long days. He was doing his round of press interviews, which must have been a very lonely exercise when you know that you are promoting a turkey. He had had enough of being cast as an anti-hero destroying the world. 'I want to be taken seriously, for fuck's sake. It's no longer about the money.'

Our 'private' meeting at the Beverly Hills Hotel would be seen and commented on by everyone in town. His mere acceptance of the place as a suitable venue made it clear that he was being very serious about the possibility of changing agency. He wanted to be snapped and I was providing the picture opportunity. I was the new boy but I was learning fast; I listened to the splatter of gossip in the corridors of the office and digested everything. It was more like a village than a town out there.

The actor smoked and drank and I ordered a salad and smoked. As people passed the table, they either nodded or stopped and offered their best for the opening. The buzz all over town was that it was a disaster, and as if he were someone sneezing in public, most kept at a safe distance in order to avoid contagion.

I made my pitch and felt all eyes on me; I told him that I was hard working, would always be honest, never scared to tell him the truth (true). I was the new kid in town but was heading for the summit (true). I was with a talent agency that wanted to sign him (true), to work as a team (a lie), helping each other with information about every opportunity in town (lie), and nothing would make us feel better than to sit down after the long hours to discuss the possibilities of packaging him as the lead actor in an 'A' list production (another lie). Enough of these action-hero-type roles (lie), I told him that he should be recognised as a fine actor (semi-lie). I promised him that I was there to serve (semi-lie), and the more successful he continued to be, the better it would be for my career and my standing in that town (true). The Oscar was just round the corner (lie).

I ended my pitch by saying, 'It's time that you were taken seriously. These damn action films are a thing of the past. You have to be seen by the world as a gifted actor. Give me the chance to help.' This was an inspired end to the pitch. It was repeating everything that he had told me he wanted earlier in our conversation.

'I have not received a call from my agent since the screening. Not fucking one!'

'Disgraceful!' I replied.

'I *am* a great actor and need that support.'

'Absolutely you do.'

'Heck, it's easy when things are going well, when your movie is raking in the cash, number one at the box office, and the flashbulbs are popping, but when the tide turns, that's when you see who your friends are and who should be guiding your career.' He was growing more agitated.

'Could not agree more.'

'I have been checking you out,' said the actor.

'Yes?' I replied nervously.

'Not much on you as yet. Unknown quantity, but . . . I want to sign. I want you to be my agent. I like you and I like your talk and I have an instinct you are going to the top. I want to share the ride!'

We shook hands, stood and gave each other a hug. The entire Polo Lounge knew what had just happened. I had secured my first big signing. I was elated. I looked at my watch and it was eight o'clock in the evening, far too early UK time to call my parents back in England. I wanted to share my jubilation with my mother.

* * *

It was like being bundled in a cashmere blanket; my first signing had provided the same sense of luxurious comfort. I was driving down to Topanga to celebrate my mini triumph

(I don't want to overdo it here) with my girlfriend and also to meet her parents for the first time. The sky during my drive was a deepening blue, and as my foot touched the gas, I whooped like a madman into the open road ahead. The scent of pine that had drenched my car gave way to stronger odours as I sped through Pacific Palisades. The smoke of barbecues combined with the smell of leaking oil from a local gas station to give me a superficial high, encouraging me to drive faster. I reached the ocean and turned right on to the Pacific Coast Highway, and then, after a few miles, right again up Topanga Canyon. The landscape, increasingly beautiful as the houses petered out, gladdened my eyes and a gentle breeze brushed my lips. Topanga was a fertile wilderness, an extravagance of nature to match my soaring spirit.

The house was a rambling hideaway down an ill-kempt drive bordered with sycamores and pines. A US army jeep was parked alongside February's sports car. There was no intrusive sound, just the thud of heat bouncing from the valley.

February skipped out to meet me, followed by an assortment of dogs. She dived into my arms and gave me a tight hug and my heart whistled to a boil. It was a moment of pure bliss.

'I'm so happy you're here,' she whispered. Her dungarees were splashed with a rainbow of paint.

I was led into the kitchen. John Lennon's 'Imagine' drifted from an elderly transistor radio deep in the corner of the overcrowded sideboard; a jumble of plates and pans were displayed on a long wooden table in the centre of a large room. February's drawings were scattered around the walls, all slightly lopsided; it was an organised mess. I was given an ice-cold glass of orange juice taken from a huge 1950s-style fridge. While we talked, February danced about like a happy excited girl celebrating her birthday. We spoke again of my previous evening's success and I told her that Douglas had been hiding in the house since the time I arrived.

'How embarrassing! Do you think he saw everything? Oh God, how awful! It sounds as if you're staying with a deranged pervert.'

'He is certainly that, but you'll like him. He's been fantastically generous and has said that I can stay as long as I like. So let's say he's a charming pervert. If such a thing can exist.'

February's mother, Helen, interrupted our conversation. There was no handshake by way of introduction, only a warm welcoming hug. She had a body like her daughter's and her eyes were on fire. Wow, what a mother and what a sublime, cool vibe! In the course of conversation, Helen spoke of her days as a hippy. I pressed her to say more and my eager questions may have given away the fantasy I had of living in a commune, drunk on free spirit.

'It wasn't as glorious as you might imagine,' interrupted Edward – or Ed, as he liked to be known. 'I tend to glaze over when people romanticise those years.'

'Come on, baby, we had some good times.' Helen's hand reached out to her husband's. He clasped it to his heart and gave her a kiss on the forehead. Ed also gave me a warm hug. This was so unlike a stiff English reception, and instead of being uncomfortable, I marvelled at the easy informality.

At first, I had kept February's arm linked in mine, but now that her father had joined us, I rapidly released it and straightened up. A boy from my background could not be cured of his inhibitions in one short lesson. And now, Ed himself, dressed in khaki shorts and grey T-shirt, gossiping about sex in Hollywood, momentarily challenged my middle-class conditioning. I recognised it was the 'meeting the parents' scenario that had brought out the bourgeois in me. Ed made gestures with his hands for emphasis and had the habit of checking with his wife's eyes when he had finished a sentence. It was clear from the beginning that they shared a deep spiritual rapport.

As the parents prepared lunch, February led me outside.

'I have a present for you, Sam.'

February had a studio a short walk behind the house, a low elongated building raked by the sun. The distinctive smell of oil paints wafted on the gentle warm air off into the wilderness. What a place to work, to lose yourself in the imagery of soil and unsullied nature.

February opened the door and beckoned me to follow. The light fell directly on to a wooden easel; a canvas covered with a cloth rested on its ledge.

'This is for you, my darling.'

And with her delicate hand she lifted the cloth to reveal a portrait of my brother Thomas. February had copied the photograph that I kept by my bed. It had been taken of him on his last day at public school: below his handsome face, his top button was undone and his black tie lowered down his shirt. Everything about him looked towards the future. The oil painting was so fine, so lifelike and so obviously him, that for a fraction of a moment, I thought he was alive and gazing right back into my eyes. I choked, and as when I heard the news of his death, my legs gave way and I fell to my knees as if to pray. February ran to me and knelt by my side, understanding and sharing my distress.

'I did it for you because I love you. I love you.' And she wiped away my tears and held my shaking body with a tenderness that wrung my heart.

Hikes under low white clouds far into the canyons helped purge some of my grief. February's parents were adorable and kind and made me feel part of their family. The landscape infused renewed optimism into my veins, and when I stopped on one of our walks and pushed the spikes of a cactus into my hand, I marvelled as drops of my lifeblood fell to the soil and an army of ants hurried to investigate. How my mood fluctuated from hour to hour! How I tried repeatedly to recapture the heavenly moment when I first arrived . . . February had the instinct of when to leave me alone with my thoughts. They still tended to drift in a rudderless way. Solitude had been ingrained in my psyche ever since I slept away from home in my hard, narrow boarding-school bed. She had felt guilty about the painting, but I reassured her that it was probably the most touching present I had ever received and sometimes an experience such as that can help the healing process; I held her during the night through my broken dreams, and pressing close her naked body, thanked the universe for introducing me to so generous a soul.

When I returned to Los Angeles late on Sunday afternoon, I was calmer and stronger than twenty-four hours before. February stayed behind to finish some work and the entire family gave me an affectionate send off, with dogs barking. I left the painting behind; I was not ready to have Tom's face staring back at me from that canvas just yet.

* * *

'Well done!' Marvin started to clap and the other agents followed.

I had announced at the weekly meeting that I had secured my first signing and he was a big star. Yes, as predicted his film nearly bankrupted the studio, but he would always command healthy fees in, say, Italy. He was a name and my commission would and should be fat. My fellow agents were very supportive when I asked for their help in searching for a good project. 'Of course, all you have to do is knock on the door,' they assured me in unison, with the exception of poor Mr Greene, who had, as expected, been fired on the Friday. He had failed to sign Roman Polanski and in a final act of desperation had tried to secure a meeting with John Belushi, who didn't show up and left him waiting in the Polo Lounge. A terrible lingering humiliation followed, because he had announced to the manager that as soon as Mr Belushi arrived he was to 'bring him right over'. The manager then told someone, who told someone, and by the time he left, alone, the whole town knew about it.

'Fool!' I overheard a co-worker say. 'If he thought that John Belushi was going to take a meeting in the Beverly Hills Hotel, then he was more of a idiot than I thought he was.'

After that, there was never a mention of his name, and like rapacious relatives dividing the effects of the deceased, his erstwhile colleagues chewed over which of Mr Greene's clients they thought they should hang on to. Many were dismissed as either yesterday's news or names that could not bring in enough commission. There was no room for the romantic gesture or even good taste. It was a 'bottom line' discussion, the only language many those in that room could understand.

The meeting wrapped up with targets for the following week. Christopher Reeve, Sissy Spacek, Chuck Norris were top of the list. 'I will go for Norris!' yelled Susan before anyone could have a say.

'OK, Susan, you go for Norris, but before meeting him don't forget that he practices a martial art that has a strict ethical code. I suggest you first learn his ten rules by heart; here are some of them.' Cowen picked up a sheet of paper and recited: 'I will develop myself to the maximum of my potential in all ways; I will forget the mistakes of the past and press on to greater achievements; I will look for the good in all people and make them feel worthwhile; if I have nothing good to say about a person, I will say nothing; I will always be as enthusiastic about the success of others as I am about my own; I will maintain an attitude of open-mindedness; I will always remain loyal to God, my country, my family and my friends . . . You get the picture?' asked Marvin, nodding curtly at Miss Gralstein.

'Yep. I will go for Christopher Reeve!'

* * *

No one was answering the buzzer. I pressed and pressed again but there was still no answer. I was standing at the gates of a film star's mansion. Claudia Tyrell had had two box-office hits in the last year and success had taken her from a trailer outside Asheville in North Carolina to a millionaire's home on Bellagio in Bel Air.

I had been asked by Mr Cowen to escort the young star to a party in Malibu. It was to be a personal appearance at a 'bash' being thrown by his accountant. 'She is going to be paid in cash and in return all she has to do is walk in with the host and stay for an hour. For that she is to be paid a hundred thousand dollars. He will hand the money over to you during the event.'

It seemed like a good job. I buzzed again and this time the black wrought-iron gates silently parted. I hurried back to my car and drove up a knoll to the porch of a substantial Palladian-style house. Before I even entered, I was struck by its air of desolation and the still light added to the loneliness.

A Spanish maid opened the door and showed me into a drawing room bereft of soul. The house was sparsely furnished, and as I called out, my voice rebounded off the walls. The room was huge and contained a single large sofa and a television blaring out the patter of a game-show host. There were no pictures on the wall and only a single photograph in an expensive silver frame – of a couple, who must have been her parents, smiling outside a movie house showing her latest feature – stood on top of the television. I picked up the frame and was studying the photograph when I heard someone behind me say, 'Hi, I'm Claudia.'

Tall and willowy, with a beautiful long neck and soft brown hair falling behind her ears, she was far thinner than she looked on the screen. This rising star, who had become famous for playing an athletic action hero, was, in fact, timid and brittle.

'Do you like the house?' she asked.

'Very comfortable,' I lied, and she smiled.

'I only bought it last week. It's my very first.'

'Bit grand for me,' I answered, looking at the tall ceilings.

She wore a maroon dress, short and light, that danced as she walked. Her Greek sandals showed off her lightness of step. She was far more dazzling in motion than in repose.

* * *

Another flawless day, not a cloud in sight and the warm air poured through our open windows. Claudia's face softened in the gentle wind and she looked spaced out but content. Her eyes were closed and I gazed at her fine features. This is the face that fascinates the world. Her eyes suddenly opened and caught me and I turned away.

'I hate doing these sort of things but in one hour I will have earned more money than my father did in the last ten years. Not fair, is it? But that's the business. You have to sell and sell to reach the top.' She seemed disenchanted already with the whole process and she had only been acting for three years. She had entered a beauty pageant down in North Carolina that by chance was being attended by a casting director in search of an actress for a new NBC drama series. 'Find an unknown' had been her instruction. She found Claudia, not to play the part of a female detective, but to star as the super hero. Two hit movies later, and with the third in the series given the green light, life should have been at its happiest.

The host looked like my father's accountant back in England. They even shared the same name, Paul Springer, which was most odd. Unbearably pale for someone who lived in sunshine all year, he dressed casual in an uncasual way. He had invited some of the biggest moneymakers in town – not the stars of the screen, but the Hollywood executives, lawyers and agents; these were the big fish who controlled the business side of the industry and Mr Springer was the one who looked after their spoils. 'A genius!' declared Cowen, when he gave me a rundown of his business activities, most of which seemed dreary to me. This was Springer's PR event of the year and he needed a star to be part of the gathering and symbolise his success. The caterers had been working all day. From the vans parked outside, it looked like the money had not solely been spent on the star. I was certain that he had worked out some tax break, but the mode of payment nagged like a mosquito bite; a leading accountant paying cash just didn't add up. An avenue of candles planted either side of the steep drive marked the way to the front door. His house overlooked the Pacific Ocean and was being picked out, although it was still only mid-afternoon, by twirling spotlights, theatrically dancing around the white exterior.

The entrance was to be carefully staged. Mr Springer and Claudia would wait for their cue from game-show presenter Gene Rayburn and walk hand in hand (that was important) into the main room to the sound of the Knack and their hit 'My Sharona'.

'Too expensive to hire,' Springer had muttered. 'Disappointing,' he said, 'as their manager *is* a client.' The guests were an uninspiring collection of grey people swigging back the expensive champagne. The tone of the whole event was enough to give one indigestion.

Gene Rayburn, the master of ceremonies and presenter of *Match Games,* was well cast. I had caught his act on Claudia's television only the hour before. In his long introduction, he built up to the entrance of Hollywood's latest star with old jokes and pleasant smiles. The invited were becoming restless with nervous energy and the impact of an afternoon's drinking shortened the time they were prepared to put up with this tedious act.

A waiter in a well-timed whisper murmured that our host would like to see me.

'Tell that Gene Rayburn just to introduce us!' Mr Springer was getting irritated.

'Mr Rayburn,' I interrupted his monologue, 'they are dying backstage. Mr Springer says just get on with it!'

The game-show host checked his ego, and with a pretend drum roll and a popping sound from the mouth, he said, 'Ladies and gentlemen, please give a warm welcome to our host with the numbers – and Claudia Tyrell, his friendly sex symbol, sex kitten and, from what I hear, sex mad.'

'My Sharona' blasted forth and out came the accountant and the Starlet, Springer soaked with perspiration, Claudia scowling at our MC. The party applauded as the music died and Springer grabbed the microphone. He made an uneasy speech, thanking all for attending and saying what a special honour it was to have his 'best friend' Claudia fly in from location just to be with him at his party. For $100k, what do you expect?

The party then altered gear slightly as a jazz band tucked in a corner scrumptiously opened with 'Summertime'. I talked to faceless accountants and worked the room, occasionally looking at my watch to check on time. We were meant to be there for only an hour, but each minute hung heavier than the last, like another weight added to a load slung from a hook in one's flesh. Claudia was making little effort to mingle and sat in the corner, on display like a piece of valuable china, puffing on a cigarette and paralysed with boredom. The expression on her face suggested she had swallowed something putrid.

'She isn't earning her money.' Springer had dragged me to his bedroom upstairs and was complaining. A smell of cheap aftershave pervaded the room.

'From what I understand all she needed to do was to walk in with you and stay for an hour. It's time for you to pay, Mr Springer.' I was beginning to sound more and more like Uncle Louis.

He got down on to his knees and dragged a leather briefcase from under the bed. He flicked it open, working a combination of 1950 (I was looking over his shoulder), and revealed a ton of cash – the $100k. I was not sure of the etiquette, so I picked up one bundle and flicked through it. It looked like $10,000, so I replaced the green notes and sealed the case.

'Don't you want to count it?' asked the accountant.

'That won't be necessary. Thank you, Mr Springer; if in the future you need another celebrity, please do not hesitate to call.'

I was about to open the door, briefcase in hand, when he beckoned my return. There was a silence, a hesitation in thought and speech.

'Yes, Mr Springer. Anything else?'

He was sweatier and paler than before. He asked whether I wanted to sit down.

'That won't be necessary.' I repeated my new phrase.

'I am ready to pay two hundred and fifty thousand dollars to have . . . ' he coughed, 'to have sex with the actress. We could do it here, upstairs, and it will not go on for longer than an hour.' He bit his lip and the smell of unwashed underpants wafted in my direction. He was waiting for my reaction and I inwardly shuddered at his request. Like an executioner picking up his axe, I framed my reply.

'Five hundred thousand dollars and I will ask.' The monster inside was stirring again. I lit myself a cigarette.

'Please don't smoke in here.' I ignored his request and took a deep drag and blew out the smoke. Oh, Uncle Louis, if you could see me now.

'OK. OK. Five hundred thousand dollars, you bastard. That's a lot of money.'

'Take it or leave it – and in cash, Mr Springer. We are talking about one of the most famous women in the world, not some cheap trick on Hollywood Boulevard. I know somewhere in this house you have it.'

It didn't take him long. 'Agreed. But no one must ever know!'

I narrowed my eyes to express contempt for his stupidity.

We shook on it, his hand feeling like a buttered kipper, and I left in search of the Starlet.

Down the stairs I walked, but halfway down I stopped abruptly. Was this the first sign that I was turning into a mobster? Was I taking after Uncle Louis? I balanced the internal debate with the fact that I was only doing it for Claudia. Was I gambling with her virtue? Had I changed that much since I first arrived in town? Was the temptation that great? Or was it life's rule to take risks whatever the consequences? The uneasiness of the afternoon marked a fork in the road. Do I turn into a callous, uncaring, lying son of a bitch who grasps the ends whatever the means, or an honest man who ignores the temptations that lie scattered in his path? This was the real world, not the world of frivolous schoolboy pranks. The danger was being contemptibly oblivious of the fact. Surely one could occasionally confuse the two? That I had to ask these questions smacked of emotional bankruptcy.

By the time I reached the hall, I had settled the matter in my mind. Always put the offer on the table and take it from there. I recognised that the Devil had edged closer. It was up to me whether or not I befriended him.

* * *

'Claudia, may I have a word?' She was still in her corner, but at least now was talking to a few of the guests. I beckoned her outside and we stood overlooking the serenity of the ocean.

'That's three hundred thousand dollars in cash . . . '

'That's a lot of money,' she replied.

'It will be quick, that's for sure.'

She turned away and looked out. She leaned forward, with her elbows on the wooden railing, and rested her chin on her hands. She had had a few drinks and her mood was brighter than earlier in the afternoon. The nature of the offer had sent her drifting into the past. A mouthful of heavy blue Cuban smoke travelled from a fat man, some yards away, who was talking up a tax break. The smoke floated by her face and startled her back to the present.

'I haven't ever told anyone this, but when she was my age my mother walked the streets. I have been waiting for *The Enquirer* to find out, but as yet nothing. I bet she never had an offer like this though.' She laughed to herself. Her early life had been strewn with humiliating circumstances. The memory of her mother's past weighed on her mind like an enormous boulder which the passage of time had not worn away. Indeed, the burden was as heavy as ever. Unsurprisingly, she reacted to the offer like a seagull taking flight as a wave crashes over the rocks. Straightening her shoulders and recovering her focus, she said, 'Tell him NO!'

* * *

Springer was waiting in his bedroom. He had not moved since the offer had been made. I told him that there was no deal and that we would now be leaving.

'You know they are all fucking whores, Alexander,' spat the accountant.

'Clearly not this one,' I replied.

The car was waiting outside, and with briefcase in hand and Claudia by my side, I climbed into the back and drove away.

'Welcome to Hollywood,' she said as we departed.

I looked away towards the sea, the harsh gleam blinding me so that I had to shield my eyes, and distanced myself from any discreditable aspect of the role I had played that afternoon.

* * *

I tried to phone home at least twice a week. It seemed days were passing quickly, and when I spoke to my parents, it was usually about February and little else. After each call I had a pang of homesickness, but as soon as I stepped into the lemon light of the sun, the sudden melancholy was banished on the currents of soft Californian air.

It was early on Saturday evening when the phone rang in my bedroom. I'd missed calling my mother as they were in the South of France, and I immediately thought that they were ringing, although it was late their time.

'Hello . . . who is that? . . . Billy?'

'Yes, it is. Did I wake you?'

'No, it's not my bedtime yet! Anything wrong?' I asked.

'You sure I didn't wake you.'

'I'm sure. In fact, I was about to go out to dinner.'

'The reason I called,' Billy hesitated for a moment and I could hear him lighting a cigarette, 'is I have some news.'

'Yes?'

'Some news,' he repeated.

'Are you sure you're OK, Billy?'

'Yes, I'm fine.'

'Tell me, Billy . . . tell me.'

'It's Margaret. She's killed herself.'

'What did you say?'

'She hanged herself, the poor soul. Jackie called round this afternoon and asked me to let you know.'

I listened, but I couldn't take it in. I grabbed a half-smoked cigarette.

'Hello, Sam? Are you there?'

'Yes, I'm here.'

'She wrote you a note. It's in an envelope . . . Sam, are you there?'

* * *

After the visit to the clinic and clearing Sam out of her life, Margaret lay in bed with a fairly high temperature. One morning her fever was so high that she lost track of the order of events. The spell of her illness faded to a distant memory and the days to come loomed over her menacingly.

Although she was safe in her bed and surrounded by her precious things – the photo of her parents, her favourite copy of the Tatler *(a flattering photo appeared of her in the Bystander section), her battered teddy bear – she was elsewhere in her mind surrounded by dark threatening shapes. She could not rid herself of the welcome that was given her when she walked into the clinic. The lady at the desk had a ginormous nose surrounded by a pygmy head. She was ugly and unemotional and made no effort to put Margaret at ease with what she was about to face. Margaret was convinced the woman had a small Book of Common Prayer, hidden beneath her desk, from which she would intone as soon as a patient was called. In her fever she saw the face of the Devil smirking at her decision. How could she be judged like this? She was not prepared to bring up a child alone: that is not the way things were in her life. It was a simple decision, surely? Everything was made easy for her to reach the decision to abort. Surely, that was a sign? It was the correct decision and that was the end of it. The nagging doubt was natural; she believed it would soon disappear. The right man would come along and they could be a family. Yes, she saw a happy family gathered round the table in the house in Gloucestershire; that would be perfect. She had a vivid dream that night of her father, in heavy unlaced boots, coming down for breakfast. He had nicked himself with his razor and blood gushed from his face. Margaret tried to staunch the blood, but failed, and in doing so her father's shirt was soaked and a mess. 'Can't you do anything right?' her father demanded angrily, and she cowered away in the darkness of a corner.*

She woke the following morning with her fever partially abated. There was no one she wanted to tell of her misery. Margaret had for years kept her innermost feelings locked away and this was not the time to lay them bare. She missed work that week, which was unusual. Jackie called, offering to bring over some food, but she lied and said that her parents were taking care of her. She had some tinned soup, which she heated, and some bread, which she toasted. It was a day later that she dragged herself out to the corner shop to stock up.

She had almost forgotten that she was due to visit the

parents at the weekend. By the Friday the fever had subsided enough for her to go, but she made the excuse she had a cold and didn't want to pass it on. Instead she was the prisoner of her mind and of her small dreary apartment. She sat alone and in anguish, her physical strength drained, and the fever re-emerged. As her temperature rose, unreasoning terror seized her and she saw herself growing old with no friends and no comfort of love. She had always half-believed that this was her destiny, but it needed this week to convince her.

The following week, she went to work in an altered state. She looked a little tired to the outside world, but that was all; it was on the inside that she couldn't cope. She had not rid herself of the previous week's delirious fears. Her unfulfilled life became a spectre haunting her every move. But, as was her habit, she buried the torment and let it fester.

Margaret went to visit her parents, and when they picked her up from Cheltenham railway station was relieved that her mother did not comment negatively on her appearance. In fact, she remarked that Margaret looked well and was glad to see she had made a full recovery. This made Margaret more confident and the encouragement brought back a little of her lost strength. Her father made no comment on her appearance, and although relieved at this, a new sense of depression overtook her – how out of touch her parents were with her state of mind. When alone, Margaret looked in the mirror and was horrified to see how gaunt and tired she looked. She brushed her hair savagely in frustration and loathing at the sight of her reflection. Her high cheekbones reminded her of her mother's, and although she was far taller and stronger than her mother, whose frame was slight, she had begun to recognise more of herself in her than ever before.

The weekend followed its usual routine of kippers for breakfast on the Saturday, with well-toasted thick white bread and strong coffee. Afterwards, Margaret and her father took a brisk drive in his blue Volvo into the busy Cheltenham town centre to buy something or other. That day, it was garden equipment and the new Frederick Forsyth novel, which her father was eager to devour. They spoke little in the car. Margaret longed for her father to say: 'Life may be tough now, my darling girl, but I promise it will get better. You are the most beautiful girl in the world and I love you.' Instead he repeatedly raked his wiry grey hair back from his narrow face, drew on his cigarette ever so lightly and said nothing.

It was on the Sunday, over a lunch of roast pork, that her father mentioned to Margaret that she should expect a call from the son of a former business associate. 'He's a lawyer who has recently moved to London to start a new job, and he hasn't many friends.'

The idea of meeting someone new gave her a peculiar sensation. Perhaps this was the man she had been waiting for? Perhaps that is why she chose to lose her child? Her head started to fill with visions of her white wedding in the local church. This had been her dream ever since she was a child, and revisiting it lifted the black cloud she had felt immersed in over the previous days.

She did not have to wait long for the call. His voice was a bit overbearing, but there was a sense that he was full of amusing and frivolous ideas. They had a long conversation and by the time Margaret hung up, she felt a good deal better. The only disappointment was that he had to go to Geneva for a week, or maybe two, to advise a client.

'I'll be in touch as soon as I get back and we'll arrange a dinner,' and oddly he burst out laughing. Margaret put it down to excitement.

'Looking forward to it,' Margaret told him, and indeed she was.

It was six weeks later that Alan Darby Mills eventually

called back. Margaret had been kept in suspense like a patient waiting for test results from the doctor.

'Sorry it took me so long to get back to you, I have been so busy!' he guffawed. 'Let's go out Thursday?'

'That would be lovely,' Margaret replied.

He did not offer to pick her up and instead they met at the restaurant. Pontevecchio on the Old Brompton Road was an oversized Italian restaurant with a glass front and a deluge of noise. Alan was waiting at their table drinking a gin and tonic when Margaret arrived. Her first impression was not overwhelming – and that is being kind. He looked squeezed into his suit and beads of sweat fell from his top lip; he was disgusting.

'Hello, old girl!' he said by way of welcome.

Margaret looked very beautiful that night. She had gone to have her hair done like Audrey Hepburn in Breakfast at Tiffany's *and wore a figure-hugging red dress. As she walked to her table, every man's eyes followed her. But Margaret was blind to that, so focused was she on making the dinner a success.*

'One really has to mix with the intelligentsia. I am meeting more and more stupid people.'

'How right you are,' replied Margaret, not believing anything she was saying. He was a conceited bore and she knew it. She asked herself what her life had come to. Disappointment almost choked her and at one point she thought she would have to walk outside to get some fresh air; he began to make her flesh creep. She could not wait for the dinner to end; each moment seemed like an eternity. Outraged to find herself in this position, she swore never to go on a blind date again. 'What am I doing with my life? Waiting for someone like this? Oh, dear Lord, do I deserve such bad luck?' she prayed silently. She hardly exchanged another word with him and when he dropped her home and

tried to kiss her she nearly slapped him full in the face. His breath reeked like a dog's ass and drifted in the air for so long afterwards that she was convinced the next morning she could still smell it. When she had slammed the door on him, she leaned against it and put her hands to her face and cried and cried. There had been few tears over the weeks and she told herself it was healthy and cathartic.

Margaret's loveless desolation continued however. Even Jackie, who was her closest friend, didn't realise what she was going through, but that was because she was struggling with her own problems. Therefore, Margaret grew more confident that no one saw her misery and this oddly became a source of comfort. Mrs Kurzner, who normally missed nothing, failed to recognise anything wrong, except for making the occasional comment that Margaret looked tired. The after-effects of her fever lingered still, and physically she was weaker than she had ever been, but she refused to visit a doctor for a check-up. She was now walking the narrow path of calculatedly covert self-harm. Her final lunch with her parents in a small inconsequential restaurant near Piccadilly Circus was short tempered. Her father was in a surly mood following a previous day's appointment with his bank manager. It had been an unsatisfactory meeting and his annoyance spilled over into their lunch together. When Margaret upset the wine on the white tablecloth, he yelled, 'Can't you do anything right?' The words and the tone, and the sight of the red wine soaking into the linen, triggered her memory of the nightmare she had endured during those feverish mournful days. It was probably then she decided that she would not see another full day on this earth. Her face betrayed no hint of this momentous decision, it remained fixed, breathtakingly beautiful, caught in the frozen frame of time.

She kissed her parents goodbye with no emotion – her wretched parents, so near to the end of their lives. To lose their daughter was a blow neither was going to be able to recover from. If Margaret had been asked how she felt at that time, she would have answered, 'I feel just fine.' The world of the dying is a very private place.

After breakfast, Margaret threw a blazer over her shoulders and strolled down Wandsworth Bridge Road. The September morning was still and warm; London was enjoying a series of these lovely days. Her step was brisk and as she walked she seemed to hear the murmur of voices. Mr Khan, the jovial newsagent, was rejoicing over some cricket results that had filtered through his overused transistor radio, placed on the top shelf among the porn mags. He had already folded the Daily Mail *before Margaret had reached the counter. It was a quiet news day, the only excitement being the sentence of five years for the teenage boy who had fired six blanks at the Queen in the Mall.*

By the time she had reached Berkeley Square, the traffic was building up and Margaret had quite suddenly to take a step back from a speeding blue Mercedes. 'Steady,' she had thought, and when she reached the door to her office she admitted that she was lucky not to have been hit by the passing car.

'How pretty you look,' Mr Kurzner had said as she came into the room bringing their morning coffee. He had never said anything like that before and it quite startled Margaret. She had grown accustomed to Mr Kurzner's unobservant ways. He gave the impression of being miles away whenever she walked past. Jackie was as usual typing away and only broke off to step outside for some fresh air. 'Like to join me?' she asked, but Margaret made the excuse that she needed to call her parents.

Her reply had been impersonal and her manner formal, as if to an acquaintance rather than a close friend. Her parents were out when she called as they had gone into

Cheltenham. Margaret had noticed on her visit the previous weekend that there was a sense of despair about her future. She hated the fact there was regret in her father's voice. How she wanted him to be proud of her!

Margaret decided not to leave a message, but instead replaced the receiver and started to write three short letters. One to her parents, another to Jackie and the third to Sam. And here life to all intents and purposes came to a halt, no more agonised puzzling, no more forward planning. Her decision to end her journey had been made and her words on three scraps of paper justified her action. Even in her final hours, justification was important.

Late that afternoon, she called California to speak to Sam. She had got his number from the London office. Gregory answered. 'He's not in,' he said, without checking. She didn't leave a message; she left nothing, not her suffering, nor her torment, not even her name.

Her goodbyes to the office were upbeat even, some would say, 'happy'. Charles, who had been working on the switchboard for a month, rose from his seat. He offered her a mint to suck on the way home. Margaret accepted and made her way down the stairs for the last time.

The early evening was so still it was like setting forth into silence itself. The hustle that marked the beginning of the day had left no trace. She took the number 14 bus to the corner of Beaufort Street and went into Farmers Brothers, which was opposite the ABC Cinema. There she bought herself a three-strand twisted rope. She set off on foot, deaf to the faint sounds of traffic, back home to Friston Street. On opening her door, she left her bag on the dining table and went into her bedroom. To the casual observer she would have seemed very relaxed, with nothing out of the ordinary on her mind.

She had found a deep hook that had been many years in the ceiling and round that she tied the rope, making sure it was short enough and securely fixed. She moved her bed to the side wall and brought in the stool that she sat on for her morning tea. In her bedroom, at half-past six, Margaret hanged herself. In the room where she and Sam had made love; in the room where they'd created a child; in the room where Sam relinquished part of his soul; in that room darling Margaret took her own life.

* * *

The response from the other end when Billy asked, 'Would you like me to open the letter?' was one of assent. Taking the sheet of paper from the envelope, he read:

> *'Darling Sam – I have been lonely for too long. I am in truth a coward and could not face another day of my prolix life. You are a good person, Sam. I don't think you realise how good and generous you are.*
>
> *Don't be sad now. Don't blame yourself for anything. What happened between us was my choice as well as yours. Whoever you fall in love with, she will be a lucky girl. Perhaps you will mention my name one day. I would like that.*
>
> *Be safe, Sam.*
>
> *Love, Margaret.'*

'Thank you, Billy, for letting me know. It can't have been easy.'

I hung up and picked a burning cigarette out of the ashtray. As I was trying to bring it to my mouth, it slipped from my fingers, but I retrieved it before it burned down the house. I walked along the drive and out of the gate. I felt sad and frightened: sad because I had not done as much as I could have done and frightened because death loomed hideously close once more. I drifted along the road, on the lookout for some sign of life, but the road was empty and peaceful. The sun was going down behind the tall trees, but the warmth of the day remained. The weather should be punishing me, I thought: I should be lashed by the rain and battered by the wind. The shock of the phone call prevented rational thought. She was unhappy when I last saw her, but that was understandable. Surely everyone who went through that experience was unhappy for a while. Obviously, she did not have the strength to recover from it . . .

'Oh dear God, what have I done? Margaret, Margaret!' I stopped at a fork in the road and burst into uncontrollable tears.

My legs were seized with cramp and I sank to the side of the road and stretched them. The blurred image of Margaret crept to the front of my mind. Her haughty way of keeping the office staff in order and her vibrant sexuality that took my breath away each time she walked by. I scanned my visual images of her and choked with tears when I reached one that pressed too close to bear. I told myself that Margaret had chosen to fall asleep.

I leaned my back against a large redwood tree and brooded, until I heard a car approaching. It was February, driving to meet me as planned; she had slowed down.

'Are you all right, my darling?'

'I'm OK, just a bit tired.'

'What are you doing there?' she asked.

She came to sit by my side and the stalks of grass that surrounded us tickled my arm. I told her what had happened and February listened with concern. She didn't try to make light of my connection with Margaret; instead she held my arm and when I shook with grief she held my hand more tightly than before. As the temperature fell, we put our arms round each other and I shared with her thoughts of Margaret and cried silently into the night.

* * *

Dear Mr and Mrs Wingate – As morning breaks, I find your daughter's memory etched into the quiet of the day. The slightest of winds breathes over the grass and caresses the brick of the house where I now live. As I write this letter in the warmth of a Californian garden, I hear the sound of the restless trees and with the beauty of the light I am reminded of your daughter, my dear friend Margaret.

I am uncertain if I was spoken of, but we worked together in the theatrical agency in Berkeley Square. It was there she encouraged my ambition and spurred me on, through the days and months, to realise my potential; for that alone I will always be grateful. I remember her forehead wrinkling as she drank her morning tea and how she would scold if I failed to put the top back on the milk bottle (gold top, of course!). I was often jaded when I reached the office, but her unfailingly firm attitude would tolerate no slacking. I admired the way she spoke to the clients, always gauging their moods, remembering their interests and finding an amusing anecdote to fill any lull in the conversation. I still hear her laugh, see her blink as she smiled, recall how she used to scratch her head if she ever grew slightly embarrassed, how she pushed back her hair just before she entered the room.

And yet with all this, it seems I knew little of your daughter, and my regret is that I didn't search deeper. My thoughts and prayers are with you during these days and I hope in some way my confused scribbling conveys how much your daughter was loved. Your tragic loss is our loss and our loss is the world's.

Yours sincerely,

Sam Alexander

I folded over the airmail-blue writing paper and tucked it into a matching envelope. I stamped it with a twenty-five-cent stamp and placed it on the table by my bed, the address written clearly in black ink. But in the end, it was another letter I failed to send. It was a letter that didn't tell the whole truth. For I left out my role in her final days, and on reading it through one more time, disgust at my lies crawled across my conscience like a rabid dog preparing to vomit.

* * *

Douglas had returned from Vancouver after visiting an old girlfriend who, in the past, Fey said, had hung around the house like stale tobacco and drink. 'They nearly got married, but he pulled out, so to speak, a week before. He is a born bachelor.'

Since our introduction, I had seen little of Douglas. When I left for work he was still asleep, and by the time I returned, he had usually locked himself up in his quarters with one of his prostitutes. They appeared so regularly that I took them as much for granted as the morning sun. His generosity was humbling and I sensed he enjoyed my so-called friends using his pool or crashing out in front of the television. He had rung from his end of the house asking whether I would like to travel with him to Las Vegas (he had some business to do there). And how could I be so churlish as not to accept? He had been a most indulgent host. Elvis Presley, casinos, Frank Sinatra, boxing, could there be a better place for entertainment in the world? It would also distract me from dwelling on Margaret's death and going over and over what I might have done to prevent it. February knew that I needed space to regain my equilibrium and encouraged me to spend some time alone. She had been empathetic with my distress and I loved her all the more for that.

Douglas and I took a private plane for the forty-minute flight from Van Nuys in the San Fernando Valley to Vegas, where Caesar's Palace was to be our billet for the weekend.

I love hotel rooms. Whenever I walk into one, I feel comfortably isolated from the outside world, all alone with my thoughts and elated by the freedom. I immediately scouted the mini-bar, poured myself a drink and switched on the television to find the local network. I luxuriated briefly under a hot shower, before I grabbed my drink and flung myself on to the fresh, crisp, white sheets. I never think of the former occupant; it is as if the room has been waiting for me since the hotel opened.

Douglas went to his quarters as soon as we checked in. 'I will see you, when I see you,' he said, with hardly a glance in my direction. He had spoken little during our short flight and spent most of the time reading his financial papers. I had not found his behaviour rude because when he did look up and make conversation it was always entertaining and warm.

The desert heat was so intense that the outside world was a no-go area, so after a while, I set about exploring the interior of this monstrosity of garishness and opulence. I was dressed in a white suit. I thought it might be the form if I was about to gamble away my savings. I put on my brown suede shoes, with laces still done up, and in front of the mirror I knotted a fake college tie I'd picked up from a fancy store on Rodeo Drive. The wearing of my old school tie was strictly forbidden after my expulsion, and my observance of this antiquated rule was a gesture of reconciliation with my alma mater. 'Good to have an old school tie, old boy, they appreciate it over here,' Commander Boeye had advised.

I had lost track of time, but I was hungry; before tackling the tables, I decided to seek out a restaurant. A saloon bar was serving the great American burger and that suited me. The place was full of powder-caked middle-aged women, dragging on their cigarettes and spluttering with girlish laughter. I saw an oriental man, in a suit not unlike mine and open shirt, silently praying; he was looking for a miracle and he was looking for it here in Vegas. I drank my terrible coffee and studied the motionless fan on the ceiling; they probably kept it switched off on purpose, hoping to force the punters back to the tables. Just as I was struck by this thought, however, the fan choked into action, causing the papers of a writer on the neighbouring table to ruffle. Without taking his eyes off his work, he grabbed a full bottle of Coca-Cola and placed it as a paperweight on the fluttering pile.

I signalled to the wide-smiling waiter for the check and as I waited a girl with bright-red hair, red red hair, and dimples *so* deep approached me.

'Do you want to spend some cash?' she asked, bending close so that her perfume enveloped me.

'Absolutely I do. First roulette and then blackjack.'

'Let's go then.'

And Ruby, who seemed very knowledgeable about the right tables to play on, took my hand and led me to an empty table. The slick croupier changed my cash into more chips than I really wanted, but I had an exotic by my side and did not want to let her down. The green baize had a hypnotic effect on me. I had a vague understanding of how roulette was played, but was still unsure how the odds worked. I had gambled away cigarettes in my 'crow's nest' room at school. I tended to play the colours because even a fool could work out that it looked like a fifty-fifty chance. I caressed my pile of chips and checked myself before putting the whole damn lot on red; it was double or nothing. I watched the ivory ball jangle its way round the spinning wheel, seeming to pause before it dropped into the number 7. Number 7 and it was *red*! My companion smiled, but was not that impressed . . . I was though. More, I wanted more! My pulse raced as I put all my winnings on red. Once again the ball found that colour, this time number 18. I had quadrupled my money and did not want to stop. Ruby was getting irritable, as if she had another appointment, and started to tug on my sleeve.

'Come on. Let me play, baby.' I didn't answer but mimed a fireman shovelling coal on the footplate of a steam engine. An undesirable character looked suspiciously at us, smoking his cigar with disdain. An elderly woman, plastered with make-up and tight-lipped, cursed out loud and then suddenly roared with laughter. I was more relieved at their silence being broken than curious as to what the hell there was to laugh about; both looked as if they were losing. How seductive the slow slash of one's throat had become. Everything in this vast theatre of greed was geared to seduce the stranger to gamble his money away and inevitably lose.

'Do you want to spend some extra cash?' I had been playing for half an hour and my agitated companion was whispering once again into my ear. I had won and won and won again.

'But, baby, I think I am spending enough. Don't you?'

She sighed so deeply I could see a lungful of breath leave her mouth, like a horse breathing in winter.

It was only then that realisation of the situation came sharply into focus.

'So you're a hooker?'

'What the hell did you think I was?'

'I thought you liked my company.'

'You must be kidding, asshole. You can't be that naive! Now give me some of your winnings.'

I grabbed at my pile of yellow and blue chips and handed

her two $100 counters, with my ego bruised. She spun on her heel, authoritatively held up her finger and headed in the direction of a pot-bellied gambler playing blackjack on a neighbouring table. For a second, I admired her proficiency in finding her next client. It was a shame; I thought she liked me.

I had sat on the same chair for what seemed like hours (in this place with no clocks), happening on lucky numbers and fascinated by the recklessness of the compulsive gambler. Many whom I sat with had more than drained their bank accounts, yet were unable to move from their seats as the hours ticked by and their plight became ever more hopeless. By the time I left the table, I was ahead by the two hundred dollars I had given my hooker earlier in the evening!

I returned to my vast bed alone and missing February. I tried to reach her, but she was out, and so I spent the hours flicking through the channels in search of comfort. How quickly one's mood changes: only hours before I felt seduced by the room, now I was as deflated as if I had reached an orgasm and lost interest in life.

* * *

The tour of Caesar's Palace was short, notwithstanding its immense size. It took in the casino of course, themed restaurants, a theatre (with a season featuring Andy Williams) and the fountain that Evel Knievel failed to clear in the 1960s. My host Douglas had gone missing. I had had no call, no sighting.

I ate lunch alone in a Roman-themed restaurant, with Julius Caesar on the place mats and dishes, Mark Antony on the glasses, a few outsiders (but stars) like Cleopatra featuring on the napkin rings and Hercules on the cutlery. There was no sign of Brutus. I was enjoying my isolation though; other than my verbal exchanges with the hooker and a loving 'I miss you' conversation with February, I had said little. The constant ringing of slot-machines kept loneliness at bay. The chiming became your friend, or at least a companion.

We planned to leave on Sunday morning, so I decided that after a quick hit at the blackjack I would try to find a ticket to Frank Sinatra's Saturday-night concert. I walked by a table of haggard gamblers who, if I were not mistaken, had been there the night before. I had in my hand five thousand dollars' worth of chips. I had emptied my account and decided to take a monumental gamble of some sort. I changed my mind about the card table I was heading for, and returned to the roulette wheel. I decided to stake everything on an individual number. Number 6 was Margaret's number. Number 6 Friston Street. So be it, I decided. As the ball turned and bounced, I promised that if it found the number 6 slot, I would see it as a sign and ask February to marry me. I had been considering it ever since I left California for the desert. I was in love and needed a family. I was also mighty young. What better than to create my own kin? Now I had thrown the decision into the lap of fate. As I gazed at my life, in the shape of a bouncing ivory ball, a tap on my shoulder completely distracted me.

'Hello there, Sam.'

It was my dear Uncle Louis, taking a break in Las Vegas (where else?), and I gave him an enormous hug. I was so overjoyed to see him that my eyes stupidly watered and I admitted to myself how homesick I had been. I thought I heard a murmur of astonishment behind me, but I was too diverted by my wonderful surprise to pay any attention.

'Uncle Louis! Uncle Louis!' I squeaked, as if I were urging on a winning horse.

'My dear Sam,' he smiled and put his arm round me lovingly.

'This is the best surprise ever! I hadn't realised how much I missed you.'

'Maybe not the best surprise, Sam.'

'What do you mean?'

A single light shone on the table I had just been playing at. A fortune in chips was stacked up in my place. My number had come up! I was shaken by this stroke of supreme good fortune, delivered by the inscrutable hand of fate.

Louis nodded to the pit boss and the chips were gathered.

'He will cash them and bring the cheque to your room. Better have a cheque – less easy to spend.'

'But they don't know my name.'

'They know your name; don't worry about it.'

I wondered how much I had won, but believe it or not, I thought it might be rude to ask.

We headed off to find a coffee and I spoke of my new love and the shenanigans of the agency business. I decided to keep the pain of Margaret to myself. Uncle Louis did not need to know everything.

'You seem to fall in love quickly,' he observed.

'I have only fallen in love twice,' I replied, beginning to sound young again.

His own relationship was 'healthy', and he said that he was happy sharing his life. 'Far too young though,' was his closing sentence. He was careful not to bruise my heart with tales of how much my parents missed me; I saw him watch his words. He had been down to our house for lunch and we joked about Aunt Flo and chuckled at the news that Rupert had recently got engaged.

'What are you doing tonight?' he asked.

'I have no plans.'

'Oh yes, you do. You'll be coming to see the Chairman of

the Board himself, Frank Sinatra. We have the best seats in the house.'

*   *   *

We were sitting in the Main Room at the International Hotel. This was where Elvis had sung and reminders of his career were difficult to avoid; a considerable bronze statue of the King overshadowed the entrance to the venue. My uncle had invited three shadowy friends as his guests. They were all well suited; one of them was particularly bulky, with a square face and deep-drawn wrinkles round intensely blue eyes. He was impatiently snapping his fingers for extra champagne. 'More, more,' he scolded, and the trembling waiter just kept on pouring. Joey, sitting next to me and looking not unlike my uncle, lit a cigarette. He inhaled deeply and poured the smoke through his nose over the cackle of conversation. 'You mean they took out his eyes?' yelled the third in a stentorian voice. He looked like an ex-pro, with a spread nose and ears resembling car wing-mirrors. His double chin and elongated upper lip gave his face a sorrowful finish. My uncle adopted a rare expression and glared at him for making such an indiscreet remark. Joey gave me a wink and, after a noticeable silence, the conversation resumed.

The lights went down and the band started to play briskly through the tumultuous reception. The conductor, a tall pasty-faced man, turned and gave the audience a complicit grin – and with that an announcer invited the biggest music star in the world to come on stage and sing 'I've Got You Under My Skin'. In his golden voice, with faultless timing and sublime phrasing, Sinatra sang effortlessly as if he was in someone's front room, moving around the stage as easily as the lungful of his cigarette smoke dancing high in the ceiling.

During the show, usherettes walked around offering drinks and smokes. Joey called one over to buy a packet of Marlboros, and with his money, I saw him slip the girl his room number, scribbled down moments before. She was slight, tanned and had small features. Her healthy complexion glowed in the light from her tray. She said nothing on receiving the note; she simply tucked it into her sequinned bikini pants.

As Sinatra sang 'That's Life', he stepped off the stage and made his way to our box to shake hands with my uncle. Uncle's friends gave an approving grunt; I was impressed. The two-hour show flew by, and the old songs took me back to the days when my parents played Sinatra records at home.

After the lights went up, we were steered backstage into Ol' Blue Eyes' dressing room; people stepped back and heads nodded as our group walked by; I was riding on a wave of euphoria. Sinatra had already changed into blue blazer and grey flannel trousers. Smoking a cigarette, he poured the drinks himself, and as he spoke a faint blue plume escaped from his mouth and competed with his eyes. He was generous and had time for everyone. His jokes were a little lame but, of course, we guffawed all the same; it was the rule to laugh at the star's bad jokes; it was Frank Sinatra after all.

'And you are . . . ?'

'I am Louis's nephew Mr Sinatra sir.'

'How are you doin', kid?'

'I loved your show, Mr Sinatra. Thank you, sir.'

He did not answer directly. 'You got a good boy here, Louis.' It was like getting the nod of approval from the headmaster.

'I didn't know you knew Frank Sinatra, uncle,' I said later.

'There are a lot of things you don't know about me, Sam.'

And he was right. In truth, I knew very little, except perhaps what was important. He was a generous loving uncle. I had an urge to confess that his shadowy world had caught my imagination and ask whether he could expound on that side of his business and even involve me. But I would have been kidding myself; I wasn't prepared for that life. I had to deal with my own darkness and to have new moral challenges to wrestle with in the slow hours of the morning would have been beyond me.

I left my uncle in the casino so he could carry on with whatever he had flown in for.

'Good night, gentlemen.'

'You look after yourself, Sam.' And he squeezed my cheek and his friends offered their hands.

'Can I pay for my ticket, Uncle Louis, now that I am in the money?'

He shook his head with an affectionate chuckle.

I returned to my suite, poured myself a large drink, switched on some music and gazed at the lights of Vegas below. I phoned February and said that I loved her, and when I hung up, I thought of Margaret and her dreadful final hours. 'Look after her, Tom!' I called out into the night sky, and at that moment Frank Sinatra came on the radio singing 'I've Got A Crush On You', recorded live at The Sands. I lowered my head and allowed myself a sad smile.

It was only then that I caught sight of the envelope resting on my pillow. It had a crisp cheque inside for $145,000. A hundred and forty-five thousand dollars! I opened the mini-bar and allowed myself a small, solitary celebration with a bottle of champagne. I drank it slowly, revelling in its taste and scent and looking out over the city as the sun came up and the lights went out.

I met up with Uncle Louis at breakfast, to thank him again. And true to my promise, I went in search of an engagement ring with a slice of the winnings. My uncle, of course, had known someone who knew someone who could help me find the ring. I made Uncle Louis swear not to tell my parents and he agreed by pointing two of his fingers skywards and mumbling an Italian-sounding prayer – very Cosa Nostra.

* * *

'Would you ever be so foolish as to become my wife?'

I had no hesitation in asking the question. I was living for now and felt a calm that comes from knowing that I was doing the right thing at the right time; I already knew that life could be tragically short and there were no rules where time was concerned.

I sat opposite February in a clean white shirt. I gazed at her perfectly composed face. The energy between us seemed to light up the entire room. I sensed eyes peering over with curiosity, aware that something important was happening. We were meant to fall in love with each other. I may have been young, but I was absolutely sure I wanted to share my life with this generous, loving girl and I was not prepared to lose her; the fear was overwhelming.

My mouth began to dry and I ordered a beer to fix my mouth and cool my throat; after several swallows I gained enough courage to reconstruct what I had planned earlier in the evening. I touched her hand and pulled a crimson box from my pocket.

The ring, a sort of miniature version of the Briolette of India, slipped on to her finger. Here was February before my eyes in a frame of gold.

A radiant look came into her face, and she said, 'Yes, my darling Sam, I will be your wife.'

I rose from my chair and kissed her on her mouth; I pulled away and saw her face; how I loved her.

The stares from the neighbouring tables turned into applause and the restaurant cheered. Gregory Peck, passing the table, asked to see the ring. 'That's stunning,' he said. And I wanted to say something like, 'Thank you, you're my favourite actor and I loved *Philadelphia Story*,' but resisted.

'February, I called your parents this afternoon and asked for their permission.'

'They like you, Sam! They think you are soulful; that you have a gigantic soul!' and she laughed with pride. 'They might be a couple of ageing hippies, but I'm sure they appreciated the gesture.' She took hold of my hand. 'I'm so glad we met, Samuel. Do you know? – from that first night, I knew we would be together.'

'And so did I.' I shut my eyes and opened them again, and yes, the vision remained undisturbed. Above my astonishment that she loved me was the overwhelming feeling of thankfulness. I felt like a shipwrecked sailor who has finally sighted dry land.

'Let's call David.'

'If we have too,' sighed February, but I was not listening to her tone. I was still young, and what better way to share good news than to call your best friend?

Within the hour, the obtrusive noise of his Harley Davidson rattled the Chinese restaurant. He did not wait to be shown to the table, instead a hapless Chinese waiter was pushed to the wall. David approached the table, unzipping his leather jacket, his smile a pained liverish grimace.

'Please excuse my friend,' I said apologetically to the manager. 'He's happy for us. I promise he means no harm.'

And he was dangerously high and overjoyed. 'They are getting married!' he shouted to the other tables, an unlit cigarette hanging from his mouth.

'They know,' I told him, embarrassed and becoming

increasingly concerned by his erratic behaviour and marked decline.

He leaned over and gave February an over-generous kiss on her lips.

'Hey, cool it,' I said in a warning voice.

He didn't answer, instead he headed off to the bathroom; a few minutes later he returned.

'Are you OK?' February asked.

'Yes I'm fine, gyppy tummy . . . must have been something I ate,' and pulled a face as if he had sucked a lemon.

She passed him a napkin and he wiped his dripping face.

'I would like to propose a toast.' He banged on the table, and shaking the remnants of white wine from his glass with the nonchalance of an old French-horn player shaking spittle out of his instrument, he filled it with champagne. 'To my friends, my dear friends. I wish you all the happiness in the world,' and he started to weep.

A misguided waiter chose this moment to ask whether we would like more to eat. The question filled David with fury and in one swipe he took revenge for his inadequacies on the unlucky waiter. He stood up and pinned the man against the wall with a hand round his thin neck. I pulled David away and escorted him from the restaurant and into the street. He sank to the ground and started muttering like an old hobo.

What a night to get engaged!

I returned to the restaurant and paid the check. I apologised, but they wanted nothing more to do with us. 'Go and don't ever come back,' the manager said curtly.

February had bundled David into the back of the car and we drove to his rented house on Mulholland opposite Woodrow Wilson. I opened the car door.

'I am sorry,' he said lamely. His voice had long lost its charm; now it was as discordant as a piano being tuned.

'Sorry are you? You're a fucking disgrace and a fucking

junkie. You helped spoil one of the most important nights of my life . . . thank you very much.' February tried to reach for my hand, but I resisted. 'Now get out!'

And without a word, Lord Amersham staggered to his front door.

'Darling, go after him. Make sure he gets in. He needs you now more than ever.' February pushed me out of the car.

I took the keys off David, switched on the lights and asked if he had more drugs. He emptied his pockets and put three packets of cocaine and heroin on the table; the insanity of it all! He sank back in a chair as I gathered up his stash and walked towards the door. I turned and saw his body dying from abuse. 'You were taking more drugs in the loo at the restaurant, weren't you? That's how my brother finished up – in a stinking public loo. You look like him now. Do you remember, we buried him in the Oxfordshire soil? I don't want to bury you as well . . . ' And desperate for air, I returned to the car where February was waiting.

* * *

February had left Sam asleep in bed, early the morning following David's fight, to check on whether he had survived the night. She had dreamt that David was dying and his final breath had woken her with a start. February did not want Sam to suffer any more desolation, he had suffered enough. She hadn't grown to like David; his relentless heroin and cocaine habit led to behaviour that was hard for anyone around him to endure. 'What the hell does Sam see in that asshole?' she asked herself.

'Oh, come on, come on!' she urged the traffic lights out loud. The drive across to Mulholland was beset with restrictions. She had not seen a single car, so the paradoxical slowness of the journey irritated her. This was unlike her;

February had always remained calm whenever faced with a challenge. She had noticed the change in herself and deduced that being in love was to blame. The radio was playing Bob Dylan's 'Simple Twist Of Fate' and she turned up the volume to take her mind off the image of David lying dead on the floor. How was she going to break the news to Sam? 'Come on, come on!' she stormed.

On her arrival she dashed from her car, leaving the door open. She was not conscious that she had also left the engine running and the radio on. The temperature had risen during the course of her journey, but as she rang the bell, everything around seemed cool and peaceful. She pressed the button again and heard the chimes, but again no answer. Damn, what was happening? Maybe he was asleep and she was just being foolish. February stepped back from the low wooden house that in its facade had no window. The view was from the back and it was impossible to climb over the fence to reach the backyard. Then, as she was about to give up and perhaps call the police, she tried the handle on the door and it turned easily. David was slumped on the chair where Sam had left him. His mouth was shining with saliva and his pale face was without expression. He looked as dead as anything February could ever imagine. She walked slowly towards him, and as she lowered her ear to his face to hear whether he was breathing, he suddenly moved. In a pool of light, David lifted his head and stared into February's enquiring eyes. He was filled with self-loathing and self-reproach. He felt swollen and empty at the same time. The loneliness of a night spent in the most abject state of mind was reflected in his ravaged body. He wanted to die that night and was surprised to find himself alive. He winced as he tried to move, and an empty whiskey bottle fell from his hand. February had gone to fetch a glass of cold water. She poured a little gently into his mouth and he swallowed it down like John Mills's character in Ice Cold in Alex. *Gradually the water began to revive him, and the golden morning sun caught his face and poured treacle over it.*

'I need help,' he wept. 'Please help me.'

Lapsing once more into a semi-conscious state, David slid from the chair on to the floor. His body smelled of burning chemicals and decaying food. It was a horrifying mixture, and as February rushed to dial 911, she had to turn back to check if he was still alive. The sun moved behind a tree and his skin returned to a deadly whiteness. How God-awful a human being can look, February thought, pitying the wretched plight of Sam's best friend.

* * *

When I woke to find myself alone, I presumed that February had gone to the market to buy something for breakfast. The sheets smelled of her body and I wrapped them tightly around me before I finally stretched and got up. I showered in cold water and shook my head under the torrent to jolt me out of my bleariness. I pulled on my jeans and a dark-grey Hanes T-shirt. I switched on the kettle as I needed to swallow some coffee; it was a typical Sunday morning, filled with the stillness that characterises the last day of the week. How awful David had been the previous night. How was it that I had not recognised the extent of his addiction? I looked at the near-empty packet of cigarettes, and was tempted to have an early-morning smoke, but heaved at the idea and instead screwed the packet up and threw it in the bin under the sink. As the water boiled, I cursed David – as I had cursed my brother – for his weakness. The sun poured through the kitchen window and I basked in its warmth. The house was empty; Douglas had once again flown out of town. I would have to find another place to live now, as February and I would be moving in together. We had not even discussed it, but now we were engaged, it would seem sensible. I'd better call my parents and break the news. I was sure they would be happy and it would even encourage them to fly over to meet my future bride. Yes, things would be fine and I planned to call as soon as I finished the rich coffee that was about to kick-start my system.

As I walked towards the swimming pool, with mug in one hand and a biscuit in the other, I realised that for once I hadn't dreamed of Margaret; it was the first time since I heard the news. I had tried to shut the memory of the tragedy away in a box, but it haunted me.

'I hope you approve of February? I love her and want to spend my life with her.'

I was talking to Margaret aloud, believing she was hearing every word. I behaved in the same way when my brother died. I thought of having a cigarette and returned to the inside of the house to pick one out of the bin. The phone was ringing as I stepped back into the kitchen.

'Hello, baby . . . where are you . . . ?'

* * *

Cedars-Sinai Medical Center is a great mausoleum of a building on Beverly Boulevard. February's voice had been calm. 'He's fine, he's alive,' she had said. 'He's being treated right now. Ask for the Emergency Room, I will be waiting for you.'

February's welcoming embrace reassured me. 'It looks as if he's going to be OK.'

The hospital was already busy although it was a Sunday morning. All days are the same in places like this. The recollection of the night I had spent with my brother after he had overdosed sent a tremor of pain through my body. February had gone to get a coffee and as she put the warm cup in my hand I thought of the Good Samaritan who had found me a blanket when I crashed outside my brother's room in a cold corridor. My brother had lived that night and I had left my teenage years behind. Light-headed from the latest blow, I looked at February and asked how she had discovered the news of David's collapse. I held her as she told the story of the morning. After she had finished, I kissed her and felt the pressure of her lips. The sensation calmed me down, but when she moved away I let out an audible wail, knowing that she had saved David's life.

A doctor with crinkly grey hair and hound-dog eyes approached us: 'Your friend is out of danger now. He'll be kept in Emergency overnight for observation. In time he should be allowed to return home. I would suggest, however, that when that time comes he's not left alone. He should have company; he's about to begin a difficult period of rehabilitation.'

The world I cherished as fine and safe was slipping away from me again as February and I walked into David's hospital room that day. We saw a ghost lying on his back, with arms by his side and wearing white hospital pyjamas. It was my brother's death that enabled my father finally to open his heart; David had hated the fact his father died without saying he loved him. His retreat into drugs and his slow burn to destruction was a 'fuck you' to the world.

He took my hand limply, his palm wet with sweat, his eyes sunk deep into his skull. 'This was the last thing you needed!' The words fell from his lips between heavy, irregular breaths and sudden spasms of pain. 'Thank you, thank you.' He was looking at February, who stood by my side. 'You saved my life and I need you to know that I am humbled by your . . . ' He turned away, buried his face in the pillow and wept.

'We are here for you, David,' said February. He looked up and released the deepest of deep breaths.

He was not conscious of the outside world for days that followed. He did not move from the hospital. His wealth allowed him to go through his cold turkey in care. We would visit together after work, and over the following week he miraculously gained more and more strength. February would bring over tapes and books for him to enjoy. They would be piled on the side table next to a frame in which his father's drawing had been put. She really was the friend he needed during those days. I could see that she was taking my role. I was unable to summon the strength to play my proper part. This was too close to my recent history and I was not ready to face another death, and one so similar to my brother's.

February was natural and filled the room with lightness and stories. She alone was bringing David back to life. As she spoke, my mind drifted to the morning when she came out of the shower, hair falling over her face, dripping globules of water into my mouth, eating my lips like a sea anemone; I felt blessed in the gloom of those days.

* * *

My luck at work was at least still holding. I had closed my first seriously *big* deal and had a dozen clients; none was as successful as my first signing, and it was he who brought in my initial haul. I had promised that I would find a good script that would stretch his unique acting skills, but promises are hard to keep in this town. In the end, we accepted a role in a violent, salacious, degenerate, gun-slinging movie set in Texas, which had all the hallmarks of appealing to the lowest common denominator; in short it was going to be a massive 'hit'. He was to be paid four million dollars for six weeks' work. Yes, four million, which meant my ten per cent commission (or rather the agency's) was going to be four hundred thousands dollars: enough to pay for my existence for at least two years. Surely my job was safe now? Gregory was not convinced.

'They will expect more of the same. You can't rest for a moment, or else you'll be out.' He jabbed his finger into my chest.

'But isn't there a time when you can pat yourself on the back and put your feet up?'

'No! There are the dead bodies all over town of those who subscribed to that sentiment. When the town reads obituaries in *Variety*, they don't say, "How sad Bert Stein died last week," they say, "I thought he died years ago." So be careful!'

I heard what he said. The impossible was possible now and ambition was the driving force. And yet at the back of my consciousness there was a perception of ringing, a form of tinnitus that was hard to pin down.

'Go sign a star!' Gregory interrupted my abstraction. 'In this office, it's the best therapy.'

* * *

'He would really like you to go with him for his first meeting,' February persisted.

'Look. The last night I ever spent with my brother, I sat by his side at a Narcotics Anonymous meeting.' Angrily, I turned my back on her and walked to the swimming pool with a half-smoked cigarette for company. Why was she interfering? She had done enough, hadn't she? She had saved his life, for God's sake! I cursed her for trying to involve me in David's crisis.

'Sam, I know that you're finding this difficult . . . but he has no one. I'm sure you care for him and I believe he wants to get well.'

'And I thought exactly the same about my brother, but the bastard lied to me . . . he fucking lied!'

I ducked my head and hid my face against her hair. My shivering slowed and ended with a single, violent shudder. The pure desolation turned into a release, and, in those moments, I had taken a further step on my long road to being healed.

* * *

It was not unlike the meeting that I had attended in New York City with my brother that Easter evening. Ten rows of tubular chairs seated the many who needed to share their pain or listen to tales that reflected their own tortuous road. The room was in the valley by the side of a golf course in a bright neon-lit function room. Tobacco smoke rose in clouds from every row.

By chance, a twenty-two-year-old English girl called Sophie had been asked by the secretary to chair the meeting. If she hadn't been at the front talking about her years of addiction, she had the type of face that would never have been noticed. She was very nice, friendly in fact, but had never mastered the art of making friends. The simplicity of her demeanour made her tale even more poignant.

Sophie had been taking drugs since she was sixteen. She had started to use them because she wanted to be accepted as part of the 'cool' gang at school. That was how it began, and from smoking hashish at school, she moved in 'record time' (her words) to fixing heroin, using her diabetic brother's syringes to inject into her veins. 'The rush was invigorating, my heart was joyful and the near-fainting sensation that lifted me to an exquisite high is something I miss today.' She spoke as if a black veil had been lowered over her and she was in mourning for that remembered ecstasy. She sipped water from a glass and went on to confess the depths to which she had sunk to obtain a fix.

She ended on a note of hope and excitement, resolutely looking forward to her 'clean life'.

The secretary, the 'host' in charge of the proceedings, was an earnest character with oily hair and gold-rimmed spectacles. He was very grateful to Sophie for her honesty. 'Much of what she described has struck a chord with the rest of us,' he said, and thanked her for being frank about missing the high. 'It's a feeling,' he said, 'that many of us share.'

I empathised with the man who sat to my right and admitted that he felt unlovable and therefore in return was unloving. 'I don't believe that this is the true me,' he wailed, and a woman in the front row stood and made her way to his side to give him a tender hug.

The secretary announced it was 'newcomers' time', and that meant an opportunity for those who were attending a meeting for the first time to speak. There followed a muffled silence only disturbed by the scraping of a chair. I looked ahead, trying not to influence David's decision as to whether to open his mouth or not. Just when I thought he had chosen to keep quiet, David raised his hand tentatively, much as he did when we sat together at the back of the class at school. 'My name is David, he said, 'and I am an addict.'

'Hello, David, welcome,' chorused the meeting.

'I have been clean for sixteen days, and this is my first meeting, and it's good to be here.'

'Thanks, David.'

'I don't want to share for long tonight. I used to feel sorry for those who didn't drink or smoke grass because the way they felt when they got up in the morning was as good as it was going to get all day.' The room muttered and shifted uneasily, as if all had experienced similar sentiments in the past. 'I don't want to share my dysfunctional family or my slow descent into the gutter. But I do want to share my thanks to my best friend and his girlfriend for saving me. My best friend's brother died in a public loo, I mean urinal, in the heart of New York City four years ago and his death devastated his family; my dear friend has not been the same since. He mourns his brother every day. I even went to the funeral and saw him buried and the sorrow of that day still haunts me. But even with that cautionary tale before me, I fell into the same trap, and without any consideration for the feelings of my friend, I would readily take drugs in front him and even encouraged him to take them with me. I am ashamed of myself for that, deeply repentant, and I want to say with all my heart that I am sorry and I love you and hope you learn to forgive me.'

I truly believe that it was not until that moment that I actually realised how much I cared for David. He was a friend from school, a companion who rebelled against the system. We called each other 'best friends' and I enjoyed his company, but I was not very sure I liked him. His vulnerability and honesty, from that night forward, nourished my heart; I clenched my teeth, fighting back the tears.

His words clearly hit the spot with those who had disregarded the feelings of others while taking drugs, and I could sense the minds of many clicking to the images of those close they had hurt. I rose and held my friend in front of these strangers; I inwardly thanked February for her guidance and wisdom. If it weren't for her, my stubbornness would have prevailed and I would probably have been at home watching a quiz show.

To close the meeting, everyone joined in the Serenity Prayer: 'God grant me the serenity to accept the things I cannot change; the courage to change the things I can; and the wisdom to know the difference.'

The pack gathered outside to continue their smoking and to engage with friends about general matters. David and I made a quick exit to the car park. We gave each other another hug and parted with, 'See you tomorrow.' All that needed to be said had been said at the meeting. I was grateful for his words and proud of the strength he had shown.

February was waiting for me at home. She had made dinner and laid it out on a table by the swimming pool. The moon slid out from behind a tree and shed its silver light on the water; the air was still warm. It was a full moon, and as I watched, it seemed to come suddenly on a level with my eyes. We were face to face, and the moon's was so plain, the sort of face you dread sitting opposite on a long train journey – a face that smiles like no one ever smiled before. The moon is always of interest, ever changing, unlike the sun which we take for granted until it sets or is eclipsed. The moon was far more in tune with my life, the perfect pallid face wanly smiling at my devastating sadness. As February and I sat together, and I recounted what had been said at the meeting, I thought how blessed I was to be with my future wife under the moon's watchful eye

* * *

Mother was looking through the open windows into the rain-cleaned air. She enjoyed the trees at that time of year, although many were already bare. The empty fields, with dull wet light behind the hedges, gave her an inexplicable sense of security.

The house was warm, perhaps too warm, given my father always complained about the price of heating and the waste of money. She did not care about those things any more. Her days, once my father had gone to London, were dead days. It had surprised her that she was so unable to shake off Tom's death. She, of course, never expected to bury it completely, but the weight still pressed constantly on her heart. Everything seemed to remind her of him, whether it was the mint growing by the kitchen that as a little boy he used to love to pick and crush for Sunday's lamb, or the lawnmower that he once broke by crashing it into a tree. She had at first derived solace from these memories, but as time went by she came to feel more comfortable in the world of the dead than that of the living. Her heart had been broken. She kept this fact to herself. She didn't want my father to know. He was regaining some of his strength and she did not want to burden him. It was Aunt Flo who knew the depth of her sister's grief and spent more and more time in her company, steering her away from her love of death.

* * *

I rang the house that day. It was my mother who answered. We spoke of my work and I asked about the house, Violet and Harold, and of course about my father.

'He's not home yet. I know he'll be disappointed to have missed your call.'

I decided to break the news anyway. She could tell him over dinner and they could toast our good health together.

'Mum, I have asked February to be my wife. I love her, mum, and I want to spend the rest of my life with her.'

The announcement sounded a little clichéd, but I didn't care. She seemed genuinely happy, and her voice came alive with questions about where and when.

'We have the photograph you sent us in the drawing room. We'll need to get a far better frame now,' she joked. 'Your father will be so happy. Oh, this is such wonderful news, Sam!'

'You don't think we're too young?' I asked, in search of a drawback to shoot down.

'Sod age! If you're happy and want to be with her, get on with it. We all know that time can do cruel things.'

I went on to talk about February's parents and their

house in Topanga. And my mother heard the contentment in my voice and I think it gave her joy on that day.

'We'll be over to see you in the States next month and we'll all be together as a family again.'

As she went to replace the receiver I heard her shout to Violet: 'Sam's getting married!'

I had been nervous about making the call, had found excuses. But now it was done I felt calm, as if I had reached a staging post on a long journey and dodged a number of accidents along the way.

* * *

David had booked a table at Lanskeys, a new dining club on Third Street and La Cienega. He had made a small investment some time ago and very quickly it had become the place to be, another place to be seen. He was eager to show off his successful investment and assured us that being surrounded by booze and probably drugs would not trouble him. He reaffirmed his desire to stay clean and I applauded his resolution.

The room was long, luxurious and dimly lit; the style was 1920s French bordello and tables were adorned with white linen and art-deco lamps. The carpet was pseudo leopard-skin and on the walls a collection of small figurative oils hung against bronze lacquered panels. At the far end, directly in view of the front door, was a prodigious photograph of the Hollywood sign. It reminded me of the day February had led me there blindfold. A large bronze sculpture of a woman dancing, with a veil covering her face, dominated the space.

David ordered champagne. He saw me frown and whispered that it was fine. Our booth, upholstered in buttoned leather, was the first on the right. As each star walked by, David rose and shook hands presidentially.

Warren Beatty, Jack Nicholson, John and Bo Derek, Dudley Moore, and when the radiant rising star Elizabeth McGovern said hello, a ripple of excitement ran round the room. The place was abuzz with gossip, laughter and cash. February, dressed in a supple electric-blue gown, grabbed my hand under the table and we started to struggle with our fingers until she squeaked with mock pain. David sat with his date, a sultry Spanish actress who looked and acted bored. She sat with her hands on her lap and her hair falling forward, languidly blowing smoke from her full cherry-red lips.

I stared at February and she stared steadily back. She was disarmingly unaware of people looking at her. 'I am happy, are you?' I asked.

'Yes, I am. I'm very happy,' she answered, fiddling with her engagement ring.

My eyes danced around my friend's club, which seemed packed with celebrities. The deep sense of peace that been with me all day sharpened my perception of the richness of life. David drank his seltzer and seemed comfortable being the sober host, good humouredly shaking hands with everyone. Over the last week his frame had filled out and the muscles that had been evident in previous years were making a comeback.

February was talking to a stranger and kept her hand clamped to my leg, as if she was never going to let go, and I felt secure that she was close. Her citrus scent floated and curled around my head. I would from time to time lean forward and move her blonde hair clear and kiss her soft neck. The distant sound of jazz could be heard above the general hubbub.

Before the first course of our dinner was served, I decided to go to the bathroom. There was just the one restroom, which meant there was a queue. After each exit, a stout Polish woman with stumpy legs would retrieve the used towels and replace them with fresh ones. She was generously tipped and her expression was friendly. Her behaviour provided a distraction for those awaiting their turn. As I edged forward, I felt a hand on my shoulder. David's Spanish date had been standing behind me all the time. We said an embarrassed hello and as our eyes met I noticed how blue hers were.

'You have a very beautiful girlfriend,' she said rasping out the words as if she had smoked all day.

'I don't deserve her!'

She gave a quick half-laugh and shook her head. There was a pause and then she took something from her bag. It was a little piece of paper, light blue, with the texture of blotting paper. 'Try this,' she said concealing the gift from the others in the queue.' It will give you the most fantastic night.' She slipped the small paper into my palm and I said nothing. As the Polish attendant signalled, I offered my turn to my Spanish friend, but she insisted I went first.

For so much action, the bathroom was remarkably clean. The white marble basin was spotless, as was the loo. As I stood and took a most satisfying piss, I felt the drug calling. I looked at the fragment of paper and dropped it on to my tongue. By the time I had finished the paper had dissolved in my mouth.

'Oh, what the fuck have I done?' was my immediate reaction. I mopped my face and dried it off. I looked into the mirror and was reassured; a tan can do wonders for your appearance. With sudden efficiency, I wiped over the sink and threw the towel into the basket. I gave the attendant twenty bucks, and as I returned to my table, David's friend gave me an exaggerated wink.

I heard music, classical music, being played. It was a perfect performance – the soloist performed faultlessly and the brilliantined conductor hardly had to direct his orchestra because it was so well trained; true professionals never fall flat. I heard the music like I never heard music before, but then, I asked myself, was the perfect performance really the best . . . ? At this point, my train of thought was interrupted.

'Would you like some more champagne, sir?' I didn't trust myself to reply. The waiter poured and I watched the bronze crystal drink fall into my tall glass. David pulled me to one side. 'Hey, Mamen just told me you have dropped a tab. It shouldn't take effect for at least half an hour and it's very harmless stuff,' he said unconvincingly. 'Anyway, I have a surprise and thought this would be a good time to tell you . . . while you're still on Planet Earth.' He beckoned February over. 'Listen, guys, you know how deeply grateful I am for everything. Well, I couldn't decide what I could do to repay you. So I thought and thought and then it came to me in a flash.'

'Oh, shit,' I thought.

'Tonight, down on the beach, you are going to get married and I am going to be your best man!'

I was stunned and February froze. The psychedelia kicked in at the news. The room started to spin like a revolving Smartie tube.

'You've always said how short life is. I've booked the priest and the registrar.'

'What about our parents, friends . . . ?' asked February.

'You can have a huge celebration when Sam's parents visit in a few weeks. This is an opportunity to get married now, today, tonight.'

The drug had shifted gear. February seemed a little tipsy, swaying slightly. 'Are you stoned?' she asked.

'Just a little!' I lied.

Then she grabbed my shirt and pulled me towards her, and letting out a gasp of laughter she said, 'Shall we do it? Shall we get married tonight?'

My legs trembled and I felt a slight knocking at the back of my head. Like someone hammering a picture hook into a soft wall. I needed to give an answer or I was going to jump on to the table and perform a most embarrassing act.

'Yes, my darling, let's do it tonight. Our parents will be thrilled!'

And the three of us did a group hug and I plunged headlong into another dimension.

* * *

February's head was resting on my shoulder; the noise had grown more intense. The psychedelic high had me confused between what was real and what was imagined. David pulled his chair close to mine and became tactile and loving. He had suddenly regained his beauty. He was always the best looking of us. We began to reminisce about our schooldays, laughing and sniggering at stories that no one but us could understand; we remembered the friends and adversaries long vanished and yet still fresh in our minds; the bullies who had blighted our days with a sadistic pleasure. In my mind's eye their faces were the faces of demons. I knew that they were related to Satan. Why did I allow them to create all that fear and wreck those years? Was I that impotent? How did they gain such ascendancy over me? Where were those bastards? I was angry and eager not to let the past drop away.

'Come on,' David said, seeing my mood and speaking like someone preaching the Twelve Steps. 'Our life is fantastic. We're living in this breathtaking city, with the coast minutes away, the mountains and skiing just as close and the wonders of nature all around. We are privileged, not because of our education or our families' wealth but because we are here, living in the present and realising it. Forget those years. It's not worth it.'

The waiter offered food, but I had lost my appetite. February remained at my side, badgered constantly by strangers. I thought of Lana and tried to remember how I had felt at the time of our relationship. I loved her; she was my first love and I knew that I would love her for the rest of my life. I held February's hand, assured that I had fallen in love again. How could someone like me attract such fantastic women? With a mixture of disbelief, insecurity and satisfaction, I whispered tenderly in February's ear, 'I love you my angel, I so love you. Can you feel it?'

She turned and kissed my lips and said, 'Yes, my darling one.'

As she spoke, my mind snapped to the loss of my brother and to my parents asleep six thousand miles away. With my bloodstream so full of sugar, I was still woozy, but I heard myself say, 'By the morning, you will be my wife, February. February Alexander . . . it even sounds right.' We held each other excitedly – a bit afraid, like children about to catch a helter-skelter ride. The craziness of it all appealed to us.

The music shifted from jazz to disco. The tables were pushed to the walls and a tangled mass of bodies, writhing like snakes, danced to Blondie's 'Heart of Glass'. The room started to spin and I retreated to a corner, arms clinging to my body to stop it losing its shape. David was schmoozing his Spanish contessa; men were dancing badly, the women vamping shamelessly. I felt the walls closing in. February was dancing with a stranger; how extraordinarily she moved! I loved her, I loved her. She beckoned me over, but I preferred my voyeuristic role. The flabby man she was dancing with was licking his lips, his tongue lolling from his panting mouth, and my soon-to-be wife was smiling back, tempting his hungry soul. I felt an irrational pang of jealousy across the smoke-filled dance floor. This vexatious emotion rarely revealed itself, and its stab was like the sting of blood running down a burned leg. It was unbearable. I needed to remove myself from the room, the stench of carnality was suffocating. I left to fetch some air from the street, still warm under a star-studded sky, and the tranquillity of the night restored my troubled soul. After a while I felt a strong arm over my shoulder. It was David, curious as to exactly where I was heading. The doormen of the club stood to attention in formal long coats like two Grenadier Guards on sentry duty outside St James's Palace. David caught my dismay at their incongruity.

'Brilliant idea,' I said sarcastically.

'We have got to get going soon. The priest is waiting.'

'The priest? Fuck me! Where is he waiting?'

'At a producer friend's house in Malibu.'

Where was February? I was beginning to feel abandoned. My insecurities heightened by my altered state, I was prey to a whole series of misconceptions. I went back into the club and pulled her off the dance floor. The sweaty man was panting from exhaustion and excitement.

'Sorry to break up your dance,' I said; 'we are off to get married!' and we ran out of the club like the couple in *The Graduate* escaping the church.

* * *

The house overlooked the ocean; oh, the insanity of it all! We met our priest, with guitar strapped to his chest, as soon we stepped from the car. He had been waiting for the happy couple to arrive. He was a young man, who told me God was on our side and wanted us to have the most peaceful of lives. There was a smidgen of Irish in his accent. At weekends, apparently, he played at the local hotel where he would regularly be cheered by the tourists. He had dreamed of the Hollywood Bowl but, in the end, God had won the day.

I had not a clue of the time but it must have been early in the morning as there was that stillness in the air that only exists when the majority sleep and silent forces are at work. I again needed air so I immediately walked out on to the deck. The stars had disappeared and I sensed the seething of the sea close to where I was standing. It was as if a veil of smoke from cooking fires was drifting before my eyes; there was no clarity. The temperature had dropped and I began to shiver, gazing into the obscurity and drawing deeply on a cigarette. I thought this would be my last experience of personal solitude; soon I would be married and loneliness would be a thing of the past. How little I understood.

David broke into my reverie to show me the wedding rings, which had been bought the previous afternoon from a reputable jeweller on Rodeo Drive. He tucked them into his pocket. 'They are very safe there,' he said. The sight of the two bands triggered a minor panic attack and I excused myself and hurried to the loo, where I retched until I vomited into the sink. I found a spare toothbrush and brushed vigorously, removing every trace of my purge. I looked at my reflection, shaking my head, trying to control my limbs and mind. Just as I was leaving the bathroom, I noticed an Oscar placed discreetly by the basin. How absurd was that? I held it aloft – 'Wow, that's heavy!' I thought – and smiled at my reflection.

Many of the guests looked very happy, chatting among themselves, waiting for the main event. The Oscar winner buzzed about being the perfect host. He looked remarkably youthful, and when David whispered that he was in fact sixty, I simply could not believe it.

'Are you really sixty years old?' I had to ask.

'I sure am. Want to know my secret?'

'Absolutely!' I replied.

'I go to a clinic in Geneva and they inject me with monkey glands. Been doing it for five years. Terrific, eh?' and he indicated his crotch as a sign that was working too.

'Yes, amazing. I have an uncle who might well be interested. You wouldn't let me have a number would you?'

* * *

The priest clapped his hands. He beckoned me forward and David, in best-man role, stood by my side. Harry Nilsson, a surprise guest, began to play 'Clair de Lune', and my heart started to beat like a drum. I stood paralysed. I had not noticed at first that February had walked to my other side. How adorable she looked with flowers threaded into her blonde hair. She knew the trick of living for the present and I envied her. I was distracted by the swelling sound of the waves and caught my reflection in the glass door that led on to the deck. The drug was doing its stuff.

Our fingers interwoven, we listened as the priest recited his lines with a crisp clarity, like the performer he obviously was. February was asked whether she took 'this man' to be her husband, and she did not hesitate: 'Yes, I do.' I tightened my grip on her hand as I was asked my question in turn. I felt a surge of emotion as I made the vow. Parting from February would be more terrifying than death. 'Yes, I do,' I said, and David gave us our rings and we slipped them on to each other's fingers.

We kissed, at first lightly and then with passion. The room started to applaud and Harry Nilsson played his hit 'Without You'. Corny some might say, but for us, it was bloody perfect.

'How romantic,' approved the priest. He was talking to a small academic-looking, clean-shaven man, with a slight tremble. It was the local registrar, who was only too pleased to be part of the festivities; he said, 'I thought at first it was a celebrity, but it doesn't matter. It was a lovely service.' How busy David had been.

'Sign here, please,' and the two of us scribbled our signatures with a flurry of loops.

'I enjoyed that,' February said as she replaced the top on the pen.

We were keen to get to bed. Harry Nilsson had finished playing his hit so was playing someone else's. Our host, the producer, was glued to the piano and David had gone missing, as had the Spanish beauty. We could thank him in the morning.

David had shown us the bridal chamber earlier. The curtains fluttered in the first breaths of morning air. The walls were the milk white of a hospital ward; yellow flowers were stuck into a vase which stood on the side table, along with a well-thumbed copy of *The Great Gatsby* and a burning candle. The bed was larger than the average person's apartment and above it hung a family portrait of our friend the producer, his pretty wife and two cheerful boys; it was in deplorable taste. Someone – probably David – had scattered yellow and red rose petals over the sheets, and the room was filled with the scent of apple and cinnamon. At last, I held my darling February in my arms for the first time as her husband, biting into her skin which tasted like the figs I had smelled throughout the night. I ran my fingers through her hair and she moved her hips forward to meet me. My love for her was pure, without blemish. As we consummated our marriage I whispered in her ear, 'From now on, you are the reason I exist.' And she held me tight against her and I took deep solace from the sense of being reborn.

*   *   *

8 November 1981

My first thought the following morning was, 'Where am I?' I had curled up in a ball as if it were freezing outside, which it was not. I touched my face, checking that it was still connected to the rest of my body; it was, so I breathed a sigh of relief. My head was pounding, I felt as if I had a knife stuck in my side and my coated tongue was stuck to the roof of my mouth. The red digits on the bedside clock read 09.24. I couldn't believe it was so early; I remembered it had been a very late night, the sort that usually cancelled out the morning. I rubbed my eyes and caught a glimpse of a bottle of water, two-thirds empty. I staggered over and poured a glass.

A blonde lying in the strange bed with rumpled sheets had her head down, her long thick mane covering her face. Ah, it's February, I thought, and tried to shake my head free of its haze. The inside of my middle finger was sore and I turned the gold band to ease the irritation. 'Shit, what's that doing on my finger?'

I needed some air, so, with my love dead to the world, I pulled on my jeans and made my way on to the deck to gaze out at the sea. The debris from the night before had been cleared and a cup of tea was miraculously handed to me by the kindly housekeeper. The conversation between two middle-aged Mexican ladies abruptly stopped and the two gave me a smile and a knowing nod. I stretched my body, eager to get down on to the sand. There was no subtlety in the light, just the white glare of the early Californian sun. The sea was kind and had no waves. There was no sound; a perfect silence reigned. I was alone with the day and felt groggy. The sip of tea helped to clear my head, and feeling momentarily better, I left the deck and sat on the beach. The waves started to lap and the stillness of the morning lifted and the day started in earnest.

I felt surrounded by the beauty of nature and soothed by the mood it generated. I looked at the Pacific and held my left hand towards the horizon, trying to cover the beam of light; it was then and only then, when I saw the gold around my finger, that the previous evening came into stark focus. I remembered what I – or should I say what we – had done. I saw it as an act of self-destruction. Aghast at the reality of the situation, I sat rooted to the spot.

'Would you like something else, sir?' the housekeeper asked.

'No, thank you, I'm fine,' I lied and descended the stairs to the room in which I had spent my wedding night. February had not moved; indeed if I had not heard her breathing, I would have needed to check to make sure she was still alive. Maybe she was as high as me, last night? I finished dressing, and with a final glance at the bed, bolted up the stairs. I had only one thing on my mind and that was escape. I dissociated myself from anything I had said or done the previous evening. I looked out of the front door and saw my means of deliverance. A black saloon car's engine was running and the driver waiting.

He rose from his seat and introduced himself. 'Good morning, your lordship,' he said as he opened the back-seat door. It was clear that he thought I was David and I was not going to argue.

'Good-morning. Take me to . . . ah . . . take me to the Beverly Hills Hotel. Where exactly are we?'

'You are in Malibu, Lord Amersham.'

'Yes, of course we are.'

Ignoring a surge of guilt at my surreptitious departure, I climbed in. The Pacific Coast Highway flashed by as the car travelled faster than was legally allowed. The driver mentioned that the police were hiding everywhere to catch the speedsters, but it didn't seem to bother him. His foot was pressed on the gas and we were on Sunset Boulevard within half an hour and soon travelling up the hill to reach the hotel. Life had come to get me, and I needed it to give me space to try and work out why last night had happened.

* * *

'Welcome back, Mr Alexander. What a pleasure to see you again. We were not expecting you . . . ' I recognised the bright-faced man as one of the committee that had welcomed the Knight earlier in the year.

'No. Actually, I'm living out here now . . . and I wanted to pay a visit, as a means of celebration, to the hotel that first welcomed me.'

'And what are you celebrating, sir?' he asked.

'I got married last night!'

There was a pause and a cough. 'Congratulations, sir. And your wife?'

'Oh yes, my wife, she . . . she is on her way.'

'Very good. We have a suite available. Suite 302. I hope that will do?'

I nodded and provided a signature and identification. He rang the desk bell to summon a porter.

'Welcome to the Beverly Hills Hotel. Your luggage?'

'Ah, of course . . . my luggage. It will join me later.'

'Like your wife . . . sir?'

'Yes, like my wife.'

* * *

It was the same room I had stayed in before. I hung the 'Do Not Disturb' sign on the door and immediately opened the window. The breeze was so warm, so comforting. I leaned out and let the currents of air caress my face. The hiss of fountains and the gentle sound of rippling water were easy on my aching head. It was here that February and I had first met and spent time together. It was like returning to your favourite coffee bar and sitting at 'your' table, reading the morning paper and feeling secure. I needed that sensation.

I rang room service and asked for an orange juice and a pair of swimming trunks. The juice was thick and filling, the trunks a perfect size. I wanted just to stretch out in the sun. The poolside was still relatively quiet, and Fernando, the amateur Spanish soccer player who had become my friend on the last visit, found me a deckchair next to the pool. I apologised for having no cash for a tip.

'No problem, Señor Sam, you will see all the entertainment here. As individual seats go, probably the best in the house. The cabanas are right in front and the showers just over there.'

We had bonded over our shared passion for football. His only regret about moving out to California was that he was unable to watch his beloved Real Madrid play. 'I miss it so bad that I'm thinking of returning.' He was not kidding.

Elizabeth Taylor walked into view with her politician husband. Fernando ran over to make sure her cabana was perfect. I lay down and watched the scurrying and panic over her entrance. I always liked Elizabeth Taylor from afar; she had this 'fuck you' attitude. She sat on her chair as if it were a throne and looked out to see if she knew anyone who should be summoned to her court. This could entertain me for hours, I thought.

The pool was empty of other swimmers and looked delicious; I dived in and swam two lengths without taking a breath. Fast and then faster, with each chop of my arm pushing away the need to face up to the consequences of my egregious behaviour.

The tents filled quickly and the list of stars would have made Cecil B. de Mille envious. The day was perfectly clear –

no smoke, no smog to yellow the pure light. The hotel operator was the sole irritant. Her voice grated, summoning names to pick up the house phone. The bigger the star, the louder the murmurous gasp from the now heavily populated pool area. I felt the sun warming me and I sighed with contentment and let my skin soak up the rays. The action occupied my mind. I had no intention of moving or even asking for an umbrella. I started to drift into a dream, but was roused by a voice offering a drink. Couldn't the 'extra' pool boy see I was asleep? I was irritated by his lack of sensitivity. I may have been barbecuing myself to a cinder, but that was no concern of his. I asked for the coldest Coca-Cola that had ever been poured, and it was brought within a second and demolished even faster, the ice numbing my mouth. The celebrities continued to be called and I was beginning to think that it was quite vulgar to have your name announced. A low profile was a far better choice in life than celebrity status.

I called the operator from the house phone and said that if anyone asked for Sam Alexander, not to call out my name but just my room number, Suite 302. I was not expecting anyone to know where I was, but I still liked the idea of being anonymous. It was approaching lunch and I signalled the waiter to bring me a hamburger and some French fries. This was the life I dreamed of as I lay in my narrow bed at my public school. It was there that I had experienced the harrowing violation of being singled out as a victim. The bullies barged into my room without a knock and sneered at my plea to be left alone. That was not that long ago. I could still feel the stab in my guts from the prefect's thrust. I dived again into the blue pool, the water soaking my now burned skin. As I emerged at the other end, I grabbed the side.

Why had I got married? I may have been in an altered

state but, for Christ's sake, I knew what I was doing. Didn't I? Perhaps my irrationality was inevitable, given my unhappy state of mind. I knew that I had not buried the loss of my brother in the Oxfordshire soil on that winter's day. My life since then had swept me along on a tide of events beyond my control. Beautiful February, so kind in all she had created for me, had fitted perfectly in to the scheme of things. Why should I run away from that? I was lucky. David was being a friend. He saw I needed a family. But it was too rushed. What would my parents think? I wouldn't tell them just yet. They didn't need this sort of news, well did they?

The waiter brought over the hamburger. It didn't look very appetising. The lunchtime sun and the cooked meat didn't go together well. I was famished though, and sank my teeth into the bun, having covered it with ketchup.

'Would Suite 302 please pick up the house phone?'

At first, I was too engrossed in tucking into the salty French fries to hear my room being called out.

'Suite 302. Telephone.'

The insistent voice eventually caught my attention and it was only then that I realised that the hotel was calling for *me*.

I had one more bite and walked to the cabana at the other end of the pool by the stairs. 'Who is the guy?' I heard a murmur ripple round me as I passed. Hollywood loves mystery and unwittingly it looked as if I had created one.

I picked up the phone and before I said anything turned to look back. The eyes of the entire poolside were staring right at me. How strange, I thought. I am nobody.

'Sam, is that you?'

'Yup, who's that?' I answered.

'It's David, you damn fool. Why did you run away? We were worried about you. February has been in tears all morning. She's very upset. Thank God for the driver, he told me where to find you.'

I had no words.

'Listen, stay there. I'm coming over.' And the phone went dead.

He needn't have worried; I wasn't going anywhere. I was too busy soaking up the sun – and I hadn't finished my burger. I thought of February's tears as I walked back and I yearned for her.

A gentleman with thick grey hair, heavily tanned, thin legs and oversized Joe 90 glasses stood over my food. He spoke with a voice that could penetrate fog.

'And you are . . . ?'

'Sam Alexander, sir.'

'I am Lew Wasserman,' and he offered his hand.

Lew Wasserman of MCA, the 'Pope of Hollywood'! The genius who'd realised that big actors could pay much less tax by turning themselves into corporations. Yes, he was a powerful man.

'I like your style, kid. I've been coming here for years and you're the first guy I've known to ask for his name not to be announced. What are you doing out here?'

'I'm an agent . . . ' I told him my story, of how I had travelled from answering the phones in a London office to working big-time in Beverly Hills.

'Take this. Call my assistant on Monday and make an appointment.' He had scribbled his number in pencil on a pink sheet of the hotel writing-paper. He returned to his cabana and rejoined the stars who were his guests for the day.

* * *

David ordered a soda water. 'Make it a double,' he quipped, and after gulping it down, he launched into me. It was quite different from anything I had heard from him before. His sobriety had given him a *gravitas* that was wholly new.

'Don't blame February. She loves you and I know you love her, you fool.' His words shamed me and I felt unbearable remorse. I was thinking of my wife and the weakness I had shown; of how lucky I had been to be given opportunities that for most people come only after a struggle. I saw with a clarity that until now had eluded me. From my expulsion from school, my brother's death and my longing for acceptance from my father to Margaret's suicide, I had had a lot to deal with, but it was time to come to terms with the past and move on.

I interrupted, 'Where is she?'

'She's waiting for you upstairs.'

* * *

February was sitting on a stone bench to the side of the main entrance. The anodyne jazz being played in the lobby drifted out into the sunshine. My head was clear and I sat next to her, putting my arm around her waist. She had obviously been crying as her face was streaked with tears. She wiped her eyes and turned towards me.

'How is my beautiful wife? I am so very sorry,' I said and reached out my hand.

'I suppose you're going to say the reason you went through with the marriage was because you were out of it. I love you and I'm not scared to hear you say that,' she replied.

'I love you too, my darling. I need you to know that anything that comes really close to me, forces me to run away. I am not proud of that, but it's the story of my life.'

'Am I just "anything"? Am I, Sam?' February's voice broke into a sob.

'No, you are my future. I think I have been grieving too

long over things I can't change. I want to start my life anew, and not be shackled any longer to the past.'

She looked at my eyes, now brimming with tears. I held her in my arms and I could feel her trembling. I knew that her love would heal the wounds that had forced me to escape into solitude. I had no excuse left; the future beckoned.

The tranquillity of that moment was shattered by a fuss of photographers snapping Bette Davis, who presumably had finished her lunch and was returning to her car. She glanced at us sitting clasped in one another's arms. 'Love is for the young to figure out!' she said in her celebrated drawl, her famous face wreathed in cigarette smoke. At her heels, her shuffling entourage laughed obsequiously.

The crumpled Kleenex that February had been holding slipped from her hand and was wafted by the warm breeze high above the star's head. Its shape as it receded from view reminded me of a kestrel hovering in search of unsuspecting prey. I looked back into February's compassionate eyes and knew I was finally safe from harm and I did not have to run any more.